CLUB TIMES

For Members' Eyes Only

Bless you, Jake White!

I need to publicly thank Officer Jake White for helping me reach the box of tissues in the grocery store yesterday. This tall drink of water was a good man to have around when the going got rough, namely when allergy season hit, thus my need for tissues. Between nose-blowings and coughing, I did manage to ask him if he was single. He gave me a strange look, then walked away. When I threw out an invitation for barbecue, he waved his hand at me. Men...

Thank goodness hospital administrator Tabitha Monroe calmed my ruffled feathers, saying that Jake was a busy cop. I noticed when she said his name, she blushed a little and kept stuttering. Could there be love in the air, as well as pollen?

Finally, I'd like to make something perfectly clear. A spaceship from Planet Zykstra has not landed on the ninth tee of the Lone Star Country Club golf course. The group of elders who've parked their lawn chairs out on the grass must vacate the premises immediately. We're investigating possible contamination of Widow Johnson's lemonade. We realize that it's an excellent brew, but this is the limit.

Whatever the season, come to the Lone Star Country Club and soothe away those Texas-size worries with a nice sauna and lunch at the Yellow Rose Café.

About the Author

Even though her upbringing is pure Southern, **MARTHA SHIELDS** loves to write about cowboys. So she jumped at the chance to work on the LONE STAR COUNTRY CLUB series. She was disappointed but not daunted when she realized that Jake White—her hero in *The Lawman*—is a cop by profession, not a cowboy. Martha believes that being a cowboy is a state of mind. Jake knows exactly what he wants, and he's not afraid to go after it. He knows right from wrong, and isn't afraid to stand up for what he believes. It's that clear-thinking cowboy courage that Martha tries to put into all her heroes, whatever they do for a living. It's what makes her fall in love with each of them.

Martha lives in Memphis, Tennessee. During the day, she tries to make college courses sound exciting, and at night, she escapes the pressures of the day by weaving tales of romantic worlds, hoping readers can do the same.

MARTHA SHIELDS

THE LAWMAN

Silhouette® Books

Published by Silhouette Books
America's Publisher of Contemporary Romance

Special thanks and acknowledgment are given to Martha Shields for her contribution to the LONE STAR COUNTRY CLUB series.

SILHOUETTE BOOKS

ISBN 0-373-61366-0

THE LAWMAN

This edition published by arrangement with Harlequin Books S.A.

Visit Silhouette at www.eHarlequin.com

Printed in U.S.A.

Welcome to the

Where Texas society reigns supreme—
and appearances are everything.

A hostage crisis wreaks havoc
at Mission Creek Memorial Hospital....

Jake White: This unrelenting cop's mission is to bring down those who commit senseless crimes. So when he's called to Mission Creek Memorial Hospital, he has every intention of putting the maniacal perpetrator behind bars. But locking *lips* with a beautiful hospital administrator wasn't part of the plan....

Tabitha Monroe: Working side by side with gruffly gorgeous Jake White during this hospital crisis was sweet torture! Personal experience cautioned her that getting involved with a cop was a one-way ticket to heartbreak. But as the danger—and their sizzling attraction—intensified, could she resist the potent allure of this mesmerizing lawman?

Branson Hines: This psychopath is at large with two innocent victims. How far will he go if his ransom demands aren't met?

Caitlyn Matthews and Sam Walters: Will these hostages cave in to their mutual desire during a life-and-death ordeal?

THE FAMILIES

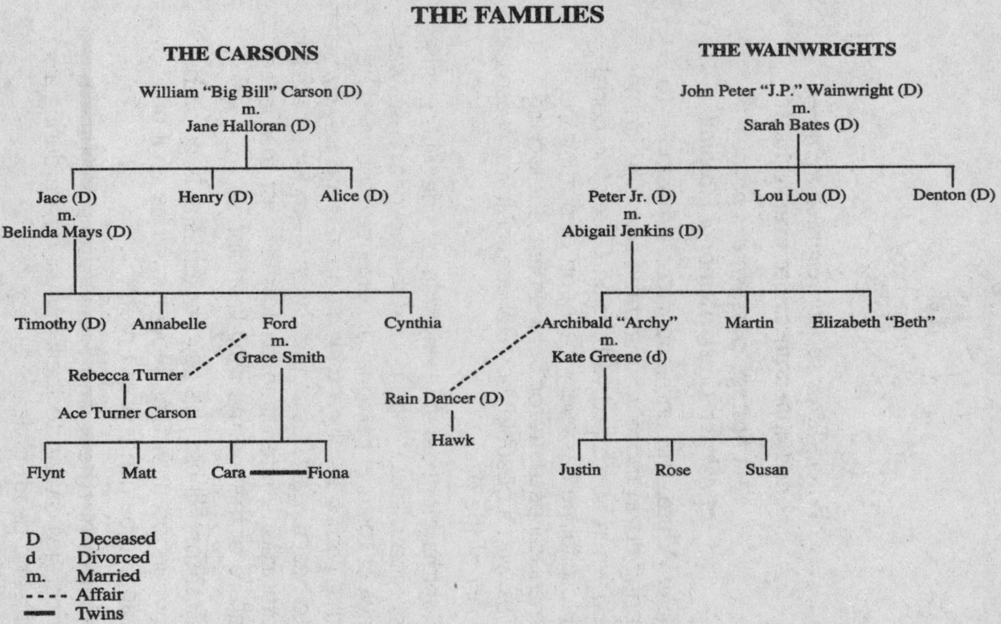

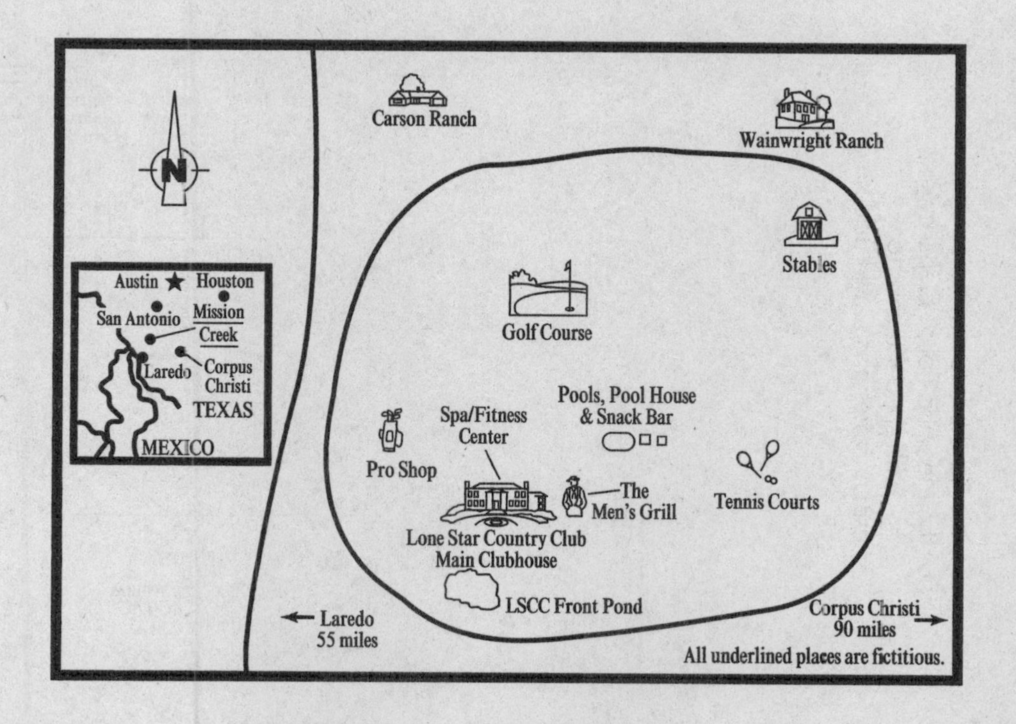
N
Austin
Houston
San Antonio
Mission Creek
Laredo
Corpus Christi
TEXAS
MEXICO
Carson Ranch
Wainwright Ranch
Stables
Golf Course
Pools, Pool House & Snack Bar
Spa/Fitness Center
Pro Shop
The Men's Grill
Tennis Courts
Lone Star Country Club Main Clubhouse
LSCC Front Pond
Laredo 55 miles
Corpus Christi 90 miles
All underlined places are fictitious.

To the brave officers
of the Memphis Police Department,
with special thanks to
Ernest Lancaster and David Baldovin.

One

Tabitha Monroe knew the instant Assistant Chief of Police Jake White arrived.

The tension filling the air changed so suddenly, so drastically, it was as if a hot South Texas wind had blown in from across the Rio Grande fifty miles to the west.

The police officials flanking her on the dais—from Mission Creek's well-staffed but hostage-inexperienced force—relaxed noticeably. They'd called Assistant Chief White in from his vacation and had been trying to put the press conference off until his return. But the media, which had been gathering from all over Texas throughout the night before, had been clamoring for information.

The transformed air held more than relief, however. On top of the fear, concern and desperation, inherent in a discussion of an armed madman disappearing with hostages, floated an element of excitement, of restlessness that seemed almost…sexual.

Taken aback by the thought so inappropriate to the situation at hand—and so foreign to her personally—Tabitha hesitated in the middle of answering a question and scanned the crowd of reporters. They'd come, it seemed, from every news agency around the country since news had leaked of yesterday's unusual hostage situation and kidnapping at Mission Creek Memorial Hospital. Her hospital.

Though she'd never met Jake White and had no idea what he looked like, she knew him the instant her gaze locked on to light-colored eyes framed with dark lashes.

Steady, strong, assessing, his gaze bored into hers and, for an instant, the rest of the room disappeared.

A delicious shiver ruffled the hairs on Tabitha's skin, which became flushed with blood shot from a heart that suddenly beat as if her morning coffee had been laced with speed.

Now she knew where the sexual energy was coming from. It was as if Jake telegraphed desire across invisible wires stretching over the heads of the crowd.

From the corner of her eye, she saw Police Chief Burl Terry motion to his second-in-command to come forward.

"Miss Monroe?"

The reporter's voice barely penetrated Tabitha's frozen stupor.

What was wrong with her? Jake White was a cop. She'd never had a sexual thought about a cop in her life. She wasn't about to start now.

Tabitha tore her gaze from the cop at the back of the room, but not before she saw him give a small "not now" wave to the chief.

They'd called him in to take command, hadn't they? What was he waiting for? For her to screw up?

You can't do anything right.

She could hear her father's voice as clearly as if he were in the room, rather than under six feet of Texas soil, the bullet that had killed him still lodged in his heart.

"Miss Monroe?"

With an effort, Tabitha focused on the crowd of reporters and for an alarming instant couldn't remember the question she'd been answering or even the reporter who'd asked it. "Yes?"

One young man in front helped her out by saying, "You were about to tell us what precautions the hospital was making to keep Branson Hines out."

"Thank you. Yes." Tabitha took a deep breath. "Mission

Creek Police Chief Burl Terry has assured me that all entrances are sealed. Everyone will be searched when they enter the hospital, just as each of you were."

"Is that going to be enough?" asked another reporter, a woman from a national news agency. "Weren't Mission Creek police guarding the hospital against Mr. Hines yesterday? And if I'm not mistaken, he escaped from the police about a month ago after almost kidnapping the son of your hospital fund-raiser—" she looked down at her notes "—Crystal Bennett."

Tabitha glanced at Jake White, who watched her intently, then at Chief Terry, who did not look pleased at having the quality of his men questioned.

Chief Terry stepped over to the microphone. "Hines was being escorted to the maximum-security prison in Lubbock by state troopers when he managed to escape. There were APBs put out, and police all over the state were looking for him. Nothing's gonna get through my boys. I guaran-damn-tee you that."

Smiling with what she hoped looked like confidence, Tabitha returned to the mike. "I have every faith in the Mission Creek Police Department."

Though she wasn't looking directly at him, she saw Assistant Chief White's tiny nod. His obvious approval made her heart swell with pride, which she quickly quashed. She was thirty-five, not fifteen. She didn't need anyone's approval, much less a cop's.

Hands raised immediately.

Tabitha pointed at another reporter, though all she wanted to do was end the press conference. She'd already said everything there was to say. "You, in the white blouse."

"Can you tell us a little more about the two hostages?" the woman asked. "Did you know them personally?"

"I *do* know them. I know all my employees personally. But I have to admit I know Caitlyn Matthews better than

Dr. Walters. She's a lovely young woman and one of the best pediatric nurses we have.'' Tabitha swallowed her emotions and continued. ''I'll do anything in my power to get the hostages back. *Safely* back.''

The sudden frown on Jake White's face alarmed her. Had she said something wrong?

''The ransom Mr. Hines is demanding is a baby from the hospital nursery, isn't it?'' a male reporter called. ''Surely you're not planning to give him one.''

''Of course not.'' Tabitha straightened. ''The demand is preposterous. There's no way we can—''

''The press conference is officially over.''

The loud announcement from the back of the room caught everyone, including Tabitha, by surprise. Since only one person could have given the command, her eyes immediately sought Jake White. He strode toward the podium, separating the crowd of reporters like Moses parting the Red Sea.

Suddenly she was twelve again, giving a report at a Girl Scout meeting that should have earned her the astronomy badge. She looked up from her notes and saw her father storming into the room. He grabbed her by her green cotton collar and dragged her from the room, growling that she had to go home and clean up the mess she'd made cooking his supper.

She never went to a meeting again.

Forcing the image away, Tabitha's eyes narrowed as she watched Jake approach.

Every head in the room swung to watch him. Cameras tracked his progress to the dais. Reporters threw questions at him as he passed.

He ignored them all and just kept coming.

Chief Terry tapped Tabitha on the shoulder. Startled, she glanced at him. Since he obviously wanted the mike, she stepped back.

''Ladies and gentlemen,'' the chief said with obvious relief, "I'd like to introduce Assistant Police Chief Jake White of the Mission Creek Police Department. Assistant Chief White is a much-decorated veteran of the Houston and Mission Creek police departments and has extensive experience in hostage situations. He's going to be the point man for the current crisis."

Assistant Chief White took the two steps leading up to the podium in one. Before turning to the crowd, he paused and met Tabitha's gaze.

Her breath froze in her lungs at the intensity in his pale green eyes. The shouting of reporters dimmed to an indecipherable clamor, background noise that seemed to have nothing to do with them.

After what seemed like hours but in reality was probably just a few seconds, Jake gave her a small smile and nod, then turned away.

Air whooshed into Tabitha's lungs, sending shards of heat spiking through her. She knew the sudden flush would be evident on her pale complexion and was thankful that Jake was now in the spotlight instead of her. No matter how rudely he'd commandeered it.

For goodness' sake, what was wrong with her? She was in the most crucial situation she'd ever been in, would likely ever be in. A situation that could make or break her career as a hospital administrator. And she was acting about as professional as a teenager ogling a boy from behind the counter of a fast-food restaurant.

In walked Jake and—

Tabitha barely restrained a groan.

When had he become Jake instead of Assistant Chief White?

What the hell was wrong with her?

She *wasn't* interested in this man, no matter how attractive he was. No matter how attracted he seemed to be to her. No matter how chiseled his jaw. No matter how his jeans stretched across his tight rear end. No matter how broad his shoulders were in the dark green golf shirt that stretched across his back and molded to muscles that had her fingers aching to—

Tabitha cut herself off with a silent curse.

She *couldn't* be interested in this man. He was a cop, for heaven's sake, right down to his bones. She would have recognized the signs even if she hadn't already known.

The arrogance. The swaggering confidence. The ability to silence a room with a single sentence. The ability to make her want to please him.

Her eyes narrowed.

There was no way in hell she was interested in this man. She was immune to cops. She'd had eighteen long years of daily inoculations.

Pulling her mind away from the past—her only defense against the emotional damage her father had done to her—Tabitha concentrated on the proceedings.

She was going to be working closely with this man for who knew how long—until Cait and Dr. Walters were safely home—so it was imperative that she keep this on a professional level.

Assistant Chief White had answered several questions about his experience with hostage situations, and when he'd said his piece, he ended the press conference. "We'll keep you informed. There'll be two daily press conferences, morning and afternoon. More if there are any significant developments."

The reporters continued shouting questions, but Jake turned his back on them. His eyes sought Tabitha first, then his attention was pulled away by Burl Terry. He conferred for a moment with his boss, then stepped over to Tabitha. He gestured toward the dais steps. "Miss Monroe."

Tabitha lifted her chin. She was not going to let him escort her out of here by the scruff of her collar. "Why did you cut me off so rudely?"

His right eyebrow quirked upward. "There are reasons. Please..."

Again he indicated the steps.

Tabitha frowned. He said please. Her father had never said please, or thank-you.

Okay, so he was a polite cop. He was still a cop. "What reasons?"

"We'll discuss them in your office."

"I want to know n—"

"Not here. You don't know how sensitive these mikes are. We have a lot more than that to discuss, but I'd like to do it in the privacy of your office. Please show me the way."

Tabitha nodded once, briefly, then stepped down from the dais. He was being perfectly logical and reasonable. She had to be the same. She couldn't let what had happened to her in the past color the present situation. The one thing had nothing to do with the other.

Stepping onto the carpet, Tabitha was surrounded by an impenetrable wall of reporters, half of whom shoved microphones in her face and shouted questions. Each tried to be heard over the others, but the result was cacophony.

Suddenly Jake's hand connected firmly with the small of her back. The electrical charge that shot up Tabitha's spine made her eyes widen and the breath catch in her throat. She couldn't answer a question even if she was able to distinguish one reporter's voice from the others.

Jake put out one arm like a shield in front of her and began pushing their way through the crowd. "No more questions now. We'll let you know if something happens."

His deep bass voice carried easily under the strident cries of the reporters who, miraculously, let them pass.

After the shock of his touch was over, when she realized it wasn't intended to be sexual—though it sure as heck felt sexual—Tabitha relaxed and let Jake guide her through the reporters and out the door.

"Tough crowd, huh?"

She glanced at him, but his attention was down the hall. "I can't believe there are so many."

He shrugged. "It's Hines's demand. Babies always make good copy."

Police officers were stationed at close intervals down the hall. They all smiled at Jake as they walked toward the elevators or told him how relieved they were he'd finally made it. Tabitha could see it in their eyes. Jake's presence made them feel safe, made them feel that everything was going to be all right.

Jake White had served on the Mission Creek Police Department for over a year, and the department had full confidence in his ability to handle the situation.

Tabitha didn't feel safe until they entered the sanctuary of her office.

Jake didn't realize he still had his hand on Tabitha's back until he paused at the door of her office and she stepped away from him.

His hand suddenly felt cold, bereft.

Jake cursed under his breath. This shouldn't be happening. The first rule of hostage negotiation was never get emotionally involved with anyone connected to the hostages. Not only was it unprofessional, not only did it cloud your vision and color your decisions, but relationships forged in crisis situations were doomed from the start.

Not that he wanted anything heavy. A failed marriage had taught him that he was too dedicated a cop to be dedicated to a family.

Still he hadn't had a steady girlfriend since moving to Mission Creek over a year ago. He missed having someone to have dinner with when he wasn't working. Someone who gave a damn whether he came home at night, or came home at all. Regular sex.

With that thought, Jake's gaze dropped to Tabitha's cute little butt swaying across the room as she retreated to the power position behind her desk. But it wasn't her butt that had first caught his libido's attention.

Tabitha turned to face him, her incredibly blue eyes wide and questioning.

It was that damned mole.

He'd spotted Tabitha's mole the instant he'd walked in the door of the conference room downstairs, and his body had reacted the same way it reacted years ago when he'd first laid eyes on a picture of Marilyn Monroe.

He'd had a weakness for women with moles ever since then. Especially when the woman who sported the mole had a lush body like Marilyn's, made for a man's hands to roam. He was not attracted to model-thin women. He wanted a woman to have curves, not angles.

Tabitha Monroe had plenty of curves. He could tell even through the navy-blue silk designer suit she wore.

There were other similarities. Tabitha had the same last name as Marilyn. Hell, she even vaguely resembled the movie star.

Tabitha's blond hair wasn't Marilyn's bleached blond, but it was shoulder length and worn in the soft curls similar to the actress's in one of his favorite photos, taken in the late 1940s. Tabitha's mouth—so close beside that feminine little mole—was wide, though her lips were pursed at the moment with what was undoubtedly worry. Her expression reminded him so much of Marilyn's pout that all he could think of doing was sucking Tabitha's bottom lip into his mouth and flicking it with his tongue.

"Assistant Chief White?"

Jake started back to reality. Reminded so rudely of the current situation and the futility of his desire, he spoke a little harsher than he meant to and before he thought through what he was going to say. "Call me Jake."

He was as surprised as she at the words that came out of his mouth.

Why the hell had he said that? Using first names was definitely not in line with keeping things professional.

Her little chin lifted. "There's no need to growl at me. You're the one who dragged me up here to lecture me on everything I did wrong at the press conference."

"I didn't drag you," he said defensively. "And I certainly didn't bring you here to—"

The sound of tinkling water distracted him. The gurgling was so out of place in an executive's office, he glanced around for the source. In a corner behind Tabitha's desk sat one of those small tabletop water fountains. Built like a mini Buddhist temple, the water ran down the steps on one side onto polished rocks below.

His attention already diverted from Tabitha, he took advantage of sanity's return and slowly looked around.

At first glance, a visitor might just think she'd overdecorated with a Chinese motif. But Jake had worked for years with a tae kwon do master in Houston, and he knew better.

Plants in colorful pots grew everywhere, including several bonsai. Mirrors and bamboo flutes hung on the walls. A menagerie of carved Chinese animals, including several dragons, were scattered here and there. A lighted fish tank hummed merrily on a green table. Round, faceted crystals suspended on the windows flashed spectrums around the room. Stones carved with Chinese calligraphy sat among the profusion.

Several conversation areas were arranged around the large office. One round, one square, one with the furniture placed randomly. Each shape was supposed to generate a certain mood, but he had no idea what. He'd never paid that much attention.

One of the groups sported a red couch, which he had to drag his eyes away from.

His gaze making the full circle of the room back to Tabitha, he grinned. ''You've feng shuied this place to death.''

The amusement in his voice wasn't lost on her, because her sky-blue eyes narrowed. ''It's not 'shoey.' It's pronounced more like a Yiddish version of 'sway.' More like 'shway.'''

''I see.'' He strolled around the room, running a finger along a jade dragon here, peering at a painting of a gnarled pine tree clinging to a mountainside there.

''I have to see a lot of people in my office. Potential employees. Worried, sometimes grieving families. Vendors. I find it helps everyone if we can talk in harmonious surroundings.''

''I see.'' Interesting. Her voice was defensive. A little too sensitive about her decor?

''It helps me, too. Very relaxing. You should try it sometime.''

Jake hid a smile by bending over to peer into the fish tank. If defense doesn't work, try offense. She was using one of his own favorite tactics.

She stopped talking, and he smiled again. Silence. The best tactic of all. And it went so well with her Zen style of decorating.

He straightened and twisted to say something, but his comment stuck in his throat when she dragged her eyes upward with a startled expression.

She'd been checking out his butt.

Heat seared through him.

She cleared her throat. ''Gardening is wonderful for reducing stress.''

Okay. So they were going to ignore the sparks threatening to set all this feng shui on fire.

Disappointed, but knowing it was the smartest thing to do,

he moved to stand directly in front of her desk. "It's hard to grow bonsai in a squad car."

"The plants don't have to be bonsai. You could try it in your hou—"

"I didn't bring you up to your office to lecture you."

She blinked, then threw the meaningless words he'd used back in his face. "I see."

Damn, she was quick. The abrupt change of subject hadn't thrown her, as he'd meant it to.

That was good. Yet it wasn't.

The only thing he hadn't liked about Marilyn Monroe was her weak sex-kitten nature. He was attracted to strong, smart women. Women who gave back as good as he gave. Women who caught on quickly to his games and played them every bit as hard as he did.

When Cindy Crawford had burst on the scene, he'd quickly switched his allegiance to her. There was a brief two-year stint of unfaithfulness—his marriage to one of Houston's prosecuting attorneys. But Jake barely counted that because his ex-wife's name was Cindy. That was what he called her, anyway, even when she insisted on the more laywerlike Cynthia.

"So why did you cut me off in midsentence and drag— Oh, pardon me. Why did you *escort* me up here?"

"I had to end the press conference because you were about to cut off any hope for negotiation with Hines, and a hopeless hostage taker is a desperate hostage taker. No telling what he'll do."

Tabitha frowned and finally sat, though only on the front few inches of her leather executive chair. "You mean by telling him I won't give him a baby from the hospital's maternity ward?"

"Right." She really did catch on quick. He was impressed...and turned on as hell.

Damn. He needed to get out of here and cool off. Luckily

he had the perfect excuse. He just had to take advantage of it before he did something stupid. Real stupid.

Her eyes focused on his face. "But I *won't* give him a baby."

"Of course you won't." Instead of walking out the door like he should have, Jake sat in one of the chairs facing her desk. "But you can't tell Hines that. Especially not on national television. He's taken hostages and threatened to kill them. If you cut off his options, he may feel he doesn't have any choice but to do that."

"Oh, my." Tabitha sucked in a tiny, horrified breath. "I haven't killed Cait and Sam, have I?"

"I didn't say that." Jake slid forward on the chair, barely stopping himself from reaching for the hands she'd splayed on her desk. "You did okay. I just needed to stop you before you went any further."

She studied him across the desk as if he were an alien whose antennae had suddenly popped from his head.

She stared so long and so blatantly, he rubbed his chin. "Is my makeup coming off?"

She blinked. "Makeup?"

"The makeup that hides my purple scales. All the best space invaders are wearing them these days."

Color tinged her cheek and she dropped her gaze to her uncluttered desk. "Sorry." Then she glanced back up. "You really think I did okay?"

He tried not to frown at this glimpse of insecurity. "Of course you did. You don't know the rules of hostage negotiation, or how to use the media to help you win. That is, you don't know the rules yet. After I check on what's being done to find Hines, I'm going to give you a few lessons."

"I attended a crisis management seminar a few years ago."

He nodded. "That's good. But believe me, you can't learn in any seminar what you're going to need to know in the next few days. You can only do it right when you've had a baptism of fire."

"I definitely want to do it right. I have to."

"You will. Don't worry. I'll be beside you every step of the way."

"Every step?"

"Well..." His mind filled with images of where "every step" might lead them, like straight to the red couch against the wall.

Damn, he had all the self-control of a thirteen-year-old.

Jake frowned. If there was one thing he prided himself on, it was his self-control. "Maybe not *every* step."

They stared across the desk for several long seconds, the only sounds the tinkling water fountain, the hum of the fish tank and the whoosh of heavy breathing.

Realizing the heavy breathing was his, Jake slapped his thighs and stood. "I need to check on things."

Tabitha's spine straightened, making her several inches taller in the chair. "What things?"

"Search tactics. Security measures. Telephone recording equipment."

"Whose conversations are you recording?"

He hesitated before saying, "Yours."

"Mine?" Her eyes widened. "You think he's going to call me? Because I'm in charge of the hospital?"

Actually, there were several reasons Tabitha had made herself the focal point for Hines during the press conference. Jake was ninety-nine-percent certain Hines's calls would be to her. But there was no point in worrying her now. There would be time enough to explain how things worked...and sometimes didn't. "That's part of the reason. I'll explain everything when I get back. Be here. I don't want you going anywhere without me. Understand?"

She frowned. "I can't just—"

"Oh, yes, you can and you *will.* You'll do everything I

tell you. You'll sit when I tell you to sit. You'll eat when I tell you to eat. You'll stay where I—"

"Wait just a gosh darned minute!" Tabitha stood to face him. "I have a hospital to run, with over a hundred employees on every shift who—"

"You have two employees who need you much more than all those hundreds put together." Jake leaned toward her. "Two employees who are God knows where, shoved into God only knows what conditions. They're definitely suffering mental anguish, but there may be physical pain, as well."

Tabitha sat again, hard. "Don't say that. I can't stand to think of them tortured."

Satisfied that he'd put the fear of God into her, Jake straightened. "Stay put. I'll be back in a little while."

"What if he calls?" She shivered.

To keep from reaching for her, Jake turned toward the door. "He won't. It's too soon."

"How can you be sure?"

"Trust me."

Silence accompanied him to the door, as did a feeling of eyes burning into his back. At the door, he couldn't resist turning. Sure enough, she was watching him, though she wasn't concentrating on his butt.

Calling himself all kinds of a moron for feeling disappointed, he asked, "You okay?"

She blinked, as if surprised to be asked. "Of course. I'm always okay."

He nodded, understanding more than she knew. She was a control freak just like him.

Great. Two bullheaded people who had to pussyfoot around each other because all they wanted to do was rip each other's clothes off. They couldn't even acknowledge their desire, much less do anything about it.

This was not going to be an easy job. Interesting, but definitely not easy.

"Assistant Chief White?"

"Yes? You can drop the 'Assistant,' by the way."

She nodded. "Do you really believe we'll have them back in a few days?"

"I hope so. Hines doesn't have too many places to hide."

Her clenched fist struck the pad on her desk. "Jeez, I hate this! I feel so helpless."

"I know." That was one feeling he knew very well.

"If I had Branson Hines in my office for just five seconds, I'd—"

"Feng shui him to death?"

Tabitha's gaze flicked guiltily around her office, then she let a deep breath out on a sigh. "Sorry."

"You'd turn him over to the closest police officer, like you should." Jake smiled encouragingly. "Don't worry. We'll get your employees back."

"Promise?"

He hesitated.

"No. You can't promise," she said. "Anything can happen."

"That's true."

Her frown deepened. "At least you didn't try to lie to me."

Jake wasn't above lying. Sometimes lying was kinder and made his job easier. With a sick feeling, however, he realized he didn't want to lie to Tabitha. With an even sicker feeling, he realized he probably couldn't.

"I've got to get out of here." He hadn't meant to say the words aloud.

Her wince was barely noticeable. "Fine. Go."

Cussing inwardly at his sudden lack of self-control, he growled, "Stay in your office."

"Why should I, if Hines is not going to—"

"Stay." Before she could utter another syllable, Jake turned and strode from the room.

* * *

Jake returned two hours later in a much better mood.

He was riding a high that came from finally having something substantial to do, after a year of doing nothing but chasing drunk cowboys down jackrabbit holes.

He'd known when he'd taken Burl's offer that he'd be twiddling his thumbs for a couple of years. Burl had known it, too. That's why he'd locked Jake in with a two-year contract. But the Mission Creek police chief had been so desperate for good leadership after the money-laundering scandal in the force here, he'd given Jake an offer he couldn't refuse. Not only was it a substantial raise in pay, but a promotion he might never have gotten in the rigid hierarchy of the Houston Police Department, with all their civil service guidelines. Small-town departments operated by their own rules, and Jake had come with enough verifiable credentials to satisfy the harshest critics.

Jake never thought he'd have something like hostages to sink his teeth into. Not that he was glad it had happened. Still, since it had, he was glad he was the one with enough experience to take command.

This was going to look damn good on his résumé.

Jake paused at door to the anteroom outside Tabitha's office. The secretary's area was abuzz with activity, crawling with uniformed officers and technical experts setting up the communications command post.

Not that they had much in the way of communications equipment. Hell, the wiretapping machines were so old, they would have to do a manual trace on all calls.

As frustrating as the sorry state of the MCPD's electronic surveillance equipment was, it wasn't enough to bring Jake down from his high.

That dubious honor went to Miss Tabitha Monroe when he walked into her office to find it empty. He searched it in disbelief, throwing open the doors to the closet and her private bathroom.

"Where the hell is she? Does she think we're playing a game?"

A middle-aged officer who'd been setting up the shortwave radio peeked around the doorjamb. "Did you say something, sir?"

"Where did she go?"

"Who? The blonde? She said she had to go down to the nursery."

"I see. She *had* to go." He stormed through the door.

"That's what she said," the officer called after him.

The elevators were directly across from Tabitha's office. Jake marched over and punched the call button. Neither opened immediately, so he paced back and forth between the two doors.

If Miss Monroe thought she could skip out on him any time she wanted to do God knows what, she didn't know who she was dealing with. He had a harder head and a stronger will than anyone he'd ever met.

Impatient with the slow ascent of the elevator, Jake strode to the stairwell at the end of the hall and took the stairs two at a time.

Time was important though not critical. But the frustration he'd felt when dealing with her earlier had returned and a little physical activity might help.

Jake's lungs hadn't even begun to strain when he shoved open the door to the second floor. The new maternity wing—dedicated only a couple of months ago—was a two-story structure tacked on at a perpendicular angle to the hospital's east wing. Delivery and waiting rooms were on the first floor, with the nursery and mothers' rooms on the second.

He spotted Tabitha as soon as he rounded the corner from the east wing into the addition.

The lit hallway testified that they'd fixed the electrical

outage caused by Hines to distract the staff long enough to grab hostages. Now they were moving patients and equipment back into the new wing.

Tabitha was helping a nurse push a crib down the hall. He watched her until they turned the crib sideways and disappeared through the nursery door.

Jake's eyes narrowed, and another part of his good mood slipped away.

She had disobeyed his direct order to stay in her office because of this? What if Hines *had* called?

The hospital staff moved out of his way as he marched down the hall.

He didn't blame them.

When he reached the nursery, he peered through the windowed wall.

Tabitha patted the arm of a nurse who wore a worried expression, obviously trying to soothe fears about the hostage taking. The middle-aged nurse seemed to hang on Tabitha's every word, gathering courage from whatever it was she was saying.

The evidence that Tabitha hadn't left her office frivolously—that she was doing something important, something probably only she could do—should have eased Jake's ire. With anyone else, it would have.

But as she talked he could see Tabitha's mole move, and his traitorous libido kicked in.

He cursed loud enough for a passing nurse to jump sideways, and the last shred of his good mood vanished.

The tight-as-a-stretched-wire sexual tension he'd experienced when he was with her earlier had eased while he had something more important to think about. He couldn't say it had left completely. His good mood had been built on the pleasure she'd sent zinging through his veins. But the desire wasn't so strong it bordered on painful.

In fact, his good mood had increased when he realized that, because it meant he could control it. Or so he'd thought.

All he had to do was see her and heat shot through him like fire across bone-dry grass.

With another livid curse, he walked into the nursery, stopping several yards behind her.

The nurse Tabitha was talking to saw him immediately and frowned, making Tabitha turn.

"Jake!" Her smile vanished the instant she saw him, which irritated him even further. "I mean...Chief White." She glanced at her watch. "Goodness, it's been over an hour. I didn't mean to be gone so—"

"Miss Monroe, I need to speak with you privately."

She straightened at his clipped tone. "Of course. I was just—"

He grabbed her elbow and started walking down the hall.

She tried to pull free. When she couldn't, she said under her breath, "You don't have to manhandle me. I'm capable of walking on my own."

"I know. You walked out of your office quick enough." Since he didn't want to drag her up six flights, he punched the elevator call button.

She yanked her arm again. This time he let her go.

"I have responsibilities," she said.

"Moving gurneys is in your job description?"

She yanked on the hem of her jacket to straighten what was already straight. For an instant, her ripe, full breasts were outlined clearly by the silk.

Jake bit off another curse. For something to do, he pressed the call button again. What was wrong with him? He was acting like a randy teenager.

"I'm not above moving gurneys, or whatever needs to be done," she explained tightly. "Especially now, when everyone is so frightened. It's important that they see I'm not afraid to work in the new wing. And on top of everything else that's happened, it's Saturday of Labor Day weekend. We're shorthanded."

He glanced up at the floor indicator above the elevator door and muttered, "Where have I heard that before?"

"What?"

"Nothing." He punched the call button again.

"Pushing the button twenty times doesn't help, you know."

"It helps me," he growled.

She lifted a pale eyebrow. "What's put you in such a foul mood?"

He glared at her. "Take a wild guess."

"It's not as if I left the building. I told the officers where I was going, and that's exactly where you found me, isn't it?"

The elevator finally dinged and the doors slid open. He placed an arm over one door to prevent it from closing, then jerked his head toward the car. "Let's go."

She stepped in, but not quickly enough to suit his mood, so he crowded her from behind.

She spun to face him. "What the hell is wrong with you? Am I not allowed to leave my office until Hines calls?"

He punched the button for the eighth floor. "With permission, maybe."

Two more people walked onto the elevator.

"Don't be ridiculous."

He glared at her as the elevator doors slid closed. "Do you want to talk about this now or in your office?"

A shadow of fear darkened her blue eyes for the briefest instant before she glanced away. Her jaw was rigid as she said, "You're right."

One person got off on the fourth floor, the other on the seventh.

When the elevator reached their destination, Jake indicated that she precede him. He took her elbow again as she did.

She yanked it away. "Please. I'm not a child."

His eyes raked down her body. "Yeah. I noticed."

Comprehension flooded her face, and she sucked in a shallow breath.

His gaze locked onto hers. What he saw did not help him cool off. Confusion. Hunger. Questions. But not a damn bit of revulsion, which would have relieved the situation because it would have killed his own desire.

"Afternoon, Miss Monroe." A hospital employee passed them, startling them both.

Tabitha gave the man a halfhearted smile. "Good afternoon, Sid."

"Let's go to your office." Jake didn't grab her elbow. Instead, he placed a hand on the small of her back.

She didn't pull away.

Though only a few feet, the walk to her office seemed endless. When they reached the anteroom, only one technical officer was there, engrossed in wiring pulled from a wall.

Jake closed her office door behind them.

She turned with wide eyes. "That's *not* a good idea."

"You want to talk about this with the door open?"

Her gaze shifted to a point behind him. "Talk about what?"

"Yeah, right." He stepped close. Only inches from her body, he could feel its warmth. His nostrils filled with a sweet floral scent underlying the more powerful smell of woman. "We can't ignore this. It's too damn strong."

"I—I don't know what you're talking about."

"The hell you don't. You're as hot for me as I am for you."

She shook her head. "No. I can't be. This is highly inappropriate."

"Tell me about it."

She lifted her face. "Not to mention unprofessional."

"Extremely unprofessional." He stared at the mole, just inches from his mouth.

"I don't like it."

"Me, neither. But it's there, and it's real, and it doesn't seem to be going away."

"Surely there's something we can do."

"I can think of lots of things, all of which you'd like—that I *can* promise—but none of which we can do with men right outside the door."

She backed up a step. "We can't work together like this. Perhaps you should take yourself off the case."

He smiled tightly. "The only reason I haven't, beside it being the only thing in the past year remotely interesting, is I know Burl wouldn't let me. I'm the only man he's got with any inkling of what to do. None of our men have worked in a hostage situation."

"Then what? Ignore it?"

"How long do you think that would work? Hell, we've only known each other a few hours and we're ready to rip each other's clothes off."

She gasped. "I certainly—"

"Don't go getting all indignant. I've seen you checking out my butt."

She glared at him but didn't deny it.

Encouraged, he took a step closer. "I can think of only one way to relieve the tension."

She regarded him suspiciously. "What? Sleep together?"

"A kiss. That's all. For now. Just a kiss."

She sucked in a tiny breath, and her gaze dropped to his lips.

His heart shifted into overdrive.

The tiny movement, so full of sexual curiosity, was all the permission he needed. Sliding his arms around her, he smothered her sudden "but" with his mouth.

Two

Tabitha's father had pinned her against a wall for beatings too many times for her to feel comfortable in any but the briefest, most superficial of embraces.

Jake's arms didn't cause panic, however. In fact, getting away was the furthest thing from her mind. Mostly because she was incapable of thought. Jake's arms around her were a warm cocoon, far from threatening. One strong hand rested at her waist, the other splayed across her back, pressing her even closer to his hard, warm, *male* body.

The pressure of his lips on hers—insistent but not forceful—burned away any notion more rational than where to put her arms for optimum holding power. She didn't want to end the kiss. She wanted to prolong it.

At the same time her arms wrapped themselves around Jake's neck, he deepened the kiss, sliding his tongue around the edges of her lips.

A spike of heat surged through Tabitha, causing a desperate need for air. She sucked in a quick breath, which caused her mouth to open.

Jake seized the opportunity, slipping his tongue between her teeth.

Warm and wet and strong, his tongue delved into her mouth, touching hers, then slipping around the inside of her teeth.

Tabitha slid her tongue along the underside of his and felt his moan from her lips to her stomach…and lower. She smiled against his mouth.

Jake drew back.

"No!" Surprised and highly displeased, Tabitha locked her arms into place, holding him a few inches away, barely enough for her eyes to focus on his.

She'd never seen green burn until now. Verdant flames leaped into her, making her blood boil and surge through her overworked heart to pool below, in the only other part in her body she was aware of. Not that her whole body wasn't singingly aware of his touch, of his smell, of his need. But only two places commanded the limited attention she possessed—lips that throbbed with hypersensitivity, and the mound that pressed into hard, swollen flesh.

"No, what?" he asked in a husky, rough voice.

Aroused beyond anything she'd ever known, she whispered, "Why did you stop?"

His eyes narrowed. "You smiled."

"I did?" She tried to think, but quickly gave up the effort. If she had smiled, that was too long ago to remember. "Sorry. It won't happen again."

His eyes crinkled around the edges but didn't lose their intensity. "Is that an invitation?"

"Yes, damn it." Driving the fingers of one hand into thick, soft hair, she pulled his lips back to hers. At first contact, she moaned.

Growling, he slid the hand at her waist down to cup her bottom and slanted his mouth across hers.

This time, however, Tabitha took the lead, edging her tongue into his mouth. He groaned, twining his tongue with hers in a dance so sensuous, so erotic, Tabitha lost track of which one was hers. Neither did she care.

She had one thing on her mind. She wanted to melt inside this man so the pleasure could go on and on and—

A thump from the next room jabbed into her consciousness. Into his, too, because they broke apart at the same time.

They stared at each other, both of them taking in huge

gulps of air, both amazed at the sheer power of the experience.

Tabitha wiped the back of her hand slowly across her mouth. "Why did you do that?"

His gaze followed the movement of her hand. "Oh, as if you weren't having a good time."

"Why?"

He straightened and made a visible effort to collect himself. "To prove a point."

"Which was...?"

He drove both hands through his hair, erasing the trails her fingers had left behind. She could still feel it—soft and thick and silky.

"Hell if I know." His twisted grin came slowly.

Muttering under her breath, Tabitha yanked down her jacket and retreated to the far corner of the room. It didn't help her dignity that she walked on obviously wobbly legs. But at least she felt relatively safe at this distance.

With her back to Jake, she stared into the tiny waterfall in the knowledge corner and mentally repeated the mantra she used when she wanted to calm herself.

Jake let her go, though it wasn't easy. All he wanted to do was lock the office door and pull her down onto the red couch against the wall.

But he couldn't. Kissing her the first time had been all kinds of stupid. If he touched her again, he was pretty damn sure he wouldn't be able to stop.

Dragging his eyes away from the firm, round bottom he could still feel in his hands, he shoved a hand through his hair again, this time yanking on it in frustration.

What the hell was wrong with him? He'd never done anything like this before. Never even been tempted. One of the most important rules in hostage situations was to not get emotionally attached to anyone involved—perpetrators, victims...or hospital administrators.

He needed to maintain distance, for that and several other very pertinent points, as well.

He'd read the file on Tabitha Monroe. She was not the kind of woman who formed casual relationships. She was too visible in the community. Not only was she chief administrator of the hospital, she was also its chief fund-raiser. She mixed with the cream of Mission Creek society, had a membership at the Lone Star Country Club, attended parties at the finest houses in and around town. She had a certain reputation to maintain, which did not include hot affairs with cops.

The problem was, the two of them were going to be working very closely in the next few days or weeks. Hell, he was going to be there every time she breathed. With the kinds of feelings he was having—and her, as well, if that kiss was any kind of indication—they could easily drift into a relationship that was personal rather than professional.

And Jake didn't do personal relationships. Not the kind this high-profile lady required. He simply wasn't good at any but the most superficial relationships. The two years he'd spent married to Cynthia had taught him that lesson well. His job would always come first, and most women objected to coming in a distant second.

But beyond that, even if he decided he did want something permanent, the chances of it lasting were practically nil. Case after case had proved that most relationships formed in crisis situations were doomed because they were built on adrenaline highs, rather than honest-to-God emotions.

There was no way he could get into *any* kind of relationship with this beautiful, smart, sexy woman, no matter where her mole was.

Tabitha's deep breathing penetrated Jake's thoughts, and he lifted his gaze to her silk-covered back. She stood in front of the tiny temple waterfall in the far corner, probably doing some kind of meditation.

He wondered if it helped.

Before he could stop himself, Jake moved around her desk and stood directly behind her. When he saw his hand lifting to her shoulder, he curled it into a fist instead.

Why did he feel this overwhelming need to touch her? Was it because he felt bad to have caused her to need comfort? Or was it his sudden, irrational jealousy of the waterfall?

He wanted to be the one to comfort her. But she wouldn't be reassured by his touch.

Then he remembered the kiss.

Or would she?

He shook his head. It didn't matter All he could use were words. "Look, I'm sorry if I—"

"Can't you tell that I'm trying to meditate?"

"I was just going to—"

"Why don't you check on your men or something?" She moved away from him, taking up a position right behind her desk. "Surely you have something you need to do. Go do it."

Jake smiled wryly. "Unfortunately, you're what I need to do. Since we don't have any information on the hostages' whereabouts, you're the focal point of the case."

She frowned at a jade dragon on the corner of her desk. "Because you think I'm the one he'll call."

"Right." Jake stared at the dragon, too. Was she doing something else to take her mind away from him?

Forcing himself not to react, he let a tense moment go by.

They couldn't work like this. It was going to be hard enough just dealing with the hostage situation. They couldn't cope with this, too.

Maybe he should take himself off the case.

He entertained the notion for all of two seconds.

He couldn't. If he backed out now, he'd be stuck in the south end of nowhere forever. Since he was the only man on the Mission Creek force qualified to head the team, Burl would have to let the FBI take over, and the Mission Creek police chief would rather walk naked across the desert than let the FBI take over.

And what reason could Jake give? That he'd fallen in lust with the main contact? Oh yeah, *that* kind of self-control would look good on his record. No, he had to keep his head together and his arms—and lips—to himself.

"Look, Miss Monroe, we can't—"

She pounded her desk with a fist, making him flinch.

She turned narrowed eyes on him. "You can't shut up, can you?"

"I just wanted to point out that what we did was—"

"Stupid? Adolescent? Grossly unprofessional?"

He lifted his chin. How about mind-numbingly erotic? "Right. We can't let it happen again."

"Oh, it won't, Chief White. You can bet your last bullet on that." She turned to fully face him, her arms crossed over her stomach. "I'm not interested in doing anything with you, other than my job. Got that?"

He heard what her lips were saying, but her eyes told a different story.

"Not the slightest, tiniest bit interested. Nothing. Zip. Nada."

"I see."

"You'd better 'see.' You're a cop, and I will never, *ever*—not in a hundred million years—become involved with anyone who wears a badge. If you try anything again like what you just did, I'll—"

"You'll what?"

She straightened her shoulders. "I'll take drastic measures."

Her vague threat amused him and brought sudden, welcome relief. Not only was he a fully trained member of the SWAT team, not only had he achieved the highest level of expertise in several martial arts, he outweighed her by about sixty pounds. "What are you going to do? Make like the Karate Kid and crane me?"

She went as rigid as an iceberg, and her voice just was as cold. "If you'll please excuse me, Chief White, I have paperwork to take care of."

She sat down at her desk, drew a manila folder from her in box, opened it and began reading.

He watched for a long, silent moment, wondering if she'd cut him out of her awareness as effectively as she seemed to. Every cell in his body was aware of her.

He considered yanking the folder from her hands and demanding her attention. He had several good excuses. He needed to tell her about the recording devices attached to her phones. He needed to coach her on what to say to Hines, how to act, how to keep him talking so they could get a good trace.

But he didn't. He let her win…this time. He was eighty-percent certain Hines wouldn't call that day, and probably not the next. If Hines wasn't already out of the area, he'd hunker down and let the search die off. So what Jake needed to tell Tabitha could wait an hour or so. Maybe she'd have cooled off by then.

Oh, she looked cool enough, sitting there in her serene surroundings. But there were telltale signs—shallow breathing, high color on her cheeks—that let him know she was still seething inside.

He spun around and headed for the door. He needed to do a bit of cooling off himself.

As he turned to close the door behind him, Jake couldn't resist one last look.

She seemed so aloof, so in control. But he knew better.

So she hated cops. Why? The only reason he could come

up with from what he knew about her was that her father had made sergeant in the Dallas Police Department.

But women who had cop fathers usually were rather fond of policemen. Many officers he knew were married to daughters of cops. Having grown up in the life, they understood how things were done.

So what had Tabitha's father done to make her hate them?

Determined to find out, Jake focused again on her sexy face. He wanted to walk over and wipe the frown of concentration off her face. He wanted to make her concentrate on him.

Instead, he closed the door. Very softly.

Nearly an hour later, Tabitha sat in her desk chair, listening to Jake's monologue on handling kidnappers. There were five other officers in the room, all in various stages of attention. A couple of them took notes. One added comments now and then.

Tabitha did neither. Her hands gripped the leather-bound arms of her executive chair. Her feet, cold as ice, were frozen to the floor.

She'd known, of course, that she was in charge of the situation, the one everyone was looking to, the one responsible for the outcome.

But she hadn't *known.*

She'd actually thought about how great handling this was going to look on her résumé. Oh, she'd been genuinely horrified. After all, she knew the people who'd been kidnapped. She was as good a friend to Caitlyn as anyone, and had a passing acquaintance with Dr. Sam Walters.

But not until Jake explained exactly how much danger Sam and Caitlyn were in, all the things that could go wrong, what they were likely experiencing, did Tabitha know the overwhelming enormity of her responsibility.

Where was Caitlyn now? Was she tied up in some dark basement, lying on a cold, wet floor, crying, not knowing what was going to happen? Was Dr. Walters with her, or were they kept separately? Was he comforting her?

Or was it worse? Was Caitlyn wrapped in a dirty sheet, lying cold and lifeless in a shallow grave just a few feet from—

Tabitha's nails dug into the leather. No. She couldn't go there. Jake said the probability was high that they weren't dead…yet.

She had to keep a positive mind-set. If she didn't, she would never get through this without cracking up. She needed to remember everything they'd taught in the seminar she'd attended in Dallas two years ago.

"You okay?"

Tabitha drew her mind back to the room and focused on Jake's concerned face. He stood on the other side of the desk, so calm, so in charge. Didn't he feel anything?

"You're white as a sheet," he said.

She tried to suppress a shudder. Bad choice of words.

Jake came around the desk and pried her hand off the arm of her chair. "And cold as ice."

"Sam and Caitlyn could *die,*" she whispered.

"Yes, they could." His face hardened. "I'm not going to lie to you."

Tabitha's heart lurched, and she looked away. "All it will take is one little slip on my part. Something I forget to say, something I say that I shouldn't."

"You can't think of it that way. Look at me, Tabitha." He pulled her chin up with his other hand. "You *cannot* think of it that way. You will do the very best that you can. And we're here. We're trained for this. We'll help you."

She tried to swallow but couldn't.

Jake's incredibly green eyes were intent. "You can't

blame yourself if something goes wrong. We're dealing with a man who doesn't think like normal people. Hell, let's call a spade a spade. The guy's crazy. He could get any kind of notion into his head. If he does, you can't blame yourself." He squeezed her hand. "I won't let you."

The last words, more than any others, heartened her.

His voice lowered and softened. "If I could do this for you, I would. But the last person he wants to talk to is a cop."

"I understand." Only then did she realize that he still held her hand. Though she wanted to keep it right where it was and put her other hand in Jake's, too, Tabitha drew it away. "I'm okay."

"You sure?"

She nodded, hoping she looked convincing. Again she felt compelled to tell him, "I'm certified in crisis management, you know. I took a weekend seminar at Dallas General a couple of years ago."

"Them weekend seminars ain't worth sh—"

"That's great." Jake threw a nasty look at the middle-aged officer who'd spoken, then leaned against the edge of her desk, returning his attention to her. "You'll do just fine. We're going to get them back. I have a very good feeling about this case."

"You do?"

He nodded. "We're going to be proactive, though, which means you've got to put yourself in the spotlight. Can you handle it?"

She took a deep breath, and gathered her inner strength. "Of course. I have to, don't I?"

"If you really think you—"

"What do I need to do?"

He smiled. "If you're up to it, then I'll schedule a press conference for seven o'clock. That'll give us time to prepare and the news agencies plenty of time to get it on the air for the ten-o'clock news.''

"What do I say?'' Tabitha asked.

"You're going to make it absolutely clear that you're willing to negotiate. You're not going to promise Hines a baby. You're going to be vague on exactly what you'll give him, but you want to make him believe that the options are open. He doesn't have to do anything stupid. You've got to sound like his only friend in the world. Can you do that?''

"I think so.'' She placed her shoulders back against the chair. "Yes. I can. Definitely.''

His smile was warm and proud. "Good girl. And don't worry. We'll have a carefully worded statement for you before then.''

He straightened and turned to bark orders to the officers there.

Tabitha couldn't help but be impressed with Jake's confidence, the depth of his knowledge and his ability to handle people.

He knew exactly what needed to be done and believed he could do it right. She hoped he could instill some of that confidence in her.

Left alone for a blessed minute, Tabitha rested her head against the high back of her chair and closed her eyes. She tried to concentrate on her mantra so she could find serenity, but serenity was elusive. Heck, concentration was elusive.

Too much had happened in too short a period of time. Her emotions were on overload, and her brain was in danger of shorting out.

"You asleep?''

Tabitha opened her eyes to see her secretary's gray head poking in the doorway. "I wonder if I'll ever sleep again. Every time I close my eyes, I see Caitlyn's face.''

With a sympathetic expression, Marie pushed the door

open and walked in. "It's awful. I still can't believe something like this happened in Mission Creek, of all places."

Tabitha sighed. "Crazy people are everywhere."

"That's for sure." She laid a piece of paper on the desk in front of Tabitha. "I brought the statement for you to look over. Chief White and his men finished it a few minutes ago."

Tabitha picked it up. "It's great of you to come in on a Saturday, Marie. Especially since this is Labor Day weekend."

"Oh, pooh. The only plans I had were sitting in Harry's bass boat and watching him fish. I'm just glad I could do something to help, even in a small way."

"You just being here helps a lot. Thanks." Tabitha began reading the statement she was to give in a few hours, but sensed Marie watching her. "Is there something else?"

"Can I run out and get you something to eat? Knowing you, you haven't eaten all day."

"No, I couldn't possibly eat anything. But thanks."

Marie nodded. "Maybe that nice Chief White will take you out after the press conference."

Tabitha shook her head. "I'll probably be here at the hospital until we get Caitlyn and Dr. Walters back."

"I don't think so. They're setting up taps on the phones at your house. Why would they do that unless you'll be going home?"

Why, indeed? "When are they going to do that?"

"Oh, they're doing it now. When you were in here earlier having that conference with Chief White and the others, Daniel Hammel—you know, Bessie's boy? He joined the police force a couple of years ago. He's into all that technical stuff. Anyhoo, he asked if I knew where you kept your keys. They wanted to get started and didn't know how long you'd be, so I gave them the spares you keep in my desk. I hope that's all right."

''You know the officer who asked you for them. You're sure he's all right?''

''Bless me, yes! Daniel goes deer hunting with my youngest son, Cody. Don't worry. He's not going to rifle through your underwear drawer or anything.''

''I wasn't worried about that.''

''Now that Chief White...'' Marie wiggled her eyebrows. ''The way he looks at you, I'd say he wants to do more than rifle through your drawers.''

''Wha—?'' Tabitha cleared her throat. ''What makes you say something like that?''

''I know the look a man gives a woman when he's hot for her.''

''Marie! You're expecting your first grandchild.''

''So? I wouldn't be if I hadn't been given that look once or twice.''

Tabitha felt heat stinging her cheeks and lowered her gaze to the paper in her hands to hide her fierce blush. She tried to make her voice cool. ''I'm sure you're mistaken about Chief White. Thanks for typing this. I need to read over it so I—''

''If I'm mistaken, then pigs don't wallow in mud. You never believe me when I tell you certain men would like to get to know you better, even though there have been several in here who have. Jake White is one of them. I'd stake my great-grandmama's tea biscuit recipe on it.''

Tabitha rolled her eyes. ''Marie, this is not the time or place for romance. Two employees of the hospital have been kidnapped. They're in a great deal of danger. I can't be thinking about who has or does not have the hots for me. And Chief White is much too professional a police officer—'' her voice almost cracked at the lie ''—to make a move even if he were interested.''

''I know what's going on with poor Cait and Sam,'' Marie said without shame. ''But sometimes love springs on you when you least expect it. I met my Harry at my granddaddy's funeral."

"Jake is *not* in love with me, Marie."

"Oh, it's Jake already, is it?"

"Marie, please. I need to read over this statement."

"All right, I'm going." But she muttered as she left. "How am I ever going to get her married off when she won't see what God sets down right in front of her?"

Tabitha stared at the laser-printed words Jake had no doubt written, but she didn't see them. If Marie had picked up on the tension between her and Jake, then others would, too, eventually. Marie seemed to have a homing instinct for men who were attracted to Tabitha, and wasn't shy about pointing them out. Tabitha could sense their interest, but it made her deal with them even more impersonally than she would normally have.

This was a recurring theme in Tabitha's life. Men would show an interest, and she would run the other way. Or more like it, push them away.

It wasn't hard to figure out why. What her father hadn't accomplished, Scott had. Scott was the only halfway serious boyfriend she'd ever had. But he'd turned out to be just like her father.

Both of them had been abusive—mentally and physically. Neither of them had loved her. Neither of them had wanted her love.

So now she pushed men away before they got close enough to push her. She recognized the habit, and had tried more than once to stop doing it so she could have a normal, meaningful relationship.

But she couldn't stop. Self-preservation was too deeply ingrained in her psyche. She simply didn't know how.

Tabitha straightened her spine.

This, however, was neither the time nor the place—nor

the man—to worry about any of that. Not only were there much more important things to worry about, Jake was a cop.

Sewer rats were higher on the list of desirable males than cops.

Satisfied with her decision and the strength of her resolve, Tabitha forced her eyes to focus on the words she had to say to the world.

Three

Jake knocked on Tabitha's closed door, but there was so much noise in the outer office he couldn't hear if she replied.

"It's okay, Chief White," Marie told him. "She's doing some paperwork to keep her mind off…you know. Go on in."

Jake smiled at the secretary. "Thanks, Marie. You've been a big help."

"Just doing my bit," she said. "Glad you noticed."

"Noticed? Anything my men need, you see that they get, from coffee to additional electrical outlets. You're greasing the wheels around here, and everything's running smoother because of you. So, hell, yes, I've noticed."

Beaming, Marie nodded toward Tabitha's office. "She helped, too, you know, by posting an announcement to all hospital employees to cooperate with me—and you, of course. Anyhoo, that's how come I'm so greasy."

Jake chuckled.

"Can I get you anything?" she asked.

He shook his head and pushed open Tabitha's door. "I'm good, thanks."

As he entered, he heard Marie mumble just loud enough for him to hear, "Yessir, I'll just bet you are."

Jake grinned. Older women who flirted always brightened his day.

As soon as Jake closed the door, he felt as if he'd stepped into another world. The command center in the office outside was loud and hot and filled with men checking the status of the search operation. Tabitha's office was cool and serene, the only noise the quiet hum of the aquarium pump and the trickle of water in the various fountains. The only person in the room was a beautiful woman who looked at him expectantly.

"Honey, I'm home." Jake was amazed at the words that popped into his head and out his mouth at the same time. How was it possible that they felt right?

She raised a pale brow. "Oh, good, dear. You're just in time to cook supper."

He grinned and pushed away from the door. God, he loved women with quick minds. "Have hot plate, will cook."

She blinked. "You cook?"

"I can heat up a can of soup with the best of them." He relaxed into one of the comfortable chairs facing her desk. He was not one to take it easy on the job, but it felt good to sit down.

"Right in the can, no doubt."

"Whatever works."

She stared at him for a long minute, then said, "Well?"

He sighed. His mind had been off the case for all of a minute. Too much to ask, he supposed, to have it stay there. He straightened in the chair. "We've found the abandoned ambulance on a dirt road several miles southeast of town. There were tire tracks nearby that do not match the tread on the ambulance's. They're being checked out."

"Checked for what?"

"To see what kind of tires they are. Make, model, how long they've been there. You can tell a lot from tire tracks."

"You think they're from Hines's car, then."

"Possibly, although the only vehicle he owns has an alibi."

"His *car* has an alibi?"

Jake nodded. "A questionable one. Mrs. Hines swears she was visiting her mother at a nursing home in Laredo. Trouble is, we can't get any witnesses to corroborate her story. Her mother's room is the first one by an exit that Mrs. Hines said is usually propped open, even though the home's policy is for visitors to check in. She says she came and went through that door, and didn't see anyone."

"What about her mother?"

Jake shook his head. "Alzheimer's."

"Do you believe her?"

"Don't have any choice at the moment. She's never been tied to any of Hines's crimes, and we haven't found a witness to place her here at the hospital."

Tabitha leaned back in her chair. "Humph. I wish you'd given me a go at her."

Jake grinned. "Catfight?"

She snorted in disgust. "Is there a man on this planet who doesn't like to see two women together?"

"Probably, but I've never met him."

Returning to serious, she straightened. "I'm pretty good at getting information out of people. You have to be, in this job."

"I've already given orders to have Mrs. Hines brought back in. I want to question her myself. Want to sit in?"

Tabitha brightened. "Yes, of course. You can use my office."

He shrugged. "All right with me. I won't be the only one in here, so one more won't matter."

"I *do* have a stake in how this turns out, you know."

"I'm going to be questioning other people, as well, starting in about half an hour. Want to sit in on those, too?"

"Who?"

"Hospital employees, mostly."

"Then, yes, I certainly do. You might as well use my

office for all your interviews. I'm not getting any work done, and the atmosphere in here helps people relax."

He'd witnessed that effect himself. "Fine by me."

They fell silent for a long minute, then she asked, "So they're headed for the border, you think?"

"Maybe. I never make assumptions. He might have gone that way to throw us off track, to make us concentrate there while he heads another way. We're continuing the search in all directions. We finally got a helicopter. The FBI brought it in from Houston. They're making concentric circles around Mission Creek."

"The FBI is involved now?"

"They're lending support. Mission Creek PD still has command."

"All right." She gave him a cool smile. "Sounds as if you've got things under control. At least as much as it can be under the circumstances. Thank you, Chief White."

He wanted to wipe all that professionalism right off her face. But he didn't. Not only had he sworn to her, and to himself, to behave, there was also too much to do.

Suddenly the tranquillity filling the room was oppressive, and he stood. He needed demanding, restless energy, not all this hocus-pocus. "Just doing my job, lady. Speaking of which, I'll get back to it."

"Yeah?"

Jake smiled at the familiar voice and shifted the phone so he could talk into the mouthpiece. Finally something was going right. "Kind of an informal greeting for the Houston PD's tech department, isn't it, P.C.?"

The technical wizard's real name was Paul Conlee, but everyone called him P.C. because he couldn't breathe unless it was through a computer.

"Hey, I know that voice. Jake, my man! How are you?"

Before Jake could reply, P.C. continued. "Wait a minute." Suddenly P.C.'s voice became excited. "I know why you called. From what I heard on the radio, you've got trouble. What do you need?"

"Got any surveillance equipment to spare?" Jake leaned back in the secretary's chair. Marie was out tracking down sandwiches for some of his men. "You wouldn't believe the antiquated stuff we have here. I swear, they bought it in Eisenhower's administration. To record a phone conversation, you have to flip a switch, and the tracing equipment takes three minutes. My only hope is that the perp is stupid enough to call from a phone that'll give an ID."

"Sure, man, we can lend you whatever you need. Only trouble is, we can't get it to you until probably Monday morning."

"Monday? Why the hell not?"

"We're short staffed. There's a three-day virus going around the department. I had it a couple of days ago and puked my guts out for a full—"

"You can skip the gory details." Jake drove a hand back through his hair. "If Monday's the best you can do, it's the best you can do."

"I'd drive it over there myself, man, but I'm still weak from the bug. The only reason I came into work is that no one else showed up in my department."

"That's okay, P.C. We'll get by. It's not as if we don't have any equipment. I'd ask the Feds, but they'd insist on manning their own gear since none of my men have been trained on it. And Burl wants to keep them out of our hair as much as possible. We borrowed a chopper from them. That's as far as he wants to go at the moment."

"Hey, man, I'm with you there. I'll get you state-of-the-art as soon as I can."

"Thanks, P.C."

"No sweat. That it?"

Jake hesitated, then asked, "Is Hackleman in today?"

"I don't know. I'll transfer you up there and you can see."

"Thanks."

Two rings later, a gruff voice answered, "Hackleman."

Jake swiveled the chair so he was facing away from the room full of Mission Creek officers. "Hey, Bill. This is Jake White."

"Well, well, well. You're in a crock of it over there, aren't you?"

Jake heard a distinct creak and could picture Bill leaning back in his chair so far you'd swear it was going to tip. Some things never changed.

"I've got it under control."

"Yeah, you're good at that, aren't you? What can I do you for?"

"You worked for the Dallas PD, didn't you?"

"I've been in Houston for fifteen years, so it's been a while. What ya need?"

"Did you know an officer named Al Monroe?"

"Sounds vaguely familiar. Why?"

"I just need some background on the hospital administrator here. She's Al's daughter. She hates cops and I think her father's the reason. You know me. I want all the information possible. This'll help to know what I'm dealing with."

"I'll have to make a few phone calls."

"I'd appreciate it."

"No sweat, pal. Good luck over there."

"Thanks. I've got a feeling I'm going to need all the luck I can get." Jake stared at the phone as he set it in the cradle.

He firmly reminded himself that he hadn't asked Bill for the information for personal reasons. He had a sound basis for wanting to know about Tabitha's father. Knowing as much as possible about the people he was dealing with—on both ends of the spectrum—could make a crucial difference at some point in the case. And Tabitha was a key player.

If only he could be a little more convincing.

Two seconds later Jake was still staring at the phone when it rang. The secretary had a sophisticated enough phone that it gave the caller's identification on a single-line screen across the top.

Unknown name. Unknown number.

Hines, perhaps? Using an over-the-counter calling card? Anyone could pick one up at a Wal-Mart or quick-stop gas station.

"This might be him, men," Jake said in a loud, attention-getting voice. "You ready?"

Dan Hammel, Mission Creek's version of P.C., snapped earphones into place and poised his hand over the switch.

"That's him?" Tabitha's breathless voice asked from the door.

Jake turned to find her beautiful blue eyes unnaturally wide, and her face white from a sudden lack of blood.

He tossed his head at her office. "I want you to answer it in there."

She spun and ran back to her desk.

"Wait to pick up until I signal you," he called after her.

He stood in the door between the two offices and, on the third ring, he pointed at Dan, who flipped the switch. Jake nodded at Tabitha, then walked into her office. He was followed by several of his men.

Tabitha took a deep breath, calming herself. Several emotions screamed through her. Now that the moment was at hand, she was frightened at the prospect of talking to Hines. She was also nervous. So much so, her hand trembled when she reached for the phone. The conversation was being recorded, so everyone in the world would know if she made the tiniest mistake.

But underlying everything was enough anger at the stupid, selfish man who thought he could intimidate an entire town into giving him what he wanted that her voice was strong when she gave her standard greeting.

"Tabitha Monroe. Can I help you?"

"Hello, Miss Monroe. This is Hank Haynes of the National Syndicated Press. I'd like to ask you a few questions, if I may. First, what are the chances of..."

The tension leaving her in a whoosh, Tabitha held the phone away from her ear and told Jake, "It's a reporter."

Anger flashed across his face. "The hell it is. I ordered them to stay off your line."

"What should I say?"

"Tell him to be at the press conference at seven. Say nothing else."

Tabitha complied, then hung up the phone on a man still trying to weasel a couple of answers from her. "Why do they do that?"

He came closer. "Some of them think they're above the law, but they'll find out different at the press conference when I promise expulsion for every reporter calling this number."

"Thank you." She relaxed against her leather chair as the other officers filed out, grumbling.

"You as disappointed as they are?" Jake asked.

She focused on his face. "A little, I guess. It would be nice to have this over. But I'm relieved, too."

He nodded in understanding, then made his way around her desk.

Alarmed, she stiffened upright.

Stopping behind her chair, Jake placed his hands on her shoulders. ''Sit back and relax.''

He gently tried to coax her shoulders back, but didn't force her.

''I am relaxed.''

''So relaxed your shoulders feel like concrete.'' He began to knead them.

''You surprised me is— Oh, that feels good.''

''Then lean back and enjoy it.'' There was a smile in his voice.

After a few seconds Tabitha closed her eyes. No one had ever done this for her, except when she'd paid for it. But this felt much, much better than any formal massage she'd ever had. This felt like liquid heat pouring down her body. She refused to think about whether it was from the kneading action of the hands on her shoulders, or *whose* hands were on her shoulders.

When his fingers climbed up her neck, she let her head loll forward. ''Where did you learn to do this?''

''I don't know. Picked it up somewhere along the way.''

''Do all the women you've—''

''Shh. Relax.''

Tabitha was a little miffed at him for implying she wasn't relaxed, when she'd never felt this loose in her life. ''You're not exactly Mr. Tranquillity, you know. Did you sit down one time today?''

''I sat down twice.''

''Humph. Maybe *you* need a massage.''

His hands paused briefly. ''You offering?''

Tabitha's eyes popped open at the image that flashed into her mind. Suddenly warmth flowed from more places than his hands. Jeez. She'd walked right into that one.

''In your dreams, copper.''

He chuckled and continued massaging.

* * *

"You were alone in the laundry room when Hines came down the chute?" Jake didn't even wait until the next hospital employee, the hospital's laundry room supervisor, was fully in his seat.

Raul Hernandez cast a surprised glance at Tabitha. He was the third hospital employee interviewed and if this one went like the last two, she felt sincere sympathy for the second-generation Mexican-American.

She gave Raul an encouraging nod.

He turned to Jake. "Yes, sir, I was alone. The staff had gone home for the day. The laundry is staffed seven days a week, but only eight hours a day."

"Why were you there at 5:30 p.m.?" Jake asked.

"I had paperwork," Raul explained. "There's a lot to do now that I'm boss."

Jake echoed on his comment, letting it trail off, suggesting more. "A lot to do...?"

Raul frowned and glanced at Tabitha again. "Sir, if you're thinking I helped the kidnapper, you're wrong. I didn't have time to do nothing. I was in my office in the back when I heard voices. Loud voices, arguing."

"And what did you do?"

"Well, I was about to come out of my office to see what was going on, but I saw a man with a gun. He was standing by the bin under the laundry chute, holding a gun on a doctor and a nurse. They was climbing out of the bin. When they got out, he handcuffed them together."

"Dr. Walters and Nurse Matthews were arguing with him?"

Raul shook his head. "No, sir. There was someone else there. A woman. But from where I was, I couldn't see her. He was arguing with her."

Jake straightened. "This other woman...was it Mrs. Hines?"

"I don't know Mrs. Hines. And like I said, I couldn't see the woman. She was standing by the door to the hall."

"You said she was arguing with Hines. What did she say?"

"Not a lot. She sounded nervous, and real mad. She kept telling Hines to hurry up."

Jake paused, as if mulling over Raul's answer, then asked, "You're sure Hines didn't see you?"

"Well, sir, I'm thinking if he had, I wouldn't be sitting here right now."

"So you're saying you didn't help him in any way."

Raul glanced at Tabitha again.

"Miss Monroe is not going to give you the answers, Hernandez," Jake said harshly.

"No, sir. I know. I just..." Raul was clearly confused. "No, sir. I didn't help him. I waited in my office until they was gone."

"Where did they go?"

With wide eyes, Raul lifted his hands. "How should I know that? All I know is they left, and I was happy they didn't see me."

"Then what?"

"Then I called security to tell them what happened, and they told me the guy had kidnapped the nurse and doctor. They told me not to go home, and I didn't until he told me I could." Raul twisted in his seat to point at one of the officers behind him.

The officer nodded.

Jake studied Raul, making the air so thick with tension, Tabitha felt compelled to speak for her employee. "Raul is an excellent employee and supervisor. I have heard nothing but the highest praise from the people under him."

Jake frowned her into silence, then looked over Raul's

shoulders at two officers sitting on the red couch. "That jibe with your version?"

The older one nodded. "He's consistent on every detail."

Jake nodded and turned back to Raul. "Can you remember anything Hines or the woman said about where he might be going?"

Raul shook his head regretfully. "Not that I can remember."

"Did he seem confident that he had a way to escape?"

"I didn't hear much, but from what I could tell, the guy is too crazy to think that far ahead."

Jake once again consulted the officers. "Can you think of anything else?"

They both shook their heads.

"Thanks, Mr. Hernandez. That'll be all."

"I didn't help the crazy guy."

Jake seemed surprised at Raul's cry of innocence. "Okay. If you remember anything you think might be relevant, let us know."

"I will." Raul stood. "I want the crazy guy to be caught."

"I know. We all do." Jake walked Raul to the office door.

"Thank you, Raul," Tabitha called after him. She didn't care whether Jake disapproved or not. She was not going to let Raul think she considered him guilty of anything.

Raul turned. "I want to help any way I can, Miss Monroe."

"I know. You helped a lot. The police are just trying to piece everything together. Why don't you go on home?"

He shook his head vehemently. "There's too much work to do."

"You're a good man, Raul Hernandez."

His relief was evident in his smile. "Thank you, Miss Monroe."

"I'll see you later."

When Jake had closed the door behind Raul, he turned back to the other officers. "Who's next?"

The older man consulted a clipboard on his lap. "A Mrs. Juanita Applebaum. She was one of the—"

"Hey, Chief."

Jake turned to the officer who'd stuck his head in the door. "Yeah?"

"Mrs. Hines is on her way. She should be here in about twenty minutes."

"Good. Have her wait in the outer office when she gets here." Jake turned back to the officers in the room. "We'll have Mrs. Applebaum come back tomorrow."

The younger one stood. "Good. I need to, uh, stretch my legs anyway."

"Me, too." The older man stood with a little more difficulty and followed the other out the door.

"What about you?" Jake asked Tabitha.

"I'm fine."

He meandered over and slumped in one of the chairs facing her desk. Rubbing his hands down his face, he asked, "Isn't this day over yet?"

She glanced at the clock on her desk. "It's barely five o'clock."

He groaned. "We still have a press conference to get through."

"Yes, we do."

He sighed, then stood suddenly and began to pace in front of her desk.

She frowned. He couldn't sit still for long. She watched him for several minutes, then finally asked the question that had been burning inside her since the first interview. "Why do you do that?"

He stopped dead and looked at her, obviously surprised. "Do what?"

"You've treated everyone you've questioned today as if they've done something wrong. These are all good people. They would never have helped Hines in any way."

His face hardened. "You can never be sure."

"Probably the worst thing Raul's done in his life is drive without a seat belt."

"In my line of work I rarely come across a person who has done nothing wrong."

"So everyone is guilty and has to prove that they're innocent? Remember a little something called the Constitution? It guarantees that Americans will be considered innocent until proved guilty."

He started pacing again. "I didn't say they were guilty."

"That's the way you act. It's what you make them think."

"They need to believe that I'm serious."

"You're scaring them half to death."

"It never hurts to put the fear of God into people."

She shook her head. "You are such a cop."

He stopped pacing. "What's that supposed to mean?"

"You exist in the shadows, seeing only the black in the world. You believe everyone is bad, that the world is screwed up and you're the only one who can clean up the mess."

He lifted his chin. "You make it sound as if I think I'm some superhero or something."

She quirked a brow. "If the cape fits..."

"Oh, give me a break. We have a deadly serious situation here. I should be acting like a clown?"

"You should be acting as if you don't think the entire hospital staff is Branson Hines's accomplice. Ever hear the expression, 'You catch a lot more flies with honey than with vinegar'?"

"Your point?"

"You'll get much more information out of people if you make them relax. When you hang a sword over people's heads with a thread and then growl in their face, the only thing they can think of is getting the hell out of here."

"My methods have worked until now."

She leaned back, shaking her head. "Where do they get you guys? Some tin-star factory that cranks out the same model each year? Or do you have to work at it? Do they have mandatory insensitivity training classes for cops?"

He leaned stiff arms on the front of her desk. "Why do you hate cops so much? What did we ever do to you?"

Tabitha felt her face tighten. "It doesn't matter now."

"Obviously, it does."

She glared at him. He glared back.

She was the first to look away. "Suffice it to say, this is as close to a cop as I ever want to get."

Four

What a waste of time.

Jake leaned against Tabitha's heavy oak desk as he listened to Deena Hines's whining monologue about the travails of being the wife of a convict. She should have been a country-western songwriter.

No. Country-western singer. This woman was too vain to do anything that wasn't in some spotlight.

Except maybe help her husband escape.

Jake didn't believe a word of her story, though it wasn't because of her appearance. Even at thirty, she looked as if she hadn't quite grown up yet. She was only five-three, and thin with an underdeveloped figure. At least for his tastes. Her big blue eyes looked out from a pale, elfin face that could almost convince the hardest cop she'd never done anything worse in her life than ride her bike on the wrong side of the street.

His disbelief didn't come from inconsistencies, either. He'd questioned her as harshly as he'd questioned any of the witnesses, but Mrs. Hines was sticking to her original alibi like a tick to a dog. And since they couldn't place her at the scene, they couldn't arrest her…although Jake wanted to, just to shut her up.

No, the skepticism Jake felt wasn't something he could put his finger on. It came from his gut. There was something crafty about this chirping, childlike woman with a thick Texas drawl. Something just didn't fit.

As she droned on, Jake glanced at the officers on the red

couch. Lieutenant Edwards, the older one, rolled his eyes. He'd stopped taking notes fifteen minutes ago. Lieutenant Jamieson just shook his head.

Jake looked over his shoulder at Tabitha, who sat behind her desk. She, on the other hand, was listening intently to Deena Hines, and the woman had fixed her attention on Tabitha's sympathetic ear. Was she really buying the horse manure this woman was shoveling at them?

As if feeling his eyes on her, Tabitha glanced up at him. With the tiniest of movements, she flicked her eyes toward the door.

She wanted him to leave her alone with this woman? Why? He hadn't been able to get any information out of Deena Hines, and he was a highly trained interrogator.

With a quick look, Jake ascertained that neither Mrs. Hines nor his men had noticed Tabitha's gesture.

He glanced back at her with a quirked brow. Did she think she could do better than him?

Tabitha, however, had already returned her attention to Mrs. Hines.

What the hell. He sure wasn't getting anything useful from the woman. Might as well let Tabitha try. They had nothing to lose.

Jake straightened away from the desk.

Deena stopped in midsentence. "What?"

"Please wait here, Mrs. Hines. My men and I need to talk." He looked at the officers on the couch. "Edwards, Jamieson. Conference."

"What did I say?" Deena asked Tabitha as he ushered his men out. "I didn't say anything."

"Don't worry about them," Tabitha said. "Men are all the same."

"Oh, isn't that the truth."

Pausing at the door, Jake glanced back into the room. Tabitha had moved around her desk to sit in the chair next to Deena. Jake couldn't hear what they were saying and couldn't even watch their faces, since they were facing the desk with their backs toward the door.

So he closed it and turned to find his men watching him expectantly. "Quiet, everyone."

"Should I cut off the tape recorder?" Dan Hammel asked.

Jake shook his head. "In fact, can you turn the speakers on? Softly."

Dan hung the earphones around his neck, then unplugged them. With another flip of a switch on the reel-to-reel tape recorder, the speakers blared into the room.

"Are you married?" Deena shouted through them.

Dan quickly turned the volume down. "Sorry."

"Jeez, Hammel," Jamieson whispered loudly, knocking a hand against the tech's head. "You got wax in your ears or something?"

"The headphones aren't working right. I had to turn the volume up to hear anything."

"What was that?" Deena asked over the speakers.

"Who knows?" Tabitha said without apparent concern. "Chief White is probably yelling at his men for something. He does that a lot."

The officers in the room grinned at Jake at this blatant misinformation. He just shook his head. At least Tabitha hadn't said anything about being recorded. That would shut Mrs. Hines up entirely.

Tabitha resumed their conversation. "No, Deena," she responded to the woman's question. "I'm not married. But my mother died when I was born, and I grew up having to take care of my father."

Jake perked up without being obvious. Is that why she hated cops? Had Al Monroe been too demanding? This could be better than any report from Hackleman.

He plopped down in the secretary's chair, which his men had left vacant for him, it being the closest to Tabitha's door.

Marie's husband had called just before Mrs. Hines had arrived, back from his fishing trip at the Falcon Reservoir. They were having a family get-together that evening, so Tabitha had insisted her secretary go home.

"My daddy..." Deena's voice lowered. "Daddy used to beat me."

"Oh, Deena, I'm sorry," Tabitha said. "Did you tell anyone?"

"Nobody cared back then. We were from the wrong side of the tracks, you see. My father was drunk half the time and out of work. We lived on what my mother made as a waitress at the Saddlebag."

"We didn't have much money, either."

"Did your daddy beat you?"

Tabitha didn't say yes or no, just launched into a story about how her father made her cook supper for him every night. It had to be meat, a vegetable and some kind of potato, plus dessert and had to be on the table by the time he was ready to go to work. He worked the night shift.

Then Deena told Tabitha about Branson's sexual demands.

The two women exchanged men-are-the-scum-of-the-earth stories for another ten minutes.

Jake kept looking at his watch. Where was Tabitha going with this? She hadn't gotten one useful tidbit out of Mrs. Hines, and the press conference was scheduled to start in twenty minutes.

At a quarter till seven, he stood. It was time to go back in. Deena Hines was a tough nut to crack. It happened. Probably had sociopathic tendencies, which allowed her to believe the lies she spouted. If they were lies. There was always the remote possibility she was telling the truth.

He'd taken two steps toward the door when over the speaker, Deena said, "One time—that time he killed that ugly little whore—he made me bring him cooked meals every day. He said if the cops found him, they'd send me to jail, too, 'cause he'd tell them I helped him. It wasn't easy, not getting caught, I tell ya, driving out to that old abandoned shack every day."

Every man in the room froze.

"Get her to tell you about it," Edwards said under his breath.

"I'll bet the police were watching you, weren't they?" Tabitha asked.

"You bet your sweet tooth they were."

"Jeez. How far did you have to drive?"

"Twelve miles one way," Deena complained. "Out that old washed-out dirt road toward Oilton. Blew out two tires that I had to change myself."

"Yes!" Jamieson cried softly.

"Get on it," Jake told his men. "Maybe we'll have something to announce by the end of the press conference."

The outer office suddenly buzzed with activity.

"But quietly," he said. "In fact, take your radios down a couple of floors. I'm about to break this up, and I don't want Mrs. Hines to know she said anything."

Jamieson nodded at several officers and headed for the outside door.

"Find an empty room," Jake told him. "I don't want anyone overhearing. Some overzealous reporter might make it there before we do and ruin everything."

Jamieson acknowledged the order with an abbreviated salute and left with the men carrying radio equipment.

Jake turned to the more experienced Lieutenant Edwards. "I'll let you escort Mrs. Hines to her car since I've got to get Miss Monroe down to the press conference."

"Right."

Jake made a noisy entrance into Tabitha's office with Edwards following. "Sorry we took so long."

The two women stood and faced them.

He nodded to Deena Hines. "Thank you, Mrs. Hines, for your time. We're finished for now, but please don't leave town."

"Where am I gonna go?" she asked.

Jake nodded toward the door. "Lieutenant Edwards will see you to your car."

Tabitha gave Deena a brief hug. "Let me know if you need anything, okay?"

Deena hugged her back. "All right."

When Edwards had closed the door behind them, Jake beamed at Tabitha.

"What?" she asked.

He walked over and gave her a bear hug. "You're brilliant."

"Thank you." She quickly extracted herself and retreated behind her desk. "I told you I was good at getting information out of people."

"I have to admit I had my doubts when you were taking so long. But you lulled her into spilling something she never would have told me."

She seemed pleased by his praise, hiding a small smile by looking down at her desk. "I told you that you can catch more flies with honey than vinegar."

"You sure did. I'll have to try it." Although he couldn't imagine himself doing what she'd done. Sweet and nice just wasn't his style. "One of these days."

She sat down. "You really should, you know."

He studied her beautiful, sexy face until she demanded, "What is it now?"

He sat then, too. "That kind of instinct can't be learned."

She lost her smile and a faraway expression stole across her face. "Yes, it can."

"Not from a mere job."

She took a moment to study him, then. Finally she said,

although the words seemed to be pried out of her, "I had to learn, early in life, how to read people."

When she didn't elaborate, he asked, "Why?"

"My, you're full of curiosity."

He lifted a shoulder. "I'd like to know."

Her gaze dropped to the ferocious red frog on the corner of her desk opposite the dragon.

"You said I needed to try buttering people up. Well, if it can be learned, I need to know how."

She glanced up, then down again. "My father."

"Your father taught you?"

"In a way."

Why was she being so closemouthed about this? She spouted enough of it when they were talking about him. "What way?"

"He..." She grabbed a pencil and began tapping it on the desk. "He was a cop."

He already knew that, of course, but he wanted to see how much more she would tell him. "A cop. Really? Here?"

She shook her head. "I'm from Dallas."

"So he was an officer in the Dallas Police Department?"

She nodded, still tapping.

God, they were so much alike. A few more personal questions, and he'd bet real money she'd be pacing. Though she was clearly uncomfortable, he couldn't stop. Something inside him needed to know. "He knew how to read people well, and he taught you?"

Suddenly she shoved back her chair and stood. "Don't we have a press conference to get to?"

"They won't start without us."

"Well, I need a few minutes to make myself presentable." She turned stiffly and headed for the private bathroom attached to her office.

"Vanity?" he called softly.

"I'm sure the hospital board would appreciate it if I looked my best." She pulled the door open and threw a glare over her shoulder. "You'll be in the spotlight, too, you know. You could stand to shave."

He rubbed the stubble on his chin. Because he'd been on vacation when all hell had broken loose—a vacation Burl had forced on him—he hadn't touched a razor in two days. "You offering to shave me?"

"Hmm." She gave him a considering once-over. "Placing a nice, sharp blade against your throat. Now there's a thought."

Somehow, he didn't feel threatened. "In the mood for a little blood, kitten?"

"Kitten?" She stiffened as her eyes widened in surprise, then narrowed. "I have never been—and never will be—anyone's kitten."

With that, she slammed the door behind her.

Jake was as surprised as Tabitha at the nickname that had popped out of his mouth. He'd never called any woman "kitten."

But he knew where the pet name came from, and it wasn't *Father Knows Best.* How many times had he read the phrase "sex kitten" with regard to Marilyn Monroe?

"Get a grip, White. She doesn't look *that* much like Marilyn." He shoved a hand through his hair. Fantasies were one thing, but this was not the time nor the place nor the woman. He had a job to do, damn it. He should go do it.

Tabitha walked into her office, alone for once. Jake had stopped to talk with several of his men in the hallway.

Sinking into her chair, she closed her eyes and sighed. Blissful quiet.

She'd held press conferences before, but never ones drawing national attention. Not ones with so many reporters from all over the country. Aggressive men and women who shouted questions at her from the minute she walked into the room until Jake escorted her out. The only times they were quiet were during her statement and while she and Jake answered questions.

"You done good."

Starting, she opened her eyes to find Jake in the doorway. Maybe getting her squeaky door fixed last week wasn't a good idea. "I was convincing enough?"

He moved into the room. "Cool and calm, yet sincere. Great job."

She couldn't help her smile. His praise was flattering, though, she reminded herself, his opinion mattered only because of his experience in these situations. "Thank you. I just wish we'd had some good news to tell them."

"Yeah. Wouldn't you know that shack Mrs. Hines told us about would turn up empty." He sat in one of the chairs facing her desk. "Tired?"

"It's been a long day."

"Yes, it has."

"So what happens now?" she asked.

"Unfortunately, that depends on Hines."

She groaned. "We wait."

"You hate it, don't you?"

"What?"

"Not being in control."

"Control of what?"

"Of anything—the situation, him... me."

She sat up straight. "I have absolutely no desire to control you."

"No?" he asked in pointedly disbelieving tones.

"No," she said firmly.

He smiled smugly, as if giving in to humor her. "The situation, then."

She hated being patronized. "Analyzing your opponent, Mr. Cop?"

"Opponent." He steepled his fingertips together. "An interesting choice of words."

"You've been nothing but adversarial since you walked into the press conference this morning."

"Adversaries don't kiss each other."

"Depends on how ruthless they are about gathering information, doesn't it?"

"Was your father ruthless?"

She leaned back stiffly, resting her hands on the arms of the chair. She tried taking a deep breath, but the satisfying whoosh of air deep in her lungs wouldn't come. He was just trying to push her buttons. "My father has nothing to do with this."

"No?"

"Why are you doing this? Are you *trying* to make me angry?"

He studied her for a minute, then asked, "Is it working?"

She blinked. "Is what working?"

He relaxed. "I was trying to take your mind off the stress."

"By giving me more?"

He chuckled. "You thrive on stress."

"What? Why would you say such a thing? You don't know me. We just met this morning."

He considered his answer a long minute before saying, "I *do* know you, because you're just like me."

"Just like you?" She waved her hands around the office. "Are you blind? Look around. What do you see?"

He made no attempt to look. "Whitewash."

"Whitewash? What does that mean?"

"We're both type A personalities. You just cover yours with a thin veneer of feng shui." He shifted his gaze around her desk. "No, make that a heavy coat of feng shui."

"We may both have type A personalities, but there's one huge difference between us. You're a workaholic. I'm a *re-*

covering workaholic. Have you made any attempt whatsoever to modify your type A lifestyle? Not that I can tell. But I have. What you see here is a conscious effort to change."

His gaze dropped to her hands, and he grinned.

She glanced down to find her fingers drumming on the leather chair arms. She grabbed the arms to stop her fingers.

"You hate that, too, don't you?"

She rolled her eyes. "What?"

"When you prove my point."

"Oh, shut up."

He crossed his hands behind his head, as if relaxed. But she knew he wasn't. "Besides, who said I want to change? Maybe I'm happy just the way I am."

"Then you'll be dead by the time you're fifty."

"Okay by me. Old cops are stuck behind a desk, anyway. I'd be dead inside, might as well be dead outside."

She studied his square-jawed, stubbled face. "That's all you are? A cop?"

He lifted his chin. "You bet your bamboo flutes."

She slowly shook her head. "That's the saddest thing I've ever heard."

It was his turn for narrowed eyes. "I doubt that."

"There's so much more to life than work."

"This from a woman with no hobbies, who's here at the hospital seven days a week?"

"No, I'm not. I take tai chi classes. I raise bonsai."

He stood and walked to the low files against the window and touched the pink azalea she had there. "You grew this?"

She swiveled in her chair. "Yes. I rooted it from a bush a friend of mine has in Dallas."

He squatted and studied it on eye level. "I've always loved bonsai."

Pleasure sent a calming elixir through her, which both surprised and irritated her. Why should she be happy that they had a common interest? A lot of people liked bonsai.

She donated several plants every year to the hospital bazaar and they sold very quickly, even though Crystal Bennett, her hospital fund-raiser, priced them far higher than they were worth.

Was she irritated by the fact they both admired bonsai? Or by the difficulty she was having keeping her gaze averted from Jake's thickly muscled legs clearly outlined by the pants stretched across them?

"My tae kwon do instructor grew bonsai." He looked at her, one eyebrow raised. "It takes a lot of patience."

She relaxed into a smile, not even caring that it probably appeared catty, especially when she said, "You hate it, don't you?"

"What?"

"When you prove my point."

He stood abruptly. "I'm hungry. Let's go get something to eat."

"Don't we have to stay here?"

"Why?"

"In case Branson Hines calls."

He shook his head. "He won't."

"How can you be sure?"

"I just am."

"But—"

"Even if he does, we're covered. Officer Hammel managed to get hold of a cell phone that can be recorded. He'll route the calls to it or to your house, which is also wired. I told you that, didn't I?'

"No. Marie told me."

"Oh. Sorry. Must've slipped my mind."

"I can't imagine why." She bent to open the drawer where she kept her purse. Her heart leaped, because Caitlyn's purse sat right beside hers. For a few minutes, she'd almost forgotten…

Damn Jake. He'd succeeded in distracting her. She'd proved *his* point again, but she wasn't going to let him know.

"What's wrong?" he asked.

She picked up both purses and placed them on her desk. "Nothing."

"You sure?"

"Yes."

"Okay. So where would you like to eat?"

She wrinkled her nose. "I don't think I can."

"Oh, yes, you *will.* You only ate two bites of your sandwich at lunch."

She stood in order to hide her frown. How had he noticed that? She almost pointed out that he'd had two sandwiches, not two bites, which was enough for both of them. But she realized in time how much that would reveal about her own overly astute observation. As a general rule, people noticed things like that about people they cared for.

So much for general rules.

"I'm too nervous to eat," she said. "But you go ahead. I've got something I need to do."

"What?"

"Caitlyn Matthews has a cat. I'm going by her apartment to see that it's been fed."

He seemed surprised. "Do you have a key?"

"I think so." She opened Caitlyn's purse and found a set of keys in the first place she looked, the inside pocket. "After Caitlyn was…after the incident, someone brought her purse to me for safekeeping."

"Let's go, then."

"You're going with me?"

He nodded. "Along with several squad cars."

"But I have my own car."

"Then I'll ride with you."

Five

Jake insisted on driving, even though it was Tabitha's car. He didn't think they'd have to resort to evasive maneuvers, but if they did he needed to be in control. He didn't tell her about the danger, of course, because the possibility was so remote.

To approach her in person with so many police around, Hines would have to be much more aggressive than his profile indicated. He seemed to be the kind of criminal who preferred slinking through the shadows.

Jake was surprised when Tabitha didn't put up a fight, just handed him the keys with a sigh.

Caitlyn Matthews lived in a small garage apartment in an older neighborhood of Mission Creek, just a few blocks from downtown. Her landlady was a Mrs. Brody, who'd lived in the house in front of the garage since she married nearly fifty years ago. The two-story white frame house had been built around the time of World War I. The ground floor had a deep shady porch that wrapped all the way around.

Euclid was a quiet street, with many older residents like Mrs. Brody who knew who belonged there and who didn't.

Jake approved of that. Neighbors who watched out for each other kept crime down, and older people had little else to do but watch what went on around them.

Even so, he paused to glance around before pulling into the driveway. The sun had almost disappeared below the horizon, leaving the gray light of dusk. Streetlights had already come on, throwing shadows across the yards.

A squad car waited on either end of the street and officers would watch for anyone heading toward the house. Jake had his cell phone attached to his belt so he could be warned if anyone remotely matching Hines's description turned down Euclid Street.

"What's wrong?" Tabitha asked from the passenger seat.

"Nothing." He finally pulled into the driveway. "Just looking around."

Mrs. Brody's back light was on as they came along the driveway. She waved from her back porch when they pulled up to the stairs leading to Caitlyn's apartment.

"Hello, Mrs. Brody," Tabitha called as she got out of the car. "You doing okay?"

"Oh, I'm tolerable well, but what happened to poor Cait is just awful." The older woman took the steps down from the porch very slowly. "I've never heard of such goings-on. Not in Mission Creek. And I've lived here all my life."

"Mrs. Brody, this is Jake White, the Assistant Police Chief. He's in charge of the rescue effort."

"You the one responsible for all this, young man?" Mrs. Brody asked.

"Well, ma'am, I'm not the one responsible for it happening, but I'm the one responsible for cleaning up the mess."

"Well, I reckon you've got the experience to handle it." She turned to Tabitha. "And I reckon you need me to let you in."

"Actually, Mrs. Brody, I have Caitlyn's keys. She was on the floor when it happened, so her purse was at the nurses' stand. One of the other nurses on the shift brought it to me for safekeeping." Tabitha drew Caitlyn's keys from her own purse. "But I don't know which key it is. Can you show me?"

Mrs. Brody's age-spotted, gnarly hands picked out a gold-toned key with a crisscross top. "There it is. Glad you got it. It's not easy for these old bones to climb those steep stairs.

I'll just get on back to my supper. I always eat at six, you know. Have y'all had something to eat?"

"We're fine, Mrs. Brody. Please go back to your supper," Tabitha said. "We're just going to make sure Billy's okay."

"All right, then. Let me know if y'all need anything." The old woman turned to climb the four steps leading up to her porch.

Jake and Tabitha headed toward the garage. The light on the landing into Caitlyn's apartment had come on while they were talking to Mrs. Brody. Light- or motion-activated, no doubt.

"Why did you say we're fine?" Jake asked. "I'm starving, and I'll bet she's a great cook."

"You're right, she is." Tabitha paused on the first step. "The devil's food cake she brings to the hospital bake sale would make you drool on sight. But if we ate her food, she wouldn't be able to feed herself anything but crackers for a week. She's a widow on a fixed income. She has it very hard."

Jake peered through the dim light at the house. He'd been too busy earlier checking for possible threats to notice the subtle signs of neglect—peeling paint, patched roof, missing shutters.

"You coming?"

He turned to see Tabitha halfway up the stairs. She'd twisted to look back over her shoulder, and the angle made her silk suit swath around every curve of her lithe, luscious body.

Suddenly Jake's hunger changed to a different kind altogether.

What he wouldn't give to see Tabitha in a white silk dress like Marilyn wore in *The Seven Year Itch.* The desire was so strong, he actually wondered where he could buy one.

Realizing how far he was letting his fantasies go, he shook his head. He was *not* going to get in deep enough to buy

Tabitha anything beyond dinner—and that he could charge to the department. The more time he spent with her, the more he knew she was not a casual fling kind of woman. And he certainly wasn't a permanent relationship kind of man.

"Yeah, I'm coming. Don't go in without me."

She continued up the stairs. "Going to protect me from the big, bad cat?"

"If I—" Jake's retort was choked off as his gaze lifted and landed on her bottom.

With each step Tabitha took, silk stretched across first one round, firm cheek, then the other.

He couldn't move, couldn't speak, couldn't think. All he could do was watch as each step she gained sent torturous waves of heat firing through him.

Finally she reached the top and turned. "Well?"

Jake swallowed hard. And he'd thought she was sexy just standing there. Climbing the stairs, she was the most arousing sight he'd ever seen.

He had to get a grip on himself, though the grip he wanted was her sweet little—

"Are you coming or not?"

Damn, it was going to be a long night.

"Almost," he said wryly, then took the stairs two at a time, thanking God and every angel watching over him that she didn't understand the double meaning.

She gave him an odd look—making him wonder if she had—then she seemed to dismiss him as she turned and held the screen door open with her hip so she could fit the key into the lock. "I don't want to hold the door open too long. We might let the cat out."

Jake drew his gun from the holster at his back.

Tabitha frowned at the gun. "Is that necessary? Billy is big, as cats go, but I think you can take him."

He grinned. Damn, she was fun, and in the way he liked best—smart and sassy. "You can never be too careful. Okay.

Push the door open, but stay out here until I give you the all clear."

She shoved the door open, then let the screen close behind him.

Jake stepped into the living room, giving the room a quick sweep, then performed the same search on the bedroom after flipping on the lights in the bathroom and closet that separated them. Since the kitchen was part of the living room, divided from it by a counter, there were no more rooms left to search.

"All clear," he called, holstering his gun as he walked through the short hallway between the main rooms. "But I don't see any sign of a cat."

The screen door squeaked. "You probably scared the poor thing to death. He was expecting his mama to come through the door, and you jump in pointing a gun at him."

Jake stood in the doorway between the bedroom and living room, hands on his hips. "If I'd pointed my gun at any cat, I'd have seen him. What does he look like, anyway?"

Tabitha closed the wooden door behind her. "Kind of like Morris the cat. Remember on those commercials? He's big and orange and his name is Billy the Kid."

"Billy the Kid, huh? Maybe I need to keep my gun out."

"Whatever pulls your trigger." She bent to look under the coffee table. The pose wasn't blatantly sexy, but the way her skirt stretched across her bottom again reminded him of the stairs. "Here, Billy boy. Come here, sweet little kitty."

Jake groaned.

She peeked above the table. "Beg your pardon?"

"Nothing." He dragged his eyes away and forced them back to work.

Glancing around the room for a likely cat hole, he noticed the decor for the first time. The tiny apartment was actually quite inviting, in a homey way, especially for a garage apartment. The living room could have been in Ben Cartwright's house, if one of the Ponderosa sons had been a decorator.

Adam, maybe?

The rooms were filled with what looked like Western furniture and stuff, for want of a better word. Antiques, from the look of it.

"How well do you know Caitlyn Matthews?" Jake asked.

Tabitha pulled her head from the living room closet. "Not all that well, to tell you the truth, but probably as well as anyone. When she first moved to Mission Creek, I tried to make her feel welcome. She reminds me a lot of me at her age. She's just…not an easy person to get to know."

"Is all this stuff antique?" He picked up a pair of silver-mounted, hand-forged cowboy spurs with engraved iron rowels. "It looks like it could be, but if it is, she must've been dealing drugs out of the hospital pharmacy. Stuff like this doesn't come cheap."

"Here, kitty, kitty." Tabitha opened a kitchen cabinet. "I know there's a cat here somewhere. His bowl still has food in it." She opened the next cabinet. "I asked her about all these wonderful accent pieces when I came over the first time. She goes to a lot of garage and estate sales, all the ones she hears about within driving distance. Gets some amazing deals."

"Accent pieces. So that's what the term is for *stuff*." Jake headed for the closet. "What do you mean, you know her as well as anyone? Not a friendly woman?"

"No, not really," Tabitha said on her way into the bathroom, "though she's a wonderful nurse, and cute as a button. I'm sure you've seen her picture since all this happened."

He could hear the shower curtain holders scrape along the rod as she talked in a distracted way.

"But I don't think she dates at all. And she doesn't go out with friends to shop or eat or for a night at the Saddlebag. In fact, from what I can tell, she doesn't really have any friends.''

''Well, I can tell you one thing about her,'' Jake said from the closet.

''What?''

''She's more than a tad anal retentive. All her clothes are lined up by color. They're even arranged dark to light from left to right.''

He heard the linen closet open. ''Hmm. I knew she always kept her station neat. I thought maybe it was a fluke the way she has all her spices lined up in alphabetical order and her drinking glasses arranged according to height. And this... I can understand grouping your towels by color and size, but her bath oils and salts are arranged in alphabetical order according to scent. She has dental supplies all lined up, and makeup all in a row.'' The linen closet closed. ''Jeez. I thought I was bad.''

''You're just bad in another way,'' he said.

''Thanks.''

''You're welcome.'' He grinned as he pushed back Caitlyn's white clothes—mostly uniforms—to peer behind them. ''You'd probably have a place like this, too, if you didn't have a life.'' He straightened and thought about what he'd just said. ''You don't, do you?''

''What?''

''Have a place like this.''

''Well, I'm organized, but—'' Tabitha's thought broke off as they met in the short hallway, having finished searching their respective areas at the same time.

Her bluebonnet eyes were wide as they met Jake's, and he couldn't tear his away.

Time seemed suspended as their gazes held. God, she was sexy. He wanted to feel the little nub of that mole against his lips, and his tongue, and his—

She tore her gaze from his and turned toward the bedroom, but stopped dead in the doorway and sent a furtive glance over her shoulder.

Heat flashed through him, because her tiny gesture told him that she'd realized immediately what room she was in and all that it implied, which told him that her libido had taken the same path his had.

His first step toward her, which he was barely aware of taking, sent her scurrying to the far side of the room.

"Where is that cat?" She knelt beside the bed to look under it. "Billy? Where are you, kitty?"

"I found a cat carrier in the closet."

Her head popped above the mattress. "Do you think I should take him to my house?"

Jake lifted a shoulder. "Your call, but he'd probably be safer there."

She frowned. "You think Branson Hines is going to come here?"

"No, not Hines, but other lowlifes might. It's been known to happen. They know a place is empty, so they take advantage of it."

"That's despicable. To steal from someone who's been kidnapped. Can you imagine going through such an ordeal, and then coming home to find all your stuff is gone?"

"Breaking and entering's no fun for anyone, but I see your point." Jake took the near side of the room, peering under the pine chest of drawers. "Maybe she lets Billy outside during the day?"

"No. Cait never lets Billy outside."

"No claws?"

"Oh, he has claws. She's just afraid he'll run away."

Jake nodded, then looked under the bed, even though Tabitha already had. "He's got to be here somewhere."

"I'm sure he is. He's very good at hiding, though." She looked around, hands planted on her hips. "The first time I came here, it was half an hour before I saw him. Cait said that the first time people visit, he runs and hides, but he eventually comes out. I think he's okay after that. The second time I came over, he jumped on my lap as soon as I sat down. With Caitlyn, though, he comes running to greet her when she comes home."

"Just like a dog."

"Pretty much. He even comes to her when she calls him. Every time. It's amazing."

Jake stood and dusted off his hands, though just from habit. The floor was so clean he could eat off of it. "Why don't we sit in the living room, then, and wait a while. Maybe he'll come out and investigate."

She lifted a pale eyebrow. "How about that. Sometimes cops do have good ideas."

"Yeah, I've come up with one once or twice in my life." Jake waved an arm toward the door for her to precede him.

She grinned as she swept through. "Then I won't hold my breath for the next one."

Her sweet little bottom wiggled out the door. Was she doing it on purpose? He wondered if she knew how much she tempted him…and he wondered how much he tempted her.

Tabitha sat in a red leather chair with pine arms that had horse silhouettes in several different postures painted on them.

Jake sat gingerly on a red brocade settee, which looked as if it might break if he sat too hard. It didn't complain at his weight, though, so he leaned back.

He glanced up to find Tabitha grinning at him. "Am I amusing you?"

She tossed her head, making her curls bounce around her beautiful face. "Big men are so funny. Like a bull in a china shop."

"This place is so small and cramped," he complained. "And I'm not *that* big."

"Six-what? Two? Three?"

He stretched his arm along the back of the couch. "Three."

"About two hundred pounds?"

"Thereabouts." He slapped his stomach. "Solid muscle, of course."

She rolled her eyes. "Yeah, I know."

Just that quickly, she reminded him of the kiss they'd shared that morning. Shared, hell. Sizzled was more like it.

Jake wanted to kiss her again. He wished she was sitting beside him so he could pull her against his side. He'd rest his head on her soft blond hair and let his hand caress her shoulder, then—

Damn. He had to get his mind on other things.

Despite the desire churning his mind, he pulled out the question she hadn't answered earlier. "You said Caitlyn reminded you of yourself at her age. What did you mean? You never did finish your thought. Do you have your socks folded in neat piles by color, too?"

Her smile faded a couple of shades. "No. I'm not that bad."

"Then how do you think you're like her?"

"It's just..." Tabitha suddenly found a speck on her skirt fascinating. "She's an only child who lived with just one parent. She's had a pretty hard life."

"Being the daughter of a cop is a hard life?"

She looked up, then pointedly away. "It can be."

Recognizing the stubborn expression, Jake steered his questions in another direction for the moment. "How was Caitlyn's life hard?"

Tabitha took a deep breath. "Hers was much worse than mine. She never knew her father, and her mother abandoned her when she was two. She was raised by a great-aunt, who died when she was four. So she was in and out of foster homes the rest of her childhood."

"I thought you didn't know much about Miss Matthews."

Tabitha lifted a silk-clad shoulder. "I don't know because she told me. There were enough clues in her human resources file, which I review, to make me do a little research."

Jake nodded. He could certainly understand the need for information. "Foster homes can be rough. I've processed more than a few products of them over the years. I know there are some very good ones out there. Probably most of them are. But I also know it can be pretty tough on a kid. They get care, if they're lucky, but they rarely get love."

"Yes."

He studied her lovely face as she stared thoughtfully at the polished pine coffee table. "There are a lot of things that are tough on a kid."

Her gaze rose to his. "That's true."

"Like—"

"Meow."

Relief washed across her face. "Billy boy? Where are you, silly Billy?"

An orange head peered around the end of the couch between them. Huge golden eyes studied Jake intently.

He slowly lowered his hand, palm up, toward the floor. "Hey there, big fella. Wanna come on over and—" He glanced up at Tabitha. "I don't know. What do cats like to do?"

Her eyebrow quirked. "Rub themselves all over you."

He straightened enough to put his hand on his knee. "Speaking for yourself, kitten?"

Her smile vanished. "I'm not a kitten." She straightened her suit jacket. "I'm Tabitha Monroe, plain and simple."

He already knew she didn't have a middle name. Had her father not cared enough to give her one? "Well, Tabitha Monroe, as far as I can tell, there's not a damn thing that's simple about you."

"Meow."

Their gazes dropped to the cat.

The feline appeared to be indignant, probably at being ignored.

Jake smiled. "Women. Huh, fella? Can't live with them, can't put them in handcuffs. At least, not without permission or justifiable cause."

"Cop humor?"

Jake ignored her comment and placed his hand near the floor again. "You gonna come here so we can get to know each other, Billy boy?"

The cat padded over cautiously, then very carefully stretched his neck until his nose was close enough to Jake's hand to catch a good scent. Jake felt the cold nose bump his hand several times very lightly, like a butterfly's touch.

Jake smiled at Tabitha, who watched them. "He tickles."

She smiled back. "Cats have a much lighter touch than dogs. They're a lot more subtle in their affections."

"Give me a dog's enthusiasm anytime. At least it's honest."

Billy took a small step forward and nuzzled his head against Jake's palm. But when Jake turned his hand to pet Billy's head, the cat skittered out of reach.

"Meow."

Tabitha chuckled. "He knows you're not a cat person."

Jake shrugged. He wasn't going to deny it. "You try."

Tabitha leaned over slightly and patted her lap. "Hey, Billy. Remember me? Come on, boy. Jump up here and I'll scratch behind your ears."

The cat sniffed around her ankles, then gathered his hind legs under him and leaped lightly into her lap.

Tabitha grinned triumphantly. "Just takes the right touch."

Jake lounged back against the couch. "You mean it takes a cat to know a cat…or kitten."

She ignored his comment. "And the right scent, too, I imagine. I smell like the hospital, as Cait does."

"I've been there all day, too," Jake pointed out.

"Oh, that's right. You have."

She didn't make any further comment, so Jake watched the cat stretch in her lap, enjoying the vigorous petting he received, letting her know with deep purring Jake could hear from where he sat. Tabitha scratched the sides of the furry head, kneaded her way lightly down the arched back, then wrapped her fist around the bushy tail and drew out the length.

Billy was in feline heaven. Finally, having discerned this human knew the preferred method of pleasing him, Billy settled across her lap.

"Shall I get the carrier?" Jake asked.

"Let's give him a minute to get used to me."

"Fine by me."

He watched the petting action for several silent minutes, watched her hand stroke down the furry back, imagining what it felt like, wishing her hands were doing the same thing to him.

He shoved a hand back through his hair and suppressed a groan.

"What?" she asked quickly.

"Nothing." Every damn thing she did made him want her. All she had to do was sit there and breathe. "Did you find cat food for us to take?"

She nodded. "And litter. We have to take the litter box, too, you know."

"Great."

She gave him a sideways grin. "Why don't you go clean it out?"

"What?"

"Well, you're not doing anything at the moment."

Cursing under his breath, he started to rise.

"Easy, now. We don't want to spook him."

Jake glared at the cat. It was getting all the affection while he had to clean up the damn thing's bathroom. But he stood nice and easy.

Billy turned his head to watch Jake, but didn't move from his comfortable spot on Tabitha's warm lap.

"That's good," she crooned. "You're such a big fine boy, silly Billy."

The cat blinked in what looked like orgasmic pleasure, and Jake spun toward the bathroom litter box before he did something stupid like haul the cat off her lap and crawl up there himself.

The litter box didn't smell nearly as bad as he thought it would. Caitlyn Matthews's ferocious cleaning habits extended to her cat, as well, thank God. After pulling the plastic lining over the edge, he saw that it worked like garbage bags with a pull-string closure.

Gathering it together, he walked back into the living room. "I'll go ahead and take this out to the trash."

Tabitha wrinkled her nose. "Good idea."

"Gee. Two in one day." He opened the door. "I must be living right."

"Yeah, well, don't let it go to your head."

He butted the screen door open. "With you around? How could I?"

If she replied, he didn't hear it, because he seized the opportunity for the last word and exited. From the vantage point of the landing, he looked around. Darkness had fallen while they were inside, but everything seemed to be normal. So he descended the stairs and deposited the litter bag in the metal trash can on the other side of the driveway.

Pulling the cell phone from his belt, he checked in with his men at the hospital. Everything was quiet.

Satisfied that his instincts were right, and that Hines wouldn't make a move or call until at least tomorrow, if not for a couple more days, Jake took the stairs quickly and pulled open the screen door. "Now what?"

She glanced down at the cat in her lap. "I guess get the carrier. We can gather his food and other stuff after we get him secure."

Jake nodded, then turned down the short hallway again. He pulled the small padded carrier from the shelf above the hanging clothes and carried it into the living room.

Billy's head came up as Jake approached.

"Uh-oh," Tabitha said. "He's getting tense."

Jake opened the little door. "Let's get him into it quickly, then."

When Tabitha wrapped her hands around the cat's stomach to pick him up, Billy started howling and writhing in her hands.

"Ow!" she cried as she shoved him in.

Jake closed door on the outraged cat and made sure it would stay closed. "What happened?"

Tabitha held her right hand to her mouth. "He bit me."

"Well, don't..." Jake pulled her hand from her mouth. "What are you trying to do, suck out the poison?"

"I don't know. It hurts."

She tried to draw her hand back, but Jake held on. "Let me see."

There were tiny teeth marks on the pad at the base of her thumb that seeped blood.

"It's not too bad, but we'd better get it clean," he said over the cat's caterwauling. "Let's see if Miss Matthews is as anal about medical supplies as she is about everything else."

"She's a nurse," Tabitha pointed out. "So she should be."

Jake wrapped his hand around both of Tabitha's wrists and pulled her to her feet. He turned toward the bathroom, towing Tabitha along by her uninjured hand.

Feeling like a child, she tried to back away. "I can do it."

Jake held on. "Don't make it worse."

"That's not the hand that's bleeding."

He pulled her into the bathroom. Keeping a hand on her wrist as if he was afraid she'd run away, he lowered the lid on the toilet seat and ordered, "Sit."

Since she didn't have any choice, Tabitha sat. "This is silly. It'll be okay."

He gave her a withering glance from the medicine chest. "It's a puncture wound, which means the germs sank deep underneath your skin. Seems as if you'd know such basic first aid, Miss Hospital Administrator."

"I do, it's just—"

"Ah, iodine." He glanced her. "Just what?"

Tabitha held up her injured hand as an excuse to look down, away from his see-through-her eyes. It was just that she'd never had anyone fuss over her before. Not for something so minor. But she wasn't about to tell him that. "Iodine hurts."

"Not as much as getting an infection would," he said mercilessly. He doused a cotton ball, then held out his hand. "Let me see."

She held out her left hand for the cotton ball. "Give it to me and I'll do it."

"Oh, no." He held the iodine-soaked cotton out of reach. "You'll be all prissy like a girl and not get the medicine where it needs to go."

"I am a girl," she reminded him.

"Really? I hadn't noticed. Quit stalling."

Feeling a frown all the way across her forehead, she gave up and extended her hand. She expected a first-aid assault, not the tender care with which he dabbed the medicine on her upturned palm.

She gasped as the first iodine hit raw skin.

He quickly pulled the cotton ball away and blew on the wound.

His warm breath tickled, but didn't make Tabitha want to pull her hand away. Just the opposite. She'd never felt anything quite so sensuous.

Just the thought made a shiver run along her arm.

"Does it hurt?" he asked as he straightened and applied the iodine again.

She shook her head. "Why did you do that?"

"What?"

"Blow on it."

His eyes seemed surprised as they met hers. "I don't know. Doesn't it feel good?"

"Well, yes, but I wondered if there was a medical reason for it."

He grinned and bent over his task again. "Hell, I don't know. My mom always blew on a scrape or cut when she doctored it. Didn't your dad?"

Tabitha didn't answer, and was glad he wasn't looking at her.

"As for a medical reason," he continued as if she had, "maybe it dries the iodine faster, so it doesn't hurt as long."

"That makes sense," she murmured.

As he bandaged her hand over her ignored protests, he told her about a scar on his forearm he'd gotten when he was seven. His mother wanted to take him to the emergency room and have it sewed up, but he threw a fit until she doctored it herself. Since it was deep and really should have had stitches, he was left with the scar.

"So at seven, you'd already learned the macho cop attitude," she said. "Was your father a policeman?"

"Nope. Dad sold shipping supplies."

"He doesn't anymore?"

A shadow crossed Jake's face. "No."

"Retired?"

He met her eyes squarely. "Permanently."

"He's dead?"

Jake nodded as he cut off the end of the bandage.

"What about your mother?"

"She's dead, too."

"Oh." Tabitha watched him roll the rest of the bandage up and put it back in the box. "Then we're both orphans."

"Seems so."

Neither of them said anything as Jake repacked the supplies and put them back in the linen closet where he'd found them. "Think she'll notice they were moved?"

She stood and stepped toward him, which was also toward the door. "Probably."

He didn't turn to go out, however, just stood blocking the way. He lifted her injured hand. "Feel better?"

"Yes. Thank you very much."

"You're welcome." He smiled warmly. "Want me to kiss and make it better?"

Another motherly ritual she'd heard of though never experienced. Dutifully she held her bandaged hand higher.

He made no move to take it. "That's not what I meant."

She frowned. She'd been looking forward to feeling his lips on her hand. "What did you—"

His gaze dropped to her mouth.

"Oh." She took a tiny, involuntary breath and shivered again. This time it shook her entire body.

He smiled and locked his gaze onto hers. "I see you remember."

"Re—" She cleared her throat. "Remember what?"

He slipped a hand around her waist and drew her closer. "This."

Then his lips touched hers, briefly, softly.

Her breath caught again. Kissing him brought the oddest sensation. There was a tiny shock, as if an electrical connection that had been broken was now complete.

Wanting to feel it again, she initiated the second kiss. She wrapped her arms around his neck and pulled his head down to hers.

When his arms locked into place, tightening around her, Tabitha felt a rush of feminine power, bringing a deep sense of satisfaction that she could wreak the same kind of havoc on his senses that he wreaked on hers.

Jake deepened the kiss, dipping his tongue into her mouth.

Tabitha groaned, and stood on tiptoe to give him better access.

Jake groaned this time and, placing both hands at her waist, he picked her up and leaned her back against the wall, never breaking the contact of their lips. One of his knees parted hers.

Understanding what he wanted, she tried to pull her legs up so she could wrap them around his waist, but her skirt was too tight.

He must have realized the problem, because he gathered handfuls of silk until his hands touched her bare bottom.

His whole body tightened, and his lips slid off hers. "Damn."

"What?"

"You're wearing a thong!"

Who cared about that? All Tabitha wanted was for the fire to resume. She pulled his head down to hers.

With one heave, Jake lifted her up against the wall and settled himself in the crook of her legs.

Feeling the hardness rubbing against a highly sensitized spot, Tabitha bucked against him.

"Oh, God." His lips slid away from hers again, but only to burn a path down her throat, making her lose her train of thought, her will, her determination to—

What?

There was a reason she shouldn't be doing this…wasn't there?

Was there? What reason could she possibly have for not wanting these delicious sensations dancing through her? Was she nuts?

Right this moment she wanted everything, and she wanted it to continue until she melted into the stars.

Jake worked a hand around her butt and slipped it under the back strap of her thong. He slowly worked his hand down, lower, closer to the hot, wet spot where Tabitha wanted to feel the pressure of—

Brrring.

The ringing brought both their heads up.

"What is it?" she asked, still dazed.

"My cell phone," he concluded, then captured her lips again.

The phone continued to ring.

Tabitha tore her mouth away. "Aren't you going to answer it?"

"No." He attacked her neck. "It's just one of my men reporting in."

She shoved ineffectually at his broad shoulders. "How do you know?"

He glared at her, but finally eased her down and she let her legs drop.

He grabbed his phone, then showed it to her as she pulled her skirt down. "Exactly as I thought. See the time? They report in every thirty minutes, assuming nothing has happened."

She pulled down her jacket with a snap. "So answer it."

Jake hit the talk button.

As he barked into the phone, Tabitha took the opportunity to escape into the other room. Breathing deeply, she heard him ask several curt questions.

Billy had settled down in the carrier, but peeked out at her with killer eyes.

She decided not to touch the carrier.

Jake stepped into the room. ‘‘Everything’s fine. It could’ve waited.’’

She moved into the kitchen area to find Billy’s food. ‘‘But you didn’t know that.’’

‘‘Damn, Tabitha, we were—’’

‘‘No, Jake.’’ She turned to face him across the counter.

He glared at her. ‘‘But you were—’’

‘‘No, Jake.’’

Three strides brought him to the other side of the counter. ‘‘Why the hell can’t you—’’

‘‘You’re a cop.’’

His eyes narrowed.

Having said it all, Tabitha picked up the cat food and started for the door. ‘‘Bring the cat, will you?’’

Six

Billy let out one long howl when Jake picked up the carrier, then crouched in the bottom like a ceramic Foo dog. When he stepped out onto the landing, Tabitha was already down the stairs.

"The door doesn't lock without a key, and you have the key," he said.

"We still have to get the cat litter and litter box," she called without turning around. "And some of his toys. Cats love toys."

"You're a hell of a lot of trouble, you know that?" Jake mumbled to the cat as he automatically took advantage of the view to glance around. "Why I ever suggested we take you with us is be—"

His thoughts scattered as his eyes registered movement at the corner of the house. He zeroed in on the bush there. It was still now. Had it moved, or was he seeing danger in every shadow?

"Are you coming down or not?" Tabitha asked from the bottom of the steps. "I can't get past you with—"

He cut off her impatient remark with a slice of his free hand.

"What is it?" Her voice was lower and vibrated with tension.

There it was again. Someone was watching them from the bush at the far corner of Mrs. Brody's house.

Jake set the cat on the landing and grabbed the cell phone from his waist.

One of the officers on Euclid Street picked on the first ring. "Yes, sir?"

"We've got a Peeping Tom. Converge on the Brody residence. Don't know what we're dealing with, so load for bear."

"Roger."

"Call for backup. Out."

Jake ran down the stairs.

"What...?" Tabitha sputtered.

"Get down," Jake ordered as he ran past her. "And stay down!"

Sirens sang as he sprinted across the backyard, ducking under a clothesline with clothespins still attached.

When he cleared it, he saw the bush at the corner of the house quivering, as if settling from having been shaken violently.

The perp was on the run. He wouldn't get far.

Jake rounded the corner and saw the small, dark-haired man hesitate as he hit the sidewalk, looking down the street at the squad cars racing toward him. Maybe he'd just give up and go.

No such luck. He sprinted across the street for all he was worth.

One of the squad cars peeled to a stop seconds behind the suspect, swinging around so the headlights caught him running. Both officers leaped from the car with their guns already drawn.

"Halt! Police!"

The suspect kept running, so both officers started after him.

Jake was several yards behind them. He crossed the street just as the other squad car screeched to a halt. He could hear more sirens in the distance, closing in. They would seal off the next few blocks, allowing no escape for Hines—if this was him—or his lookout.

The younger officer ahead outsprinted both his partner and Jake. He grabbed the suspect's feet just as he was heaving himself over a six-foot wooden fence. A kicking and yanking match ensued.

"Hold on!" Jake called.

Two seconds later, the officer's partner grabbed the other foot, and the two of them pulled the suspect to the ground.

The older officer turned him over and the younger one shone his flashlight on the suspect's face. "Ronny Stubbs!"

Jake halted just behind them. They knew him. Good. Since Hines was a local criminal, it stood to reason his friends would be, too, and as such, known by the Mission Creek police.

The officers parted to let Jake view a panting, wide-eyed boy who couldn't have been more than fourteen.

Jake eyed the officers casually backing away. "Why aren't you restraining the suspect?"

The younger officer blinked. "He's a kid."

Jake's face hardened. "I've seen kids commit crimes you wouldn't believe an adult would commit, that any human being would commit. So don't assume he's harmless just because he's a kid."

"He *is* harmless, sir," the older cop, Officer Clement, said.

"You know him?"

"He's a friend of Gaylon, my son."

"How old is he?"

"Well, they've just started the ninth grade. Gaylon's fourteen." Clement tapped Ronny's athletic shoes with his boot. "You fourteen, too, boy?"

"Yes, sir." The boy swiped his nose. "Last May."

"Hell." Feeling his adrenaline drop back into the realm of normal, Jake squatted in front of the teenager. "You know what's going on in Mission Creek, Ronny?"

The boy's eyes brightened. "Yes, sir. A doctor and a

nurse at the hospital were kidnapped. Do you have any clues yet?''

Surprised at the only slightly daunted enthusiasm, Jake peered up.

Clement rolled his eyes. ''Ronny's wanted to be a police officer ever since I can remember. He's always following squad cars on his bike and asking me questions.''

Several more officers ran up then, guns and flashlights pointed at the suspect.

The younger officer turned to them. ''False alarm. All we got is a curious kid.''

The new arrivals relaxed, and one of them asked, ''Free to go, Chief?''

''Yeah,'' Jake said over his shoulder. ''Get back on patrol.''

''Roger that.''

As all but the original two filed away, Jake turned to the boy. The kid was shaking. Jake patted the boy's shin. ''It's okay, Ronny. We're not going to arrest you.''

''You're not?''

''Not *this* time.'' Jake kept a smile off his face with difficulty. ''Why? Is there some reason we should?''

The boy straightened. ''No, sir! I wouldn't do anything to jeopardize my chances with the department.''

''Then don't run next time. And don't hide in bushes when the entire Mission Creek Police Department is on code red.''

''No, sir. I mean yes, sir. I mean I won't, sir.''

Finally allowing himself to smile, Jake stood and offered him a hand up. ''You live around here?''

Ronny nodded and pointed west. ''Yes, sir. One street over from Euclid. I knew you might be coming around to check on Caitlyn Matthews's apartment, so I've been watching.''

''Well, stay out of the way from here on out,'' Jake said.

"If you'd been any faster, we might have been forced to fire, and that wouldn't have been fun for you or the officer who shot you."

The boy visibly paled. "I will, sir."

Jake nodded toward the west. "Get on home, then."

The boy took off.

"Kids," the younger officer said with disgust as they followed at a more leisurely pace.

"You might be looking at the future of the MCPD," Jake said.

"God help us," the older officer muttered.

Jake left them at their squad car and headed back down Mrs. Brody's driveway. As he turned the corner, he spotted Tabitha high up on the stairs, silhouetted by the light on the landing above her. She watched the opposite corner intently, the one where he'd disappeared earlier.

She seemed worried. About him, perhaps?

Something in him wanted to think so.

Or was she worried that Hines was after her now?

Whatever. He was just glad she'd stayed put, though she hadn't stayed down like he'd told her. He was also glad she hadn't witnessed half the Mission Creek police force converging on a kid who could barely call himself a teenager.

That reminded him of her disappointment in him earlier, when he'd been questioning the hospital employees. She'd accused him of believing the worst of people.

Jake frowned. Was she right? Did he always believe people were guilty until they proved themselves innocent? What if Officer Clement hadn't been there today? Would Jake have hauled Ronny in and had him interrogated?

He drove a hand back through his hair.

Probably.

But, hell, it was his job to be extra careful, wasn't it? And with the situation the way it was, he had to check the source of every shadow. He was responsible for the outcome of this situation, and he damn well wanted to do things right.

Still, it had only been a small-town kid who yearned to play cop.

Jake straightened his shoulders and focused again on Tabitha, who hadn't taken her eyes off the other side of the yard.

Okay, maybe there was a grain of truth in what she'd said. Maybe he should start being a tad more optimistic about people, start trying to see the good before he looked for the bad.

She certainly looked good to—

He cut off his thought with disgust. One thing he didn't need was Miss Zen-on-Speed. She had her head up her feng shui.

Plus, she hated cops, and he didn't know how to be anything else.

To get away from the frown that thought provoked, Jake continued on down the driveway. After a few more yards he must have caught her eye, because her head snapped around.

"Jake!" She ran down the stairs and over to the car, where he stood. She stopped on a dime several feet away, as if she'd just realized the depth of her reaction. "What happened?"

"False alarm."

She deflated. "Another one?"

"Yep." He reached for the passenger door handle. "Wait. We still have to get—"

"I brought everything down," she said.

He looked at her, strangely disappointed. If she'd been busy toting the cat and all his paraphernalia down the stairs, she couldn't have been that worried about him. "Okay."

When he made no move to open her door, she asked, "Am I going home by myself?"

"No."

"You're driving me?"

"Yes."

She nodded, looked away, then back at him. "Are you going back to the hospital?"

"No."

A wrinkled creased her forehead. "To the police station?"

"No."

She reached for the door handle. "Fine, don't tell me. Sleep in the desert, for all I care."

His hand closed over hers. He felt a slight shiver run up her arm, and knew she was far from indifferent. "I'm staying with you."

Her eyes were wide as saucers as she looked at him. "Oh, no, you're not."

He nodded. "Hines might call."

"But I—"

"Need help and protection."

She searched his eyes. "If you think you're *sleeping* with me, you're—"

"I never said that."

She straightened her shoulders. "Just as long as you understand. Because you're *not.* You can have the couch."

"A couch will be a heavenly cloud compared to some places I've slept while on duty."

She raised a pale brow. "I can imagine."

He opened the car door for her. When she'd seated herself with stiff dignity, he closed the door and slipped behind the steering wheel. After glancing back at the cat, who glared at him from the carrier, he turned on the ignition. "What would you like to eat?"

She sighed. "If we go somewhere, we're bound to run into reporters. They're all over town. And we'll be questioned within an inch of our sanity."

"Order pizza from your place?"

"How about if I cook something for you?" She placed a

hand over her stomach. ‘‘The thought of a greasy pizza is not appealing.’’

‘‘I don’t want to put you to a lot of effort,’’ he said.

She lifted a shoulder. ‘‘I have some chicken in the refrigerator. I was going to make chicken marsala.’’

Jake’s mouth began to water. ‘‘I love chicken marsala, but I haven’t had it in...I don’t know, years, probably.’’

She frowned at him, as if she didn’t like the idea that they shared even something as insignificant as a favorite dish. ‘‘I live on Hayward Street.’’

‘‘I know.’’

She sighed and twisted to wave at Mrs. Brody, who’d stepped onto her back porch. ‘‘Somehow, I knew you would.’’

Tabitha groaned when she saw the horde of reporters lounging on her front lawn. ‘‘They’re going to ruin my flower beds.’’

The horde perked up when they saw the squad cars ahead of Tabitha’s pull onto Hayward Street.

Jake snapped open his cell phone and punched two numbers. ‘‘Back those people off onto the street. They’re trespassing.’’

He pushed a button and closed the phone.

‘‘I don’t have a No Trespassing sign,’’ Tabitha said.

‘‘Doesn’t matter. It’s private property, and they know it.’’ He eased off the gas and pulled over to the side of the road.

‘‘What are we doing?’’

‘‘Waiting to let my men clear them out. Otherwise it’ll take half an hour to get from the car to the house.’’

The squad car behind them pulled around and joined the other officers in pushing the reporters off Tabitha’s lawn. When they were lined up on the street, Jake continued toward the house.

Tabitha could hear the din of questions as they crowded

the car when Jake pulled into her driveway. But they didn't go past the officers standing guard where her driveway met the sidewalk.

Though she wasn't going to tell him, she was glad she had Jake with her. "These people are crazy."

"Nah. They just have an extremely aggressive and competitive job." Jake turned off the ignition. "Nice house."

His comment brought her back to the fact that not only was he with her now, he was going to stay with her, for God knows how long. Squinting slightly, she tried to see her house as Jake would.

She decided he wouldn't really like it. Much too picket fence for him.

The small frame house was in an older, established neighborhood of Mission Creek, just a few blocks from where Caitlyn Matthews lived. It was the first house she'd ever owned, and she'd put a lot of sweat equity into it.

Tabitha opened the car door and got out.

The reporters immediately shouted questions at her.

"Ignore them."

Tabitha reached into the back seat for the cat carrier. Then she stepped down her curved, flower-lined walkway.

She'd painted the wooden siding of her house a restful green and the door—which faced south, the best feng shui direction for doors—was Chinese red. Red was the most powerful yang color and as such, attracted the dragon's breath, which was the best kind of chi.

But Jake wouldn't know any of that. All he would see was a green house with a red door.

As she unlocked the front door for him, she wondered if she should cover it, at least for now. The chi coming at her house from the crowd in the street was surely a killing shar.

"Wait here," he ordered.

She waved a hand at the horde. "Surely no one could have gotten in past all that."

"I'm not taking any chances."

So she waited on her covered porch while he searched her house. Glancing up at the Pa Kau mirror she'd hung above the door, she wondered if it would be enough to reflect the bad energy. Was symbolic reflection always enough?

She peered into the small entryway through the screen door. How long did it take to search such a small place? Tabitha's house was about twice the size of Caitlyn's apartment, but that wasn't saying much.

It was perfect for Tabitha, however.

She had two bedrooms, one of which she used as an office. There was a living room, dining room and a remodeled kitchen, which she loved. She also had a walk-in pantry and a bathroom with a claw-foot tub. They all opened off a small square center hallway.

A moment later, Jake came back into the entryway and pushed the screen door open for her. "I see you've used the same decor as your office."

She stepped in. "Of course."

"Early Chinese import store, where prices are cheaper by the dozen."

She ignored his sarcasm and headed straight for the blinds on the front of the house. She snapped them all shut, then flipped on the air conditioner in the living room to high. The loud hum of the window unit drowned out the din outside.

With a sigh of relief, she turned on lamps in the south end of each room, then headed into the kitchen and picked up the phone. She pushed the caller ID button and whistled. "A hundred fifty-seven new calls since this morning."

Jake nodded toward the front. "Probably from your new fan club out there."

"Why didn't you warn them against calling here, too?"

He shrugged. "Didn't think about it. I'll tell them at the press conference in the morning."

She made a face as she clicked through the numbers, not

recognizing any of them. "Another press conference? Is there anything to say?"

"Could be by then. By the way, that phone is not hooked up to the recording equipment. When you answer the phone, you need to answer the one in your office. And you need to wait until I switch on the recorder."

"Okay." Tabitha scanned through the numbers.

"That's important."

"I know. I'll remember." She clicked off the phone. "I'll look through the rest later. Right now we need to get Billy settled."

"You stay here. I'll get the rest of his things in."

She smiled. "Thanks. I wasn't looking forward to going out there again."

He returned her smile and spun toward the door. "You're welcome, kitten."

Her smile faded. "I'm not your kitten."

The only answer she received was the front door closing firmly. Heaving a disgusted sigh, she knelt by the cat carrier. "How you doing, Billy boy?"

The cat stared at her with blank golden eyes, as if his cat spirit was somewhere else.

She wanted to take him out and cuddle him until he was no longer frightened, but she knew that was not a cat's way. He needed to run and hide until he felt comfortable.

Jake opened and closed the front door, then came into the kitchen carrying everything they'd left in the car.

"Trying to impress all the pretty female reporters?" she asked as she grabbed the sack of kitty litter from him.

He lowered the cat food to the counter, then bent to set the sack of cat toys on the floor. "Hmm?"

"Never mind."

He held up the last item, the litter box. "Where do you want this?"

Tabitha considered every two-by-three-foot space she had

available. There weren't that many, and most of them would be inauspicious for a cat's toilet. Finally she pointed to the closed door beside the open one leading into the center hallway. "The pantry, please."

He disappeared into the closet lined with shelves. "I'll put it in here, but you have to set it up." He came out, dusting his hands. "It's only fair, since I had to clean it out."

Tabitha rolled her eyes, then grabbed the cat litter and the box of liners and quickly had the litter box back in business.

"Do you need to show him where it is?" Jake asked.

Tabitha went to the sink and washed her hands. "He'll find it."

"Now what?"

"We let him out." She dried her hands and went over to the cat carrier. "Stand back. I'm just going to let him go."

"Will he go crazy?"

"He'll probably run and hide."

Jake nodded and took up a position on the other side of the island.

Tabitha squatted by one side of the carrier and reached for the latch. "Okay, Billy boy. You're officially free."

The door opened and nothing happened. Billy stayed put.

Deciding he probably wouldn't come out with her hovering, Tabitha straightened and turned to find Jake's gaze on her, hot and intense. Surprise made her lose her balance for a split second. She steadied herself by grabbing the edge of the counter. She didn't know what she'd done to attract his erotic attention, but she couldn't deny the tiny thrill that made her whole body smile.

"You okay?" he asked.

Jeez. He noticed everything. "Mmm, hmm."

Since she didn't feel like explaining why she'd stumbled, she turned toward her bedroom.

He followed. "You almost fell."

"No, I didn't."

"I saw you."

Tabitha spun in the doorway of her bedroom to face him. "So I stumbled a little. Big deal."

"Why did you stumble?"

Now she was getting irritated. "I don't know. Why not? I guess I stood a little too fast."

"Ahh." He planted his fists on his hips. "You felt faint, didn't you?"

"No." To get away from him, she walked into the room and switched on the lamp beside the bed.

He followed. "Then what was it?"

All these questions. She wasn't used to someone grilling her over every move she made. No one ever had. But fainting sounded better than giddy. "Okay. Maybe I felt a little faint."

"I knew it. You haven't eaten enough today to keep a fly alive."

Concentrating more on him than what she was doing, she nearly had all the buttons of her jacket undone before she realized why she'd come into her bedroom.

"Do you mind?" She looked over her shoulder so he couldn't sneak a peek if her jacket gaped. "I'd like to change into something more comfortable."

As soon as the words were out, she wished she could take them back.

His mind went right to the seductive meaning of the phrase. She could see it in the slight flaring of his nostrils.

His green eyes sparkled. "By all means."

"I mean jeans and a T-shirt."

"Mmm."

"A *big* T-shirt."

He made no move to leave, just stared at her. Probably with visions from the Victoria's Secret catalog flashing through his brain.

"So get out."

"Oh. Right." His face finally cleared, but showed no embarrassment or contrition. "I'll start supper. You need some decent food in you or you'll never make it through the next few days. Where's the chicken you mentioned?"

This was a new one. "*You're* going to cook?"

"I told you I could." He seemed surprised by her surprise. "Is that a problem?"

"Well, no. I just—" Her father hadn't so much as boiled water for coffee.

"Just what?"

She rolled her eyes. Why couldn't he *ever* let anything go? "Nothing. The chicken is in the fridge."

"I happen to be a passable cook." Jake headed for the door, finally. "I can't make the chicken marsala, but I'll get the chicken ready. Is there anything to go with it?"

"I've got a couple ears of sweet corn and some pole beans in the vegetable drawer of the fridge."

"Sounds like a feast," he called, already in the kitchen.

She followed to close the door. "And if you want to wash the mushrooms, they're in there, too."

"Roger."

Tabitha frowned as she shut the door. Was he serious? Would he really help her cook? She knew there were men who loved to work in the kitchen, but she'd never known one personally. To her, they were like some mythical creature that people claimed to have seen, but you don't really believe them. Like Bigfoot.

That image of Jake made her smile. She'd never noticed how big his feet were. She'd have to check them out.

Besides, she'd heard women say that the size of men's feet indicated the size of their—

Tabitha nipped that thought in the bud. With a huff of self-disgust, she started toward her jeans drawer, then checked the movement and glanced back at the door.

What was it he'd said?

I'm not taking any chances.

She shouldn't, either.

Stepping back, she pushed in the button on the knob of her door.

Seven

Feeling a warm gaze on his back, Jake glanced over his shoulder.

Tabitha stood in the door from the kitchen to the hall, watching him. Sure enough, she'd put on blue jeans and a huge navy-blue T-shirt with Rice University splayed across the front in big white letters.

"You went to Rice?" He already knew, of course, from reading her file. He just wanted to see how much she would tell him.

He went back to shucking corn.

She came farther into the room. "I had a full academic scholarship for undergrad, and though some say you should go to a different school for your M.B.A., their graduate assistant offer was too good to pass up."

"Rice is a top-notch school. I'm impressed."

"You should be."

He grinned at her arrogance and glanced over as she leaned back against the counter, just a few feet down from him. "It's in Houston."

"Yes, it is."

"We might've seen each other, and never known."

She looked down at the sink where a bowl of washed, snapped and stringed pole beans waited in the left side. "That was a long time ago."

"Yep."

"Do police officers go to college?"

"Some do."

"The ones with ambition."

"Yes."

"Where did *you* go to school?"

He grinned at her correct assumption and held up his left hand with only the pinky and forefinger sticking up. "Hook 'em Horns."

"University of Texas."

He nodded. "Best criminal justice school in the state."

"Did you always want to be a cop?"

"Not always." His smile faded, and he concentrated on picking silk from the ear of corn. His reasons for choosing law enforcement were personal…and painful. "The cat's gone."

She didn't blink at the change of subject, just shook her head and glanced at the empty carrier. "He's just hiding. Poor thing is scared to death. He doesn't know what's happened, doesn't know where he is, doesn't know who we are. Under those circumstances, I'd probably hide, too."

Jake relaxed back into a smile and placed the first ear of corn in the closest bowl of the double sink. "I doubt it."

She crossed her hands over her stomach, which stretched Rice over her chest. "Why would you say that?"

She'd changed bras, too, he noticed. To a sports bra, by the way it flattened the lovely breasts he'd been itching to wrap his hands around. Not that they were flat, even now. If she thought downplaying her assets would make a difference, she didn't realize how much he wanted to—

"Why did you say that?" she repeated.

He shook off the image. He certainly didn't need to go there, although he damn sure wanted to. In order to make *her* back away, he said something sure to get her dander up. "Because you're a control freak. It's a damn good thing Hines didn't kidnap you. You'd have tried something by now to get yourself out of it and more than likely have a hole right between your beautiful bluebonnet eyes.''

But her ire didn't rise. Instead, she frowned and picked up the two cat bowls. Taking them to the sink, she lifted the beans out and set the bowls in. Then she reached across him for a paper towel, and her shoulder brushed his arm.

She hesitated for an instant, just long enough for him to know she felt the same tiny shock of desire that he did, just long enough for him to catch a lungful of the warm, all-woman scent that blended with the sharp freshness of the vegetables.

''Sorry,'' she murmured, drawing back.

To keep his hands from reaching for her, he picked up the other ear of corn. ''Not going to argue with me?''

''About being a control freak? If you don't control things in your life, they can end up controlling you.'' She wrinkled her nose at him. ''You're one, too, you know.''

He wanted to pursue her intriguing comment, but knew this wasn't the time. They were both too tired and hungry. He pulled off half the husk with one hard yank. ''I guess we're two peas in a pod.''

She filled one bowl with water, then picked both of them up. ''We're having beans tonight, not peas.''

He continued shucking. ''Beans have peas, sort of. I don't know what they're called, but they're in a pod like a pea.''

She filled the other bowl with cat food. ''They're seeds.''

''Two seeds in a pod, then. Is that better, Miss Botany?''

She set both bowls on the floor in the far corner of the kitchen. ''There are usually more than two seeds in a pod.''

Shaking his head, he chuckled. ''That's another form of control, you know.''

''What?''

''Your insistence on accuracy. Egregious attention to detail.''

She lifted a blond eyebrow. ''Egregious?''

He grinned. "Longhorns can use just as many ten-dollar words as Rice farmers."

"Rice *Owls*. And I don't use ten-dollar words...do I?"

He glanced up from the ear of corn. "And I quote, 'The Mission Creek population has a higher SES than the city where *you* live. It is also a much safer place to live because we have one of the most efficacious and proficient police departments in the United States.'"

"Well, that reporter deserved it, questioning our experience and ability to handle the situation, just because we're a small town in South Texas." She grinned. "Think he knows what SES stands for?"

"Probably not." Jake set the second ear next to the first. "And, is it even true? Does Mission Creek have a higher socioeconomic status than wherever that guy was from?"

"Atlanta. And yes, Mission Creek has a higher SES than most major cities, thanks to the old cattle families like the Carsons and the Wainwrights. They valued education from the beginning, and that's what leads to a high socioeconomic status."

"How'd you find that out?"

"I work closely with Crystal Bennett on hospital fundraising. In that line of work, this kind of information is extremely important."

"I guess it explains all those ten-dollar words."

"Those weren't ten-dollar words. Six or seven dollars, tops." She sighed. "I shouldn't have done it, I know. I was trying to keep everything plain and simple, so Branson Hines would understand what I said. But when that reporter sneered his question about how a two-hundred-bed hospital and tiny police force in—how did he put it?—'the south end of nowhere' could guarantee the safety of either patients or citizens, I couldn't help it. I was tired...and tired of stupid questions. There are no guarantees in this life, and he needed to get over it. So I helped him."

"Hey, I'm not complaining. You can defend me any day."

"I wasn't—" That quickly, her animation changed to a deep, thoughtful frown, and she turned toward the refrigerator. "Did you get the chicken out?"

"Not yet. Do you have a vegetable brush?"

She stopped cold with the refrigerator open, peeking around the door as if she saw a real longhorn in her kitchen.

"What?" he asked.

"You know what a vegetable brush is?"

"Why wouldn't I?"

"Well, you're a man." Then she added with distaste, "And a cop."

"Male cops aren't allowed to clean vegetables?"

"I've just never known one who..." She frowned as she trailed off.

"Okay, I'll prove it. A vegetable brush is about yay big." He formed his thumbs and forefingers in an *O*. "It's round with stiff bristles and—"

"It's in the drawer to the left of the sink." She returned her attention to the refrigerator. "Be careful, though. The sharp knives are in there, too."

"Yes, Mom."

Jake found the brush and turned on the cold water as she brought a package of boneless chicken breasts over and began to clean them in the other side of the sink.

Though she wasn't close enough to touch, he could feel the heat of her body as he briskly brushed the corn free of remaining silk.

Her proximity and, again, her scent imbued him with as much a sense of comfort as of stimulation. In fact, the comfort was stimulating in its own comforting way. Somehow, being here with her—cooking with her, teasing her, pulling information from her—felt cozy, felt good, felt...right.

The realization was so disturbing Jake was glad for the

excuse to move away from her when he had to find pots for the vegetables. Although, as he did, he also felt a sense of loss.

"Damn, White," he murmured into the cabinet, "get ahold of yourself."

"What was that?"

He rattled a stack of saucepans. "Do you want to break the ears in half or cook them in the big pot?"

"It doesn't matter. Breaking them would be easier, I guess. I'll probably only eat half of one, anyway."

Though Jake was determined to make her eat a good meal, he wasn't going to argue with her now. He needed to get out of the house, away from all the yin energy seducing him. He needed to talk with his men—with fellow police officers—so he could remember who he was and what the hell he was doing there.

He pulled out the two biggest saucepans and set them on the counter.

He broke the ears of corn with one snap each and ran enough water to cover them. Then he poured the beans into the other pan and covered them.

"I'll let you season them." Two strides took him to the back door. "I need to see what's going on outside."

"Okay."

He refused to let her quizzical tone stop him. Without glancing at her again, he opened the door and stepped into the fresh evening air.

It smelled like freedom.

Jake's watch said it was nearly eleven o'clock when he pushed his chair back from the table. It had taken them over an hour to eat because of several interruptions by his men. One time there was a question about who would be in charge at the next shift change. The next time was by the man Jake had commissioned to bring him clean clothes.

Leaning back, he patted his stomach. "That was delicious."

Tabitha was flattered in spite of her determination not to be. She eyed his clean plate. "Thank you."

"I don't get home cooking this good too often. I have to enjoy it when I do."

"You're so at home in the kitchen, I thought you'd have gourmet meals every night."

"I'm not that good." He took another swallow of iced tea. "Besides, it's too much trouble for one person. And then you're left with all that food. You either eat the same thing every night for a week or have to worry about freezing part of it."

Tabitha pointed at the empty serving platter. "Not the way you eat."

He shrugged. "I usually grab something on the way home."

"That gets old."

"Yeah." He rubbed the back of his neck.

"Tired?"

"It's been a long day."

She stood and began stacking the dishes.

He immediately stood and pushed her hands out of the way. "I'll clean up, since you cooked."

Tabitha blinked. Cooking was one thing. A person had to eat, after all, and some people didn't like takeout. But cleaning up after a meal was another thing entirely. Totally outside the realm of most males' experience.

She picked up the serving dishes and followed.

He stopped in the doorway between the small dining room and kitchen. "What are you doing? I said I'm cleaning up."

She stood her ground. "You helped cook. I'll help clean."

He rolled his eyes and stepped into the kitchen. "You're afraid I won't do it right."

"Maybe. But I've never known, never even heard tell of

a man willing to clean up the kitchen.'' She set the serving dishes on the counter beside the plates he'd just put down. ''I have to see it for myself.''

''Suit yourself.''

Twenty minutes later, the kitchen sparkled.

''You're drooping,'' he said. ''Go on to bed. Tomorrow's going to be another long day, too, I'm afraid.''

Tabitha glanced toward the hall. This was the part she'd avoided thinking about. ''You're staying here. Isn't that what you said?''

He nodded. ''Like it or not, I need to be with you, twenty-four/seven, until this is over with.''

''Protection?''

''Protector. Advisor...'' His voice dropped a perceptible notch. ''Anything you need me to be.''

''I only have one bed,'' she said quickly.

He smiled. ''Yeah, I noticed that right off.''

Her chin lifted. ''So you get the couch.''

He shrugged. ''I've slept on worse.''

She told herself she was *not* disappointed that he wasn't insisting on sleeping with her. ''You probably won't sleep much with it like it is. There are too many dragons.'' She started toward the door leading to the living room. ''I'll move the ones right around the—''

He caught her arm. ''The dragons don't scare me.''

''I didn't think they would scare you. Dragons create very powerful chi, which can be quite disrupting to...'' She trailed off because the amused look on his face said she was wasting her breath. ''Fine. But don't blame me if you have circles under your eyes in the morning.''

''Kitten...'' His face softened, and his voice was husky as he traced the line of her jaw. ''If I can't sleep, it's not going to be because of any dragons.''

''Oh.'' She dragged her eyes away and stepped back from the touch that made her feel good and uncomfortable at the same time. "Well, then, I'll..." She cleared her throat. "I'll get you a pillow and some sheets."

"That'd be great. Thanks."

She turned toward the linen closet. "You're welcome."

"I'm going to check on my men again. They should be changing shifts in half an hour, and I'll need to give instructions to the next batch, so don't wait up."

She stopped in the doorway to the hall and glanced back at him.

He watched her with an intensity that sent a thrill shimmering across her skin.

"Don't worry," she said a little stronger than necessary, to hide her reaction. "I won't."

The house was quiet when Jake entered over an hour later. The only light on was a lamp in the living room, which illuminated a couch transformed into a cozy bed with sheets, a blanket and a pillow. There wasn't a single dragon left in the room.

Smiling, he slipped into the bathroom, where he found a still-in-the-box toothbrush with a note. "This is an extra. It's yours while you're here."

He stared at her simple, no-nonsense handwriting, trying to stamp out the glow forming around his heart. How long had it been since someone had cared so much for his comfort? Since someone had thought whether or not he had what he needed?

He hadn't even realized he'd missed it...until now.

Cursing, he ripped the toothbrush from its box. But he couldn't fault Tabitha. She was merely seeing to the comfort of a guest.

It was his own stupid sentimentality. She reminded him of a life he'd lost very suddenly when both his parents had been ripped away just a few weeks before he graduated from high school. She reminded him of...

His mother.

Jake froze with the toothbrush ground onto his molars. Memories he'd repressed for the past eighteen years surfaced like air bubbles, popping gently into his mind.

The way his mother had tucked him in every night. The hot meals she always had on the table. Chicken marsala was one of her specialties. Her unfailing humor and patience. Her cat.

He had allowed himself to remember the way his parents had died. It was the reason he became a police officer and the fuel that powered his career.

But he hadn't allowed himself to remember the life he'd lived before that day. He'd remembered his adoring parents, but he refused to remember details.

Like the way his father had helped him with his homework. The way his parents had attended every football game, applauded every academic achievement, grounded him the time he'd come home drunk.

About to choke, Jake yanked the toothbrush from his mouth and spit. Then he glared at the red plastic brush. It wasn't even sharp. How could such a simple inanimate object pierce his armor so all those memories could come flooding back?

But he knew it wasn't the brush. It was the woman who'd given it to him.

He turned on the cold water full blast and rinsed the brush, then his mouth. Switching off the light, he strode back into his temporary bedroom, stripped down to his shorts, placed his pants where he could slip into them easily, then turned out the light.

He slid between the sheets and cursed. They smelled like Tabitha.

Settling back against the pillow, he crossed his hands behind his head and stared at the ceiling.

Tabitha slept just a few feet away, her bed butted against

the wall he could reach out and touch. But he didn't touch it, didn't even look at it.

He was a cop. He worked long, grueling hours. He'd trained himself over the years to catch a few winks wherever, whenever he could. He could do it tonight. All he had to do was control his thoughts, control his—

Damn. Even his control methods reminded him of Tabitha.

And he'd thought the day had been long. It was nothing compared to the night that stretched torturously ahead of him.

A sudden bounce on the mattress shocked Tabitha out of her light doze. With a sharp cry, she bolted upright in bed.

"Meow."

"Billy." She relaxed in relief. "Jeez. You could give a person some warning before scaring them half to death."

Billy nonchalantly performed a whole-body stretch on the unused side of Tabitha's double bed.

She reached out to pet him from head to tail. He arched into her stroke, then rolled over onto his back.

She tentatively scratched his tummy. When he began purring instead of biting her, she scratched for real.

A slight creak of the hardwood floor in the hall froze her fingers on his fur. Seconds later, the barrel of a gun poked out of the darkness.

"What is it?" Jake demanded in a loud whisper.

"It's the cat." Tabitha relaxed for the second time. "He finally decided to come out of hiding."

The gun disappeared on a relieved curse, then was replaced by a lean, naked torso as Jake stepped into the room.

Tabitha's heart began racing again for an entirely different reason.

Moonlight filtering through the slats in her wooden blinds glinted off his well-muscled chest, covered by just enough hair to make her fingers ache to brush through it. He'd obviously stopped to pull on his pants but hadn't taken the time to zip them, leaving an obvious vee where a belt buckle should be.

"The damn cat," he repeated for his sleep-fogged mind. He ran a hand back through his dark hair, making the muscles ripple across his chest.

Tabitha watched, enchanted by this god of the night, as he padded to the other side of the bed, the side closest to the door. He reached out to pet Billy, who'd rolled back over so he could eye the newcomer.

"Meow."

"Yeah, yeah. Tell it to the cat god when I accidentally shoot you." Jake sat down hard on the bed and looked at her. "Were you asleep?"

She shrugged. "Sort of."

He leaned forward and placed his gun on the bedside table. "Yeah, me, too."

"It's hard to sleep when you're worried." And thinking about the man sleeping in the next room.

"I know." His teeth flashed in the darkness. "Want me to sing you a lullaby?"

She smiled. "Can you sing?"

"You'd fall asleep just to get away from the sound of my voice."

"Oh, it can't be that bad."

Their hands touched when they reached to pet Billy at the same time. Jake's stroked hers, as if her hand was Billy.

Tabitha's breath caught at the shocking warmth of his hand.

Did he mean to? Or was he too sleepy to notice it was skin beneath his fingers, not fur?

Her questions were answered when he caught her hand.

"Don't do that," he whispered.

"Don't do what?" Her voice was breathless, low.

He groaned. "Don't react to me like that. It makes me want to..."

She slipped her hand from his, though she didn't want to. "I know."

He stood abruptly and faced her, both hands dug into his hair. "We can do this. We're both professionals."

She nodded. "Yes, we are. We can. You're right."

He let his hands drop. They stared at each other through the darkness.

Tabitha put her hand on Billy's fur and stroked, though her attention was on Jake.

"I should go back to bed."

When he made no move to leave, she said, "Probably."

"Do you want me to?"

She swallowed hard. No, she didn't want him to leave her. She wanted him to hold her, to tell her they'd get through this, to make her believe everything was going to be okay.

"Tell me to go." Though his words pleaded, his voice clearly said he didn't want to.

"I..." She dropped her gaze to Billy, who'd turned onto his back again. "Tell me about cases like this you've worked on before."

He stood very still for a long moment, then with a defeated sigh he sat down on the bed. "There were a couple of cases that were similar. At least, ones where we were dealing with corporate situations, instead of families."

Tabitha leaned back against her pillow. "Did you get the victims back unharmed?"

"In one of the cases." He fluffed the pillow on his side and followed suit.

The mattress shifted with his movements, which Tabitha somehow found comforting.

"It was a shipping company where a Venezuelan national demanded to be taken back to his country."

"On a boat?"

"A ship, yes."

"What happened?"

"We sweated him out. Turned off the air to the deck he'd commandeered with five of the ship's employees. It gets real hot in Houston when you're packed into a sardine can. The kidnapper was the second one to pass out. His victims tied him up and walked out."

"But you knew where he was."

Jake joined her as she stroked the cat. "Yes."

"That helps."

"That helps a lot."

"What about the other one?"

"The other was a computer company. Software developer. One of the programmers snapped. Demanded a space shuttle be placed in the parking lot so he could take it to Mars."

"You're kidding."

"Nope. When a shuttle hadn't appeared by the designated time, he killed his boss, who was the only person he'd kidnapped, then himself."

"So he was crazy."

"The other employees said he'd always been a little weird."

Uncomfortable against the headboard, Tabitha slipped down a little, until Billy rested in the crook of her arm. "Do you think Branson Hines is crazy?"

Jake hesitated. "He has to be somewhat out of touch with reality if he thinks you can just hand him someone else's baby."

"Deena's young enough. If they want a child so badly, I don't know why they don't just try again." She could feel the hair on Jake's forearm flutter across her skin as he petted the cat.

"From what I read, she all but killed the baby they were going to have, with her vices. Drugs, smoking, alcohol."

"It certainly complicated things. Probably brought on her premature labor."

"Hines claims his baby would've been saved with all the brand-new equipment in the maternity wing you just opened. Is that true?"

"Maybe, maybe not." Tabitha yawned and slipped farther down on the bed. "We'll never know. Of course, there's no convincing him of that."

"No."

In the moment of silence that followed, Billy's purring seemed more like roaring.

"He's a loud little son of a gun, isn't he?" Jake said.

"Mmm. And look at the way he's lying. Like a baby."

"Will he stay that way if I pick him up?"

"I don't know."

Jake placed his hands under Billy's back and gently picked him up.

Billy stayed contentedly on his back and kept on purring.

Tabitha chuckled and stroked his tail. "Silly thing."

"We should search the pound for a cat like this." Jake rocked Billy back and forth in his arms. "Maybe we could fool Hines."

Tabitha slipped all the way down to her pillow. She turned onto her side, facing Jake, and crooked her arm under her head. "I think the fur would be a dead giveaway."

Jake grinned. "I don't know. From all the reports I've read, Hines sees what he wants to see."

He gently placed Billy alongside Tabitha. His hand brushed her stomach as he drew it away. He either didn't hear her sharp intake of breath, or chose to ignore it as he settled on his side facing her.

They studied each other's pale faces in the dim light. Desire thickened the air.

"Jake..."

"Shh, beautiful kitten." He reached across Billy, who

purred between them. ‘‘Go to sleep. I’m here, and I won’t let anything happen to you.’’

Tabitha smiled and let her eyes flutter closed. ‘‘Jake?’’

‘‘Yes?’’

‘‘Do I really have bluebonnet eyes?’’

She could hear the smile in his voice as he said, ‘‘Yes, little kitten, you do.’’

With a sigh, she drifted into sleep. His promise to keep her safe followed her into her dreams.

Eight

Tabitha eased into consciousness at a tortoise pace. Cushioned by a soft cloud, she came awake by slow, sweet degrees.

The first thing she became aware of was the warmth surrounding her. Not hot like the Texas sun. More like a warm bath. The water lapped soothingly on her skin, pulsing ever so gently along her spine like a heartbeat.

Her eyes opened wide.

Heartbeat?

Oh, jeez. It *was* a heartbeat. *Jake's* heartbeat.

Fully awake now, she realized she lay spooned against him. How had this happened? The last position she remembered being in was facing him across the width of a cat. A *big* cat.

There was certainly no cat between them now. She was butted against him—literally—so tight no one could slip a prayer between them. She'd deliberately worn a T-shirt to bed instead of the spaghetti-strap teddy she usually wore, just in case of an invasion like the one that had happened last night.

A lot of good the thick cotton did her now, with the hem twisted nearly to her waist. Her bottom rested against his hips; the only thing separating them was the thin silk of her panties and his—

Had he taken off his pants? She couldn't feel the thickness of a zipper.

She moved her hips ever so slightly.

He was wearing something, but she didn't think it was briefs. Her panties moved too easily against him. Boxers, maybe? Silk?

A cop in silk boxers? That image was too foreign to fully form in her mind. She *had* to be wrong.

But she couldn't worry about his choice of underwear now. She had to extricate herself, hopefully without waking him.

She considered their positions.

She was on her left side, facing the window. He lay against her, his left arm serving as her pillow, his right curled around her waist. His hand rested across her stomach and—surprise, surprise—his fingers had found the scant half inch of bare skin between her panties and the twisted hem of her shirt.

The second she realized where his fingers were, shivers danced across her skin, raising goose bumps in their wake.

Her eyes drifted closed. Was she imagining it, or could she distinguish the heat of his fingers from the general warmth beneath the covers? It seemed she could feel every slightly calloused tip brushing like an angel's breath across her skin.

Tabitha forced her eyes open.

What was going on? Was she actually enjoying the intimate embrace? Any other time someone had held her this tightly, for this length of time, she'd had a conniption and had fought to be free. Yet she'd lain here—God knows how long—without panicking, without even waking up.

This wasn't like her. Not at all.

But she still didn't have time to figure it out. Heck, she probably couldn't, with the heat fogging her brain. Every time she let down her guard she thought about the weight of his arm on her waist, or the pliable firmness of the biceps against her cheek, the hair on his legs that tickled the—

Jeez! There she went again.

Did she actually want this man?

She knew the answer to that question before it formed in her mind. Yes, she wanted him—with desire that hid like red-hot embers beneath everything she said, everything she did. Embers that burst into flames with the slightest prodding—a smile, a word, a touch.

What would he do if she twisted around and began fanning those flames with kisses, with caresses, with provocative movements of her body?

She knew the answer to that question, too. He'd made his desire perfectly clear, more than once. He'd also made it clear that he'd seen the embers inside her, felt their heat.

Tabitha almost wished she could turn around. Who would know? The world that waited outside already knew he was staying with her. If any of the reporters had suspicions about where he was sleeping, they wouldn't hesitate to splash them all over the papers, no matter what went on.

But Tabitha couldn't turn around. Her heart pounded with fear at just the thought.

She'd been so unsuccessful in every intimate relationship she'd ever had—all one of them—she didn't have the confidence to initiate anything more than a handshake.

No, it was more than a lack of confidence. She didn't know how to initiate intimacy. Her father had spurned any kind of affection at all, and Scott had turned cold the one time she'd kissed him first. He'd insisted on being the one to start their sexual encounters—and they'd always begun and ended with pain. She'd finally realized they weren't making love at all. Scott had a rape fantasy, and all he'd wanted from her was fulfillment.

She'd only dated a few men since, and never more than twice, never going further than a chaste good-night kiss.

Until yesterday when Jake had kissed her and she'd kissed him back. He seemed to like it. So…

No. She had to get up and get dressed before he woke.

Reaching back, she gently lifted his arm and began moving it back to his side.

The cat jumped on the bed with a bounce and meowed.

Jake came awake immediately, fully conscious the instant his eyes opened.

"Go away," Tabitha whispered hotly. "I'll feed you in a minute, but first I have to get up without waking him."

"Him who?" Jake asked with a smile. His voice was still husky with sleep. However, other parts of him had definitely wakened.

Tabitha started, then froze. "You're awake."

"How can a man sleep with you two caterwauling?"

She twisted to look at him. "I was not."

Her eyes widened as her hip bumped against his morning erection. "Oh."

He couldn't help smiling. "Surprise."

"You..." She swallowed visibly. "That wasn't there a minute ago."

"Did a little exploring, did you?"

"No, I just—"

She tried to ease her bottom away, but he wrapped his arm around her waist and pulled her back against him. Her softness felt so good. He wanted to sink into her and never come up for air.

He nuzzled the hair off her neck. "I wouldn't mind if you did."

"You wouldn't?"

"Not a single bit," he said in between the kisses he placed up the right side of her neck.

"Jake, we—we need to get to the hospital."

"What time is it?" He lifted his head and squinted at the clock beside her bed. "Just six-thirty. The press conference isn't until nine."

"We both need to take showers and... Oh." She sighed

sensuously as he slipped a hand under her T-shirt and ran it across the velvet of her stomach. "I don't… Oh."

He smiled at her obvious pleasure and returned his attention to her neck. "Feel good, kitten?"

"I don't… Oh, yes." She bowed her head forward, giving him better access to the sensitive tendons extending into her shoulders. "But we… I mean, don't you… Oh, jeez."

His hand slipped upward, stroking the underside of her breast. She arched back, stretching the T-shirt across her chest. His gut tightened as he witnessed her nipples forming taut little buds. He held her hips against his, feeling her movements across his throbbing heat, feeling even more blood flow in to engorge him.

He took the weight of one breast in his hand, feeling the satin texture of the pliable curves contrasting with the puckered tip. He rubbed his thumb across it and couldn't have said what turned him on more—the flexible resistance of the bud against his finger, or watching his hand caress her beneath her shirt, or the moans that emanated from both of them.

"Jake. What are you…"

"I want to make you feel good," he whispered. "As good as you're making me feel."

Wanting to see what he was touching, Jake threw the sheet off. Cool air hit his heated skin.

She had on red panties. Silk.

"Damn, Tabitha." He ran his hand over the curve of her hip. "How did you know? Red panties do a number on me."

She didn't say anything. Didn't move.

"Kitten?" He pulled his hand from her hip and pushed the hair back from her face. "What is it?"

She turned wide blue eyes to him. "We need to get up."

He placed a kiss on her shoulder. "We do?"

She shrugged away from him. "Yes."

Rising to rest on his elbow, he pulled her onto her back

and studied her guarded face. The hand he rested on her stomach felt the tension that had suddenly entered her body. "Why?"

Her gaze slid away from his. "You're the one who said we could stay in the same house and remain professional."

"I said that? And meant it?"

She didn't smile at his joke.

"Please let me up, Jake. The cat is hungry."

Jake lifted his hand from her stomach.

She rose immediately and all but ran into the hall.

Sighing with frustration, Jake fell back to the pillows.

Damn, she'd been so hot for him. Why had she turned cold all of a sudden? Was it him? Or was it the badge he wore?

He wasn't wearing it now.

What the hell did she have against policemen, anyway?

Her father, Albert Monroe, was the only connection that Jake knew of between Tabitha and police officers.

He glared at the open door.

What had the son of a bitch done to her?

Ten minutes later, Tabitha stood in the shower, letting the warm water sluice down her body. Such a simple thing, yet it felt incredibly sensuous this morning. Even with her eyes closed she could trace every path the water followed along her curves. The shower droplets were thousands of warm fingers thumping against her skin.

The senses in her entire body had been turned up several notches, and it didn't take a genius to figure out why.

Turning impatiently, Tabitha reached for the shampoo.

Okay, she was attracted to the man. It wasn't as if she could do anything about it. Above and beyond the fact that he was a cop, above and beyond the fact that they were key players in a situation that meant life and death for two people—a situation that could make or break either one of their careers—was the fact that attraction inevitably led to intimacy. It almost had just a few minutes ago.

And intimacy wasn't one of Tabitha's greatest strengths. In fact, she sucked swamp water when it came to intimacy. After Scott, she'd vowed she'd never be close to any man again. Intimacy terrified her—which meant that Jake terrified her, because the desire she felt for Scott paled in comparison to what she felt right now.

Tabitha scrubbed the shampoo deep into her hair.

What was wrong with her? People's lives were at stake, and here she was having a latent overdose of adolescent hormones.

She had to get a grip on herself. This...hunger she had for this cop was just a passing fancy. A blip on the screen of her long-range goals.

As long as she remembered that, she'd be okay. She could repel his animal magnetism. She could see his smile without having heart palpitations.

Dropping a dollop of scented liquid soap on her pouf, Tabitha rubbed it into a frothing mass of bubbles. Scrubbing her skin, she berated herself until she looked down and noticed that her skin was turning Chinese red.

She couldn't trust herself enough around him to do the simplest things like give herself a shower.

For the first time Tabitha looked forward to Branson Hines's call. She needed someone to take her frustration out on. If he didn't call, she might have to go looking for the little twerp herself, just so she could keep her hands off Jake.

Tabitha opened the bathroom door and called, "Your tu—"

She stopped dead. Jake stood in front of the stove, dressed only in his slacks. At least he had them zipped this morning. The wonderful, wake-up smells of coffee and bacon comingled with the happy sound of his whistling.

"What are you doing?" What a brilliant question. What he was doing was perfectly obvious. Instead of speechless, shock had rendered her stupid.

He glanced over his shoulder and answered her obvious question with an equally obvious answer. "Cooking breakfast."

"Oh. Right."

"Hope you don't mind."

"For me, too?"

He frowned. "Of course for you, too. What kind of a cook do you think I am?"

Never in her entire life had anyone cooked breakfast for Tabitha. Except a restaurant, and that didn't count, because she paid them.

"What's wrong?" he asked.

She made a conscious effort to raise her jaw. "Nothing."

"You act as if you've seen a ghost."

The Ghost of Breakfast Future?

"No," she said too loudly, more to negate her thought than his statement. She cleared her throat and forced her frozen muscles to move. "I'm fine. Thank you for cooking breakfast. It's very thoughtful."

And totally unlike a cop.

"You're welcome." He smiled. "It won't be ready for about ten minutes. I checked on my men first thing. Everything's quiet, both here and at the hospital."

"Good. Okay, then. I'll get dressed."

As she turned toward the bedroom, he said so softly she wasn't sure she was meant to hear, "You don't have to on my account."

Nine

"The Mission Creek Police Department's presence is certainly visible," Tabitha commented as Jake pulled into her parking space.

With just a casual glance, Jake could see seven of his men. They watched every person coming and going. The three guarding the front entrance had a big job, controlling the crowd of reporters milling around, no doubt waiting for Tabitha. "That's on purpose."

"To scare Hines away?" she asked.

Jake switched off the engine. "That, plus we want to make it clear that he has no chance to get back in here and wreak more havoc if he does something to the hostages."

"You can't keep up this protection forever," she said. "I'm sure it's costing the taxpayers a bundle."

"The taxpayers are who we're protecting." He handed her the keys. "We'll keep it up at least until Hines is caught."

"Which will be soon."

Jake approved of her positive thinking. "God willing."

As they entered the hospital, he paused to talk to the men stationed there. Tabitha hurried in, away from the cameras and microphones and questions shouted at her by the horde of media men and women.

When she disappeared, they turned their attention on Jake, but after telling them they'd have a full statement at the nine-o'clock press conference, he ignored them.

He didn't catch up with Tabitha until he reached her office

twenty minutes later. He was going over the day's schedule with the men who had just arrived to relieve the night crew in the command center in Marie's office when Tabitha walked through her door.

When the men he was talking to shifted their attention behind him, Jake turned around to find her headed out. "Where are you going?"

She stopped at the door to the hall, seeming surprised that he'd asked. "I always make rounds first thing in the morning."

"Rounds? You're not a doctor."

She rolled her eyes. "I visit around the hospital. I like to keep in touch with my people, and patients."

He checked his watch. "It's Sunday and we have a press conference in half an hour."

Her chin began a rebellious ascent. "Today, of all days, I need to check on my people. They see me every morning that I come to work. They'll expect to see me today."

He walked over to her. "Wait until after the press conference, and I'll go with you."

"After what's happened, I need to talk to the employees, reassure the ones who are frightened. It's important."

"I know, and I agree. But I can't go with you now. I have to talk to the men who are about to go off shift, and brief the ones taking over."

"I don't need you to go with me."

"Please wait." He was used to giving orders, not begging favors. "I'll be with you in a few minutes. We need to go over what you're going to say."

"Well..." She took a deep breath. "I suppose there's some paperwork I can see to."

He smiled. "Thank you."

She seemed mollified but still annoyed at having her freedom curtailed. "You're welcome."

He watched her walk stiffly back into her office. He knew

just how she felt, but it couldn't be helped. She needed protection and he needed to see if any of her employees seemed a little too smug.

He turned back to his men. They watched him with knowing expressions.

"Have a good night's sleep, Chief?" one of the younger, braver officers asked.

Jake growled as he returned. They couldn't possibly know he had slept in Tabitha's bed last night. What's more, he didn't want them to know. Ever.

"Go fishing in some other lake, Tyrrell. Now, where were we?"

Fifteen minutes later, Jake opened the door to Tabitha's office and was about to walk through when Marie's office phone rang. Everyone in the room stopped and looked at the officer closest to it.

Tabitha's wide eyes rose from her paperwork. "Do I answer it?"

Jake held up a hand. "Just a sec."

Officer Pitner looked down at the display, then at Jake. "It says 'Out of Area.' Same area code as my mother-in-law. Houston."

"Hines could certainly have driven that far. The ambulance was found in that direction." Jake pointed at Dan Hammel, who'd already seated himself at the tape recorder. He switched it on. "All right, Miss Monroe. Answer it."

Tabitha took several deep breaths, then picked up the phone on the third ring. "Tabitha Monroe. Can I help you? Yes, he is. Just a moment." She punched a button, then looked at Jake. "It's for you. Detective Bill Hackleman of the Houston Police Department."

"Right." Jake nodded at Hammel, who turned off the tape recorder. Then he turned his attention back to Tabitha. He certainly didn't want her listening in on this conversation. "I'll get it out here."

"Okay."

He waited until she'd hung up her phone, then stepped behind Marie's desk. As he picked up the secretary's phone, he blessed the fact that secretaries needed to know when their bosses were on another line. A light would come on if Tabitha picked up her phone.

"Jake White."

"Hey, White. Got some interesting information for you."

Jake sat in Marie's chair and spun so his back was to his men. "What'd you find?"

"Seems Al Monroe had a penchant for abusing prisoners. In fact, that's how he died. In the line of duty, my ass. A Mexicano he took a stick to still had a gun."

Jake's hand tightened on the receiver. Abusive police officers were all too often abusive husbands...and fathers. "Anything else?"

"That ain't enough for the broad to hate cops?"

"Yeah, that's enough." More than enough. "Thanks, Hackleman. I owe you one."

"All in a day's work, my man."

"Talk to you later."

Jake stared at the receiver as he replaced it, suddenly depressed.

As a police officer, he knew that abuse of a child hurt so deeply, the wounds stayed fresh all their lives—rarely healing, rarely even scabbing over. It took an incredibly strong person to overcome such trauma enough to lead a halfway normal life, much less forgive the person who had inflicted the damage.

He already knew that Tabitha was an incredibly strong woman. Now he knew how strong.

Now he knew what he was up against.

* * *

The press conference was frustrating for everyone, since there was no information to give the media beyond the conclusion that the tire tracks found near the abandoned ambulance probably were made by Branson Hines's vehicle. From there the trail went cold because the ambulance and tracks had been found scarcely half a mile from the Lone Star Highway, a two-lane paved road that headed east toward Corpus Christi.

The hour after the press conference, however, was very enlightening for Jake. At least on a personal level.

As he followed Tabitha around the hospital wards and service departments, he watched as she talked to her employees about what had happened and what was being done. Some of the hospital's employees seemed afraid to be at work; others realized the danger was over, at least for now.

Tabitha was amazingly good at bolstering her employees' courage. Somehow, she made each employee think his or her job was the most important in the hospital, made each employee believe that he or she was the most important employee—both to the hospital and to her. She made such a stirring speech to the kitchen crew, Jake was surprised they didn't follow her out doing a goose step to the theme from *General Hospital.*

She was one of the most well respected and beloved administrators that he'd ever seen. He actually watched people's faces light up when they saw her coming.

She knew personal details about every single one of them, asking this woman about her bursitis and that man about his grandchildren.

But it was all smoke and mirrors. He'd bet real money that not a single one of Tabitha's employees knew that she loved cats, or that she could eat three slices of bacon and two eggs for breakfast but didn't eat much dinner.

Tabitha gave the impression that she was close to everyone, but that was the same as being close to no one.

Jake knew. He was the same way.

He was popular with the guys on the Mission Creek police force. He went to the Saddlebag with them all the time, but he was always the designated driver. Jake didn't drink beer or any other alcoholic beverage, because alcohol made you lose control. And losing control made you tell people things you'd rather they didn't know.

He'd bet a year's paycheck that Tabitha didn't drink, either. As he'd learned today, she had much more to hide than he did.

As he pushed open the door to the almost-back-to-normal maternity ward—their last stop—Jake decided to test his theory. "I think I'll cook a couple of steaks for us tonight. What kind of wine would you like to go with them?"

Tabitha's nose wrinkled. "None for me, thank you. I don't drink."

He smiled grimly as he followed her in.

Two seeds in a pod.

"You okay?"

Tabitha opened her eyes and lifted her head from where she'd leaned it back against her chair. "Come in and talk to me. Please! I'm going crazy."

Jake grinned as he entered her office. "And here I thought I was giving you space so you could get some work done."

She gave him a twisted smile. "Like I can concentrate. I'm dreading Hines's call so much, I nearly have a heart attack every time the phone rings."

"Good thing you work in a hospital, then, isn't it?" He sat in the chair across from her desk. "I don't know why you're complaining. That makes just three heart attacks this morning."

Besides the call for Jake before the press conference, Marie had called to see if she needed to come in. Tabitha insisted she stay home. The other call had been from Crystal Bennett, Mission Creek Hospital's fund-raiser. Crystal had gone out of town for the long weekend with her son and her new husband, Ace Carson.

"Thanks to you for telling the reporters not to call this number, and thanks to Congress for the Labor Day holiday." She stood and twisted hard to realign her spine.

He winced at the distinct crack. "Ouch."

"Feels good." She twisted in the other direction. "You should try it."

"Maybe later."

She shrugged and wandered over to check the moisture level of her bonsai. "Are holidays bad for police departments?"

"Crime happens every single day of the week."

"Surely—statistically speaking—some days are worse than others."

"You mean like full moons?"

She glanced over her shoulder. "Are they?"

He spread his hands. "I've never noticed a difference, but I've heard it's true—statistically speaking."

Satisfied her plants were as healthy as she could make them at the moment, Tabitha turned and leaned against the credenza. "Not into statistics, I take it."

"Statistics are interesting, if you have the time. But statistics don't get criminals off the street."

"Well, they don't actually put the handcuffs on the criminals, but they can help."

"How?"

"If, like you said, crime is worse on full moons, the powers that be can schedule more people to work those days and nights. That would help get criminals off the streets, wouldn't it? If there were more cops around when more criminals are active?"

"You've got me there." He shook his head with a grin. "You're a very smart lady, you know it?"

"Yes, I do." She grinned playfully. "Helps keep the men away."

His face turned thoughtful. "Is that how you do it? Outsmart them, so to speak?"

She went still, sensing a zinger. "I was teasing."

"No, you weren't."

She started to argue, then decided not to waste the effort. For some reason, this man knew her almost better than she knew herself. "It's as good a way as any."

"Why do you want to? You're thirty-five. Why aren't you married by now, with two-point-seven kids?"

"Why aren't you?" she shot back. "You can't be much older than I am."

"I'm married to my job."

She shook her head. "That answer's too pat, too much of a cliché. Clichés don't fit you."

He raised a dark brow. "I'm sorry if you don't think so, but it's true. I was..."

"You were what?" she asked when he trailed off with a frown.

He stood and headed for the door. "I have to check on my men."

"Coward."

He stopped at her muttered comment.

She went on. "You're brave enough to stop a bullet for people you don't know, but you're not brave enough to share a little bit of your life with anyone."

He turned slowly. "What was it you said about me yesterday? Something about a pot calling a kettle black?"

She shrugged. "Okay, we both have a problem with emotional intimacy. But I'd really like to know what makes a man like you into a cop."

He studied her face, as if deciding on how much he could trust her.

"It's okay," she said. "I don't share my own secrets, and I don't share other people's, either."

He strolled toward the chair he'd just vacated, but he didn't sit down. "I'll talk if you will."

Tabitha chuckled.

"What?" he demanded.

"Sounds like a deal I would make."

He smiled slyly. "Yes, it does, doesn't it?"

Her mouth twisted. "You first."

"Uh-uh." He leaned on the back of the chair. "I didn't hear you agree to reciprocate."

"Okay, I agree." She sat back down in her own executive chair. No one had ever read her this well. It was very disconcerting. "You were about to tell me why you think you're not a cliché."

Jake sat down, too. "I was about to say that the reason I know I'm married to my job—whether or not that's a cliché—is because I was married once."

Tabitha blinked. "To a woman?"

"No, to a rattlesnake." His smile turned wry. "Actually, sometimes I thought she was close kin to a rattlesnake."

"Who was she? Tell me about her. I can't picture you as a husband."

"Neither could I. Neither could she, after about six months." He settled deeper into the upholstered wing chair. "I told you, I'm married to my job. I was gone more than I was home. Sometimes I wasn't able to call when I wasn't coming home. I didn't show up at the social events she organized. She was an attorney. Am ambitious attorney with an eye on a political career. That's why she wanted me. She even told me once that a cop with an untarnished record—one with ambitions—looked good on her résumé. That's all I was to her, in the end. A line on her résumé."

"How long did it last?"

"Two years. I came home one night after three days on a stakeout. She'd moved out. I was served papers a few days later."

"Oh, Jake. I'm so sorry."

He shrugged. "That was eight years ago. I'm over it."

She picked up a pencil and began tapping it absently on the desk, then she met his steady gaze. "Why didn't you try harder? Why didn't you at least call when you couldn't come home?"

"I told you, I'm married to—"

"Horsefeathers." She pointed the pencil at him. "When men don't call, it's because they don't think about it, or don't want to. Either way, it's a sure sign that they don't care."

He stared at her, hard.

She lowered the pencil. "What?"

He shook his head, as if clearing it. "You're right. I don't know if I ever really loved her."

"Then why did you marry her?"

"Because she talked me into it. And she had a..."

"She had a what?" Tabitha prompted. "We're sharing, remember?"

He took a deep breath. "She had a mole. A dark one, right beside her mouth. Like yours."

Tabitha touched her mole. She hardly ever thought about it. "A mole?"

His gaze latched onto her fingers. "Yes."

"You like moles?"

He chuckled, a tad nervously. "Yeah. I do."

She jerked her hand away from her face. Surely she hadn't heard him correctly. "Moles?"

"Mmm, hmm."

She shifted in her chair. "You mean like a sexual thing?"

"More or less." He dragged his gaze away from her mole and sighed. "Some men get turned on by women's feet.

Some like breasts, some like butts. And don't get me wrong, I like those, too. But if a woman has a mole, it's one of the first things I notice about her. Especially facial ones. Especially—" his voice lowered "—if they're close to her mouth."

Tabitha swallowed hard. Was it her imagination, or was she breathing a little harder than she had been? This was nuts. Was she actually getting turned on by hearing what turned him on? "I see."

"I noticed yours the second I walked into the press conference yesterday."

Her mole was itching now, being the center of attention. She forced herself not to touch it again. She cleared her throat. "So what you're saying is you're not attracted to me, particularly. You're attracted to my mole."

He smiled slowly. "That was yesterday."

She frowned. "You're not attracted to me today?"

His eyes shone with amusement. "I'm even more attracted to you today, because I've discovered there's a brain underneath the mole."

"You like smart women?"

"Especially if they have a mole."

She glanced down and discovered she was pushing the pencil back and forth between her fingers. A sure sign of nerves. She stopped immediately. This was not what she had in mind when she'd asked him to talk.

"Most men..." She had to clear her throat again. "Most men don't like women with brains."

He shrugged. "Most men don't have brains themselves."

"True."

"Your turn."

"Me?"

"Yep. I shared, now you share. You agreed. No going back."

Tabitha glanced at the door he'd left open. No one in the outer office was paying any attention to them. Darn it. "I..."

She didn't know what to say. Because she'd been soured on men at an early age, she hadn't paid much attention to them over the years. She'd concentrated on her career. She went out with a guy if he asked and she halfway liked him, if she thought she could stand him for an evening. But she'd never been attracted to one like this. So there was no pattern, no consistent trait that attracted her. She certainly didn't have anything as good as a mole.

Wait a minute. That wasn't the topic they'd started with.

Her lips curved in a pleased smile. "I've never been married."

He grinned. "I wondered when you'd backtrack to that."

She glared at him. "You got to start out easy."

"I'm not complaining." He laced his fingers behind his head. "Okay. Let's go with this for the moment. You've never been married. Ever engaged?"

"No."

"Why not?"

She smirked. "Guess I've been married to my job."

"Too pat. Try again. You're smart and beautiful. Why haven't you ever been in a serious relationship?"

"You didn't ask that."

"So now I'm asking."

"Okay. I dated a guy in college halfway seriously. Lasted a whole semester."

"What happened?"

"I decided he wasn't the guy for me."

"Why not?"

"Because he was like my—" Tabitha dropped her gaze. No, she couldn't tell him about her father. Maybe the sexual innuendoes *were* easier. "Because he didn't like my mole."

Jake was silent so long Tabitha glanced up to find his green eyes concentrating on her. The heat coming from him wasn't sexual, but was just as intense.

"He was stupid, then," Jake said finally, softly. "Your mole takes my breath away."

His statement surprised her. It took her breath away. "Thank you."

"What about later?" he asked. "Why haven't you been involved with anyone since?"

She straightened. "Hey, I didn't ask you for a recital of all the women you've seen over the years."

"No, you didn't, did you? Okay. Now for part two."

Tabitha groaned and hurried on, "After college, there was—"

"Why are you attracted to me?"

She stared at him. "What makes you—"

"Don't try to deny it," he said.

Her chin lifted. "I will if I want to."

He chuckled at her defiance. "Do I have to close the door and prove it to you all over again?"

His low comment made her gaze flicker back to the door.

"They're not paying any attention to us," he said without looking.

"I know." Even to her own ears, she sounded miserable. "Maybe if I got naked and started dancing on top of my desk—"

"Then I *would* have to close the door."

"Why?" she couldn't help but asking.

"Because, kitten." He leaned closer. "I won't share you with anyone."

"Oh."

"So...?"

"So?"

"Why are you attracted to me?"

She swallowed. "I don't know. I don't have a list like you do. I haven't thought about it that much."

"Surely you can come up with something."

Since she couldn't concentrate with his attention on her,

she closed her eyes. But that should tell her something, shouldn't it? She couldn't concentrate during the times she felt most attracted to him, either. So was she attracted to him because he paid her attention?

No. Other men had paid her attention. She hadn't been attracted to them.

But none of them had been so...aggressive about their attention.

Tabitha frowned. Aggression was the one thing she hated most. Surely she wasn't attracted to Jake's aggression.

"Thinking hurts, does it?"

She opened her eyes to his handsome, amused face.

No, she wasn't attracted to his aggressiveness. Not exactly. It was more the fact that he was interested enough to be aggressive, but he controlled it. He controlled it with humor and intelligence and respect for her.

Suddenly an incredibly powerful wave of emotion swept over her, one she'd never felt. Tenderness and desire and pleasure and—

Oh, God. Was she in love with him?

"What the hell are you thinking?" he asked.

No. She wasn't in love with him. Absolutely, unequivocally not.

She made her lips curve upward, hoping the attempted smile didn't look as fake as it felt. "I like your sense of humor, and your ambition, and your—"

He slapped his hands on her desk, making her jump. "That's not what you were thinking."

She lifted an eyebrow. "You can read minds now?"

"I can read yours."

"All right, then, psychic Jake, tell me what I was thinking."

His eyes narrowed. "I don't know the specifics, but I know I saw panic in your eyes not two seconds ago."

The panic flooded back, and she stood up to hide it. Why did he have to be so darn perceptive? She couldn't tell him about her momentary lapse, thinking she was in love with him. It wasn't true.

Suddenly, strong hands landed on her shoulders and spun her around to face him.

"What is it?" He shook her shoulders, but not hard. "Tell me."

She couldn't tell him about thinking she was in love with him, but she could tell him about the other part. Abuse was enough to inspire panic in any woman. "I thought for just a second that I was attracted to your aggressiveness."

He immediately released her shoulders. "My what?"

She put a hand on his chest to reassure him. "Then I realized I'm attracted to your *controlled* aggression."

He frowned down at her. "I've never hit a woman in my life."

She shook her head. "I didn't say abusiveness. What I meant was..." She spread her hands. "I just now figured it out myself. My own surprise is what you saw in my face."

He grabbed her hands. "Tell me what it is."

Her gaze dropped to his broad chest. "I like the fact that you're interested enough to be aggressive, but that you have enough control not to be abusive. Does that make any sense?"

He lifted her chin with one finger. "Perfect sense."

She couldn't drag her gaze away from his. His desire shone blatantly from his eyes, igniting her own. Her pulse began to race, making her skin tingle with anticipation of his touch, making her throb all over.

He grinned suddenly, with pleased self-satisfaction. "So you *admit* you're attracted to me."

He'd broken the spell with humor, in order to maintain control. He had the good sense to realize the door to her office was still open. The physical yearnings so new to her had made her forget all about it.

Grateful—and even more attracted to him—she rolled her eyes. "Duh."

He chuckled. "Intelligent comment."

She lifted an eyebrow. "Is sexual desire intelligent? From what I've seen so far, all brain activity goes on hold."

He ran a finger lightly over her mole, his voice lowering. "It does if you do it right."

She shivered. "We'd better stop this."

He muttered curses, then released a deep breath. "You're right. This is not the time or place."

His thumb lightly stroked the palm of her hand, then he stepped back. "Are you hungry?"

She blinked. "Hungry? Is it time for lunch already?"

He checked his watch. "Ten after twelve. I was going to send out—"

The phone beside them rang, startling them both.

Since Tabitha's phone didn't have a display, they turned as one toward the doorway.

A second later, Officer Pitner appeared in it. "Unknown name. Unknown caller."

"Is Dan ready?"

Pitner glanced behind him, then nodded. "Ready to go."

"Tell him to turn it on." Jake faced Tabitha. "This could be Hines."

She took a deep breath. "I know."

"You ready?"

"I have to be, don't I?"

Jake looked at Pitner, who nodded. "Anytime you're ready."

Tabitha took another breath, then stepped to her desk. Even though they'd had a number of false alarms that morning, she felt a certainty in her bones that this was the kidnapper.

She picked up the phone. ‘‘Tabitha Monroe. Can I help you?’’

‘‘Call the cops off or you’ll never see your friends again. Not alive.’’

The line went dead.

Ten

Jake knew from the sudden blanching of Tabitha's face that the caller was Hines. "Keep him on as long as you can."

She shook her head and lowered the receiver. "He's gone."

"What did he say?"

"He told me I have to get rid of you, of the police, if I want to see Sam and Cait again alive."

Jake nodded. "That's standard operating procedure for kidnappers. Like there's a manual or something. Don't worry about it."

Jake spun and headed into the outer office, which was alive with activity. Adrenaline pumped through his veins. Though it was brief, this was first contact with the kidnapper.

"Let's hear it," Jake said to Dan Hammel.

Hammel must have already rewound the tape, because he pressed a button and Hines's nasal, high-pitched voice came over the speakers.

"Call the cops off or you'll never see your friends again. Not alive."

Jake glanced at Pitner, who was on the phone. "Any chance of a trace?"

The officer shook his head. "On five seconds? Not with our equipment. I'm talking to the phone company, to see if they can get anything. Not much hope, since he apparently used a calling card, but they're trying."

Jake nodded, then turned to Hammel. "Play it again."

"Call the cops off or you'll never see your friends again. Not alive."

"Interesting that Hines called the victims Miss Monroe's friends, not her employees." Jake shoved a hand back through his hair. It helped him think.

"What's it mean, Chief?" Officer Fletcher asked. He sat on the two-way radio all day, the point man for the coordinated search that had extended to all of Duval County.

Jake lifted a shoulder. "There's no way to be sure of anything. But unless Hines is smarter than I think he is—and if he is, I'm dumber than I think I am—it means that the hostages are alive, and that he's talking to them."

"He sounded scared," Hammel said.

"And frustrated," another officer said.

Jake nodded. "It's hard to pin down anything, with only about a dozen words to go on."

Officer Pitner hung up the phone with a defeated sigh. "Nothing beyond the fact that he definitely used a calling card. The trace has to come from the originating company, and there's just no way to know which one it is. Everybody from the post office to Wal-Mart sells them."

Jake nodded. "We'll get something next time. Good work for now. Keep it up."

He pulled out his cell phone and dialed Burl Terry's cell number. The chief of Mission Creek Police Department had returned to the office directly after the press conference. Since he had no experience in hostage situations, Burl was letting Jake handle everything. He was two years away from retirement and didn't give a damn what the media thought about his role in the crisis. Since the only thing he cared about was having the job done right, all he required was to be kept informed and to be included on any major decisions.

Since the men in the room were analyzing Hines's call, Jake paced the room as he and Burl discussed it. As he turned, he glanced into the open door to Tabitha's office.

She remained standing behind her desk, the telephone receiver still in her hand. She stared at the dragon on the left corner of her desk, her face white.

"I need to go, Chief," Jake said. "I'll let you know if anything else comes up, but I don't expect Hines will call again until at least tomorrow."

Jake ended the call, then stepped into Tabitha's office. She glanced up, her face bleak.

He closed the door and walked over to her. Gently lifting her arm, he took the phone from her hand and replaced the receiver.

"Oh," she said. "Sorry."

"You're hurting yourself, not me." He massaged her stiff fingers, which had cramped around the phone, then lifted her chin. "Everything is okay. This is not unexpected. I haven't run across a kidnapper yet who doesn't insist the police be called off."

"He said he'll kill them if I don't." Her eyes finally focused on his. "Didn't he? You heard what he said, right?"

He nodded and stroked her jaw with his thumb. "They all say that, kitten. He's just trying to scare you."

She shivered. "Well, he's doing a very good job."

Touched by her vulnerability, and the fact that she was showing it to him, Jake took her hand and led her over to the red couch against the wall. He sat her down in the center, then sat next to her and wrapped his arms around her.

She resisted, but not with any force, so he held her captive until she settled into the crook of his arm with a sigh. "I suck at this."

"No, you don't."

"Yes, I do. Crisis management is part of my job, and I've gone through training. What do I do? I fall apart the first time he calls."

Jake kissed the top of her head. Her hair was soft against his lips, and fragrant with herbs. "Nobody is good at this.

Especially when you know the hostages. A couple of years ago I dealt with the CEO of a multibillion-dollar international company. He'd been trained in crisis management, too, and had actually handled several kidnapping situations. But those were people he didn't know—overseas employees. When his teenaged daughter was kidnapped, he fell apart. His wife had to handle the calls."

"Did you get her back?" Tabitha asked.

"Yes."

She hesitated. "Alive?"

"Yes, thank God. The last I heard, that guy had quit and moved his family to Idaho where he opened a fishing camp."

"I don't blame him."

Jake rubbed her arm. "This kind of thing should never happen, but it does. The only way you can train for it is to go through a real situation. And chances are that if you do, you'll never go through another one. Kidnappings happen, but not as often as most people think."

"Thank God."

"Yes."

After a moment of silence, she whispered, "What if Branson Hines does kill them because I didn't call off the police?"

"I hate to tell you this, but you can't call us off. It's a criminal case now, and we're in charge. Even if you could by some miracle manage to convince us to go away, you'd never be able to call off the press."

She sighed heavily. "You're right."

"Don't worry, kitten. We'll make our presence as unobtrusive as possible. I'll change the positions of the men here at the hospital and put them in plain clothes. That'll at least give the appearance that you're complying with his wishes."

"Thank you."

"As far as the search goes, we've scoured most of the

county. He's either hours away from here, or dug into some hole that we'll never find until either he comes out or makes a mistake. I'll make the Feds happy by asking them to search the rest of Texas. Give them something to do besides breathing down my neck."

He paused. "Does that make you feel better?"

She was still for a moment, then she leaned back far enough to look up at him. "Yes, it does. Thank you."

He lifted a brow. "You sound surprised."

Her forehead wrinkled with concentration. "I guess I am."

"Why?"

She searched his face. "You're different from other cops."

He went still. "I am? How?"

She frowned further and tried to lower her head, but he caught it with one finger. "Tell me how I'm different."

"You seem to care about people like me. What I mean is, the people you're helping."

"Other police officers care."

"Some don't."

"That's true, unfortunately." He pushed a strand of blond hair behind her ear. "But in any job you'll find people who care and people who don't."

"I guess so." Her gaze dropped to his lips. "You're also..."

Jake didn't want to push her, but he'd never seen her this open, this vulnerable. "Also what?"

"Different in other ways."

"What ways?"

Slowly, hesitantly, she lifted her hand. Extending the forefinger, she drew it toward his face.

Jake sat very still, not wanting to spook her. But every cell in his body reached toward her, willing her to touch.

Finally her finger landed on his lips, softly, like a butterfly.

He closed his eyes on a sigh and kissed her finger.

"Like that," she said breathlessly. "You seem to want me to touch you."

"I do." He opened his eyes and met her gaze. "Very much."

She lowered her gaze to her finger and watched as she drew it slowly across his lips. She gasped softly when he stuck his tongue out just enough to wet her finger as it passed.

With that one tiny noise, Jake went hard.

She was so damn sexy she took his breath away.

"Do you know what you're doing to me?"

"What?" She seemed inordinately interested, as if she really didn't know.

"You're making me want to touch you back."

"I am? You do?"

A low growl rose from his throat. "Yeah."

She shivered, but this time pleasure caused the reaction, not fear. "Okay."

Jake slowly twisted, gently forcing her back against his arm. She went willingly. Her trust touched him deeply and instead of the passionate, tongue-tying kiss he wanted to give her, he rained soft kisses all over her face.

Her hands gathered fistfuls of his shirt, holding him in place, drawing him closer.

Only when she began panting did his lips touch hers.

She gasped, opening her mouth against his.

Even then Jake didn't force anything. He slipped his tongue along her lips, then beneath them, running along the ridges of her teeth.

She whimpered. "Jake."

"Yes, kitten?" he breathed against her mouth. "Tell me what you want."

For an answer, she raked the fingers of one hand through his hair, clamped onto the back of his head and pulled him close. She opened her mouth and drove her tongue into his mouth.

The arm behind her shifted, tugging her around until their chests touched. He could feel the tight points of her breasts nudging his chest.

He sighed with deep pleasure and shifted again. This time he sat back against the couch, intending to pull her on top of him and lay them both down. He wanted to feel her weight against him, against all of him.

As he sat back, however, the cell phone he'd hung on his hip dug into it, reminding him where they were.

Slowly, with regretful kisses, he drew away, but only far enough to break the passion. He held her against him, enjoying the feel of her breath against his neck, her arm around his waist, her leg slung over his. He especially enjoyed the fact that she didn't move it.

A moment later, when his rapid heart rate had returned sufficient blood to his brain, he sighed. "Damn."

"I agree," she said. "It wasn't half an hour ago that we agreed this was neither the time or place."

He shifted again, pushing her back along his shoulder until he could see her face. She was flushed with passion, her lips were slightly swollen, and strands of hair crisscrossed her face.

One by one, he began pushing them back. "Hey, can I help it if you can't keep your hands off me?"

"Me?" She slapped his chest. "You weren't exactly fighting me off."

He grinned and hugged her close, breathing deep of her warm, fragrant scent. "No, and I won't, either. You feel too damn good."

"So do you." Her comment was so quiet, he barely heard.

She seemed so naive, so unguarded at that moment, he wanted to wrap her in his arms and keep here there, always. She made him feel as if he was the only man on earth at that moment, the only man who'd ever touched her. Though he knew it wasn't true, the possibility made him feel ten feet tall.

"Jake?"

"Yeah?"

"Why..." She shifted so she could see him. "Why are you doing this?"

He blinked. "Doing what? Holding you?"

She nodded, rocking her head against his arm.

"Because I can't not do it. Because you're beautiful. Because you're smart. Because you're brave. Because you're the sexiest woman I've ever known."

"So it's not because of my mole?"

He chuckled and bent his head to kiss the tiny nub. "Well, I have to say that your mole started it. If you have to blame something, blame it."

Her gaze lowered to where her fingers played with a button on his shirt. "Does this happen very often?"

"Does what happen very often?"

"Your not being able to keep your hands off women you're working with."

He forced her chin up so she had to meet his gaze. "Never. It has *never* happened. I want you to know that. I've never, ever done this before. I shouldn't be doing it now. I don't know why I am except—God help me—I really can't keep my hands off you."

Her smile said she was pleased with his answer. "And is it okay if I can't keep my hands off you, either?"

Laughing, cursing, he hugged her close. "You witch."

"Witch?" She pushed at his shoulder. "I am not."

He grabbed her hand and tugged it down to his pants. "It was nearly gone, but just the thought of you not being able to keep your hands off me makes me hard as a rock."

Instead of being offended, Tabitha seemed fascinated. She rubbed her fingers along the length. "I did this?"

His hips jerked under her touch. "Uh-huh."

She lifted her wide-eyed gaze to his. "Can I see?"

He nearly choked, and nearly came right there under the pressure of her hand—like a green boy. He dragged her hand away. "No."

She went still. "I'm sorry. I'm sorry. I didn't know. I just wanted—"

He rolled them both until she was flat on her back on the couch, stretched out beneath him. The eyes she lifted to his were fearful.

What had she been through, to be afraid of a little sex play? She was all over him, then afraid to move. She kissed him like a randy teenager, then touched him as if she'd never even seen a man. She was passionate, then naive. Frisky, then hesitant.

He'd never wanted a woman more in his life, but he wanted this one from the inside out. He knew at that moment that he couldn't make love to her until she trusted him enough to tell him about her father.

He lifted a strand of hair caught across her lips. "It's okay to touch me, kitten. I want you to touch me."

"You do?"

He bent and gently kissed her. "Of course I do. You make me feel so damn good." He twisted his mouth. "A whole lot better than I should be feeling in here, when one of my men could come through that door any second."

She closed her eyes and dragged in a breath. "You're right. I just..."

"Just what?"

She opened her eyes. "I'm not very good at this, either."

"Not very good? Hell, you *felt* how good you are at this."

"I mean..." She frowned. "I don't have a lot of... experience with this kind of thing."

Her admission touched him, but he wanted more. "Why not? You're thirty-five years old."

Her gaze slid away. "I just don't."

He sighed with disappointment. But he shouldn't expect miracles. "It's all right."

"You probably think I'm about fourteen, the way I'm acting."

He gently forced her to look at him. "I think you're wonderful...and soft...and sexy as hell. And when this is all over—assuming we can wait that long—I'll let you see any part of me that you want to."

Her eyes began to sparkle. "You will?"

He closed his eyes and groaned. "You're doing it again, witch."

She giggled, and the happy sound made his heart soar. He wondered if she'd ever giggled as a girl, if she'd ever been allowed to, if she'd ever been happy enough to even try. He wanted to make her giggle for the rest of her life.

"So being a witch is not necessarily a bad thing."

He growled against her neck. "Depends on what kind of magic spells she casts."

His stomach growled at the same time.

"Well, for now I can call the pizza place and in thirty minutes, lunch will magically appear."

He sat up and pulled her with him. "I think we need to get out of here."

She gasped softly and at the hopeful, promising look in her eyes, he nearly shoved her back down on the couch.

"In a very *public* place," he clarified. "I'm taking you to lunch."

She frowned. "I don't know if that's a good idea. Where would we go that the press wouldn't bug us to death?"

"You're a member of the country club, aren't you?"

She brightened. "Of course. They won't let the press in there."

He stood. "Right."

She reached out one hand and he pulled her up. "But shouldn't we stay here?"

He shook his head. "Hines won't call again today. He'll give you time to get rid of the police. At any rate, we'll have all your calls forwarded to the cell phone I gave you. If he does call, you'll get it."

"All right, then. Take me to lunch."

Eleven

The Lone Star Country Club was busy on the Labor Day weekend. Jake drove Tabitha across town in his own vehicle, a full-size truck the reporters hadn't had time to connect to her. Several squad cars had followed them and would wait just outside the club gates, close enough in case of an emergency but far enough away to be discreet.

Instead of pulling into the parking area Tabitha pointed out on the right, Jake drove up the tree-lined, semicircular driveway to the covered portico.

"Valet parking?" she asked. "A little extravagant for a cop, isn't it?"

He grinned. "What the hell."

"Nice knowing I'm a what-the-hell kind of woman," she murmured as he set the brake.

He grinned. "Better than a no-way-in-hell kind of woman, isn't it?"

She chuckled wryly. "Not always."

Her door opened then, so she twisted and let the young man assist her from the cab.

Jake handed his keys to another young man and met her around the other side. He guided her through a set of doors, gratified that she didn't object to the hand he placed on the small of her back.

The huge two-story lobby was quietly abuzz from various groups in the carefully planned conversation areas. The chatter stopped long enough to be noticeable the moment they walked through the doors.

Tabitha hesitated. "I probably shouldn't have come. I see at least three members of the hospital board here."

"Everybody has to eat." Jake applied slight pressure on her back to urge her on.

An older man Jake recognized as head of the Wainwright clan—Archy Wainwright—stood as they walked across the plush carpets. The Wainwrights were one of the founding families of Mission Creek and had donated half the land the country club sat on. They'd helped established the town of Mission Creek and the Mission Creek Memorial Hospital, as well.

Tabitha stopped to shake his hand. "Good afternoon, Mr. Wainwright. You know Chief White, I'm sure."

Jake measured the man's strong grip. "Good afternoon."

"Everything all settled at the hospital, Miss Monroe?" Wainwright's voice clearly indicated he'd caught her playing hooky.

Before she could reply, Jake stepped in.

"We're just in to get a bite to eat," he told the man, drawing his critical attention away from Tabitha. "I made the decision—and I'm sure you'll agree—that Miss Monroe needed some time away from the stress of waiting. Especially since there's little chance the kidnapper will call again in the next few hours, and since Miss Monroe's calls are being forwarded to her cell phone."

Mr. Wainwright nodded. "All right, then. Nice to know you have everything under control, Chief White. Keep up the good work."

"*We* plan to." With a tug on Tabitha's arm, Jake drew her away from the Wainwright party.

"Thank you," she said softly.

"No problem. Rescuing fair maidens from bullies is all part of the job."

"He's not a bully, exactly, just—"

"Rich and powerful and thinks he owns everything in

Mission Creek.'' Jake guided her to the entrance of the Yellow Rose Café, which sat at the back of the clubhouse.

Tabitha smiled ruefully. ''Just half the town. The Carsons own the other half.''

''Every town's got at least one.'' They paused at the hostess stand. ''Two, please. That table back by the windows will be perfect.''

The hostess glanced toward the back, then grabbed two menus. ''Right this way.''

Jake pulled out Tabitha's chair, then seated himself and took the menu from the young lady.

Tabitha set hers to the side.

''Not even going to look?'' Jake asked.

She shook her head and raised her glass of water. ''The menu hasn't changed since I joined the club. I always have the Cobb salad.''

''How are their plate lunches?''

''I don't know. I always—''

''Have the Cobb salad.'' He grinned. ''Kind of monotonous, isn't it?''

''When you like something, why change just for the sake of change?''

''Variety is the spice of life.''

She lifted an eyebrow. ''Experiments can blow up in your face.''

''Yes, but without experiments, we wouldn't have electricity, or penicillin, or plastic, or—''

''Okay, okay. Monotony Monroe. That's me.''

He lifted his chin thoughtfully. ''Has a certain ring to it, doesn't it?''

''As long as I'm confessing, I have to tell you that I make pizza every Saturday night.''

''You *make* pizza? You don't order it?''

She shook her head. ''I'm too picky about what I want

on it and how much. I end up spending as much as I would to order it, but it tastes a whole lot better."

"Well, maybe you can—"

"Tabitha?"

They looked up to find a tall, broad-shouldered man in a white straw Stetson standing over their table. Flynt Carson, heir apparent to the enormous Carson spread.

Jake shoved back his chair and stood. Though also formally polite, Jake meant the gesture more as a protective warning. He needn't have bothered.

Flynt nodded to both of them. "Tabitha, Officer White. Good afternoon. I just wanted to stop and say hello. Wanted to tell you we're all behind you one hundred percent with the situation at the hospital."

"Thank you, Flynt," Tabitha said. "I really appreciate that."

Jake relaxed.

"I'm glad you could get away for a few minutes," Flynt continued. "If there's anything we can do to help, just holler."

"The town could use some surveillance equipment made at least in the second half of the twentieth century," Jake told him.

"What do you mean?"

Jake explained.

Flynt nodded. "I'll bring it up at the next police board meeting."

"Thanks. So far I've avoided explaining what we have to the press. But if the situation goes on much longer, it could be embarrassing for the town."

Jake knew that was his strongest argument. Both the Wainwrights and the Carsons hated that the world considered Mission Creek the south end of nowhere—if the world thought about the town at all.

"If the board doesn't okay the purchase, I'll buy it myself."

"Great." Jake extended his hand with a smile. "Thanks for stopping by."

Flynt shook Jake's hand, then Tabitha's. "I meant what I said, Tabitha. And to you, too, Jake. Burl's been keeping us informed. No one could do a better job."

Tabitha beamed. "Thank you, Flynt. That means a lot, coming from one of the hospital's biggest supporters."

Flynt touched the brim of his hat. "Enjoy your meal."

As he left, Jake sat down. "That was profitable."

Tabitha smiled. "He's a nice guy. A little taciturn, but most cowboys are, aren't they?"

"That's what I hear."

"Howdy, folks." A middle-aged woman with a pencil sticking out of her bleached French twist smiled at them. The tag pinned to her white blouse said her name was Trudy. "Y'all ready to order?"

"I'll have the Cobb salad and iced tea." Tabitha pushed her menu toward the waitress.

Trudy pulled the pencil from her hair with the ease of knowing exactly where she'd left it. After a couple of strokes on her green pad, she looked at Jake expectantly.

"How's the pot roast?" he asked.

"Honey, it'll plumb melt in your mouth."

"By all means, then, put me down for pot roast."

"Have the okra with it. He just pulled out a fresh batch. And the lady peas came out of the field yesterday."

He handed Trudy his menu. "My mouth is watering already."

The waitress grinned. "I'll bring you some sliced tomatoes on the side. Can you handle all that, cowboy?"

"I can handle anything you throw at me, Trudy."

"We'll see about that, honey." Trudy winked at Tabitha. "I'll be right back with y'all's tea."

Tabitha gave him an arch smile. "So you're an incorrigible flirt."

He shrugged. "A little flirting never hurt anybody."

She uttered a sound that could have been either agreement or disbelief, then turned her gaze to the window.

Jake's smile slowly froze as what he said sank in. He studied Tabitha's lovely profile as she idly gazed at the gardens that stretched from the trellised walkway on the other side of the windows to the club's eighteen-hole championship golf course.

Suddenly Jake knew that flirting *could* hurt somebody, and that somebody was him. He wasn't just flirting with her. He was flirting with disaster, because he wanted more than flirtation with Tabitha. Much more. He wanted all of her—every smile, every kiss, every dream, every disappointment, every day, every night, *everything.*

Damn. When had it gone this far? Was he in love with her?

No. He couldn't be.

Tabitha Monroe was not a woman he could have a casual affair with, then blithely leave after the time that remained on his contract. She needed a man who loved her desperately, who wanted to marry her and settle down and be with her twenty-four/seven.

She didn't need him.

Jake ignored the pinprick that truth sent to his heart. He didn't do relationships. Did he?

No. He wasn't going to stay in Mission Creek. In exactly twelve months and twenty-three days, he was out of there. He didn't know where yet. He didn't have to worry about putting out feelers for another six months. But somewhere bigger, badder. Some place where crime—real crime—would consume his days and nights. Like they had in Houston.

Hell, she didn't even want him. She hated cops.

Though he still didn't know why. He wanted that, too. Wanted her to trust him enough to tell him about her father.

She turned to him then and asked a question about his college days.

Since that was much easier to answer than the questions he'd been asking himself, Jake eagerly bit into the conversation.

Their meal came quickly, along with another round of flirting with Trudy. He and Tabitha talked about their college days as they ate. After the main meal, while Jake ate a slice of blueberry pie, he asked Tabitha about her career.

She talked freely about her progress from midlevel management to chief administrator, seeming happy to be away from the stress waiting for them back at the hospital, glad to be talking about anything but that.

"What about you?" she asked after Trudy cleared their dishes. "Why did you decide to become a cop?"

Jake shrugged and started to spout his stock answer to this question. But he couldn't utter the platitude about helping society. Not to Tabitha. He frowned down at the yellow checkered tablecloths that matched the aprons the waitresses wore. "Why not?"

"It's not as if you just fell into law enforcement the way I fell into hospital management. You majored in it. You chose the University of Texas because of its law enforcement program. That means you knew from day one that you wanted to be a cop."

Jake absently rubbed a drop of thick blueberry juice into the tablecloth. He'd never told anyone about his motivations for wanting to be a police officer. He'd never been able to before now because it hurt too much.

"Surely there's a reason."

He glanced up at her interested face. "Don't you think we should be getting back?"

Both eyebrows rose. "Have I hit a nerve?"

He dropped his gaze again.

"I have, haven't I?" She reached across the table to cover his hand with hers. "Jake, tell me."

Jake felt his heart turn over. Such a small gesture, but he knew what it meant. She reached out to him, trusting him to accept her touch. He knew in that moment that if she reached out to him further—telling him about her father—he'd be sunk.

For the first time in eighteen years, Jake wanted to tell someone how his parents had died. He wanted to tell Tabitha everything.

"When I was eighteen, a senior in high school, my..." He leaned back in his chair. "Sure you want to hear this?"

She leaned forward. "Positive."

"It was my grandmother's birthday. She lived on the other side of Houston, on the edge of a neighborhood that wasn't too great. Anyway, my parents were going to take her out to dinner and I—in my infinite teenage selfishness—refused to go. I wanted to go to a movie with my friends instead."

"So what happened?"

He felt his face harden as he thought about the details for the first time in years. "On the way home they apparently had a flat tire, four blocks from my grandmother's house. The police were called after someone in the area heard gunshots. They found my father shoved into the open trunk—"

Tabitha gasped. "Oh, Jake, no."

"He had a bullet in his abdomen, and one in his heart."

Tabitha covered both his hands this time. "Stop, please."

But he couldn't. "They found my mother still sitting in the front seat, a bullet in her head."

She squeezed his hands. "Why?"

He turned his hands over and latched on to hers. The connection felt warm and real. "Robbery, for one thing. But the police thought it was more than that. Probably some gang initiation or rite. They never caught a single one of them."

"Oh, Jake." A tear slipped from her eye and followed the curve of her cheek. "You hear about things like that happening, but you never think it will happen to you, or someone you love. I'm so sorry."

He smiled, feeling lighter somehow, glad he'd shared his pain with her. "Don't cry for me. It happened half a lifetime ago."

"It still hurts." Another tear followed the first. "A person doesn't recover from something like that. And you were so young."

"At least I didn't get caught up in some stupid custody case. I lived with my grandmother until I went to college."

"Is she still alive?"

He shook his head. "She died six years ago."

"No brothers or sisters?"

"Just me."

"You're all alone, just like me."

He smiled sadly. "Two seeds in a pod."

She dropped her gaze with a slight frown and only then seemed to realize that they were sitting in the Yellow Rose Café, holding hands and staring into each other's eyes like a pair of lovers. She pulled her hands away.

"No, we're not two seeds in a pod. There's at least one fundamental difference between us."

"What?"

She glanced up. "I'm not out to rescue the world."

Stunned by her comment, Jake leaned back in his chair. "What's that supposed to mean?"

"You have a rescue complex. That's why you became a cop. You couldn't rescue your parents, but you can make up for not being there to help them by rescuing other people."

He turned sideways in his seat. "Okay, Mrs. Freud, I think it's time we—"

"No wonder you're so dedicated to your job." Her face became earnest as she dug into the analysis. "No wonder you can't maintain a real relationship. What superhero ever did?"

"Superhero?"

She nodded. "It probably isn't a conscious thing, but you want to be Superman. You want to rescue the entire world."

He'd never heard his motives put in those terms. He didn't like it. "I think you're full of Cobb salad, but say I did. Are cops such a bad thing to have around? Aren't you glad someone takes on the job of getting criminals off the street? What's wrong with rescuing people?"

She sat back, smugly amazed at her insight. "There's nothing wrong with it from society's point of view. From yours, however, there's a lot."

"Such as?"

"You'll be dead by the time you're forty. No one is Superman. No one can rescue the entire world."

"I know that. I never said I wanted to rescue the entire world."

"You don't have to say it. Your actions, as the cliché goes, speak louder than words. Frankly, I'm surprised you even came to Mission Creek. There isn't enough crime here to keep you busy twenty-four hours a day. There aren't enough people to rescue."

"Yeah, well, I'm leaving as soon as my contract is up."

"See? You just proved my point. Planning on going to a much bigger city, aren't you?"

His eyes narrowed. "I didn't realize you had a Ph.D. in psychology."

She waved a hand at him. "It doesn't take a psychologist to see this."

No one else had ever seen it. No one else had ever cared to dig deep enough to find the clues to his psyche, to figure him out. Not even himself.

"How many people do you have to rescue before you think your parents will forgive you?" She reached across the table again and laid her hand on his arm. "Jake, it isn't your fault that you weren't there when they died. Don't you see? It's survivor's guilt. You probably see it all the time, in your line of work."

Though he didn't like the way she was putting it, he knew she was right. But he was feeling a little too raw at the moment to admit it. He needed time to think about what she had said, to analyze her analysis. If what she said was true, it put a whole new perspective on everything in his life.

"I just noticed something," he said to distract her.

"What?" She leaned back with a rueful smile. "That I'm getting too personal?"

"Well, yeah, but we've been sitting here for an hour and a half, and neither one of us has been fidgety, or even so much as used going to the rest room as an excuse to move."

"You're right." Then she peered at him sideways. "So what does that mean?"

"Hell if I know. Maybe this place has good feng shui."

She glanced around. "Not particularly."

"Then it must be us." He was as startled by the comment that slipped out of his mouth as her bluebonnet eyes said she was.

"Us?"

Her disbelief clearly showed that she'd never thought about the two of them as "us." Neither had he, until this very moment. But it felt right. "Maybe *we* have good feng shui."

She quickly looked away. "Now that you mention it, I thought I saw a turtle in that picture on the north wall. Tortoises are very stabilizing influences, you know. Especially on the north..." She trailed away and cleared her throat. "Didn't you say something about getting back to the hospital? We do have a press conference at four, remember."

He smiled and picked up the check Trudy had left at the

corner of the table. He wasn't the only one who wasn't ready to face the truth. "Ready anytime you are, kitten."

Tabitha shushed him as she stood. "I'm not your kitten."

He walked behind her to the cashier stand.

No, she wasn't his kitten. She wasn't a stray that needed rescuing. If he didn't keep that in mind, he'd find himself stuck in Mission Creek in ten years with a whole litter of them.

Although…

Somewhere along the line, cats had begun to grow on him.

Twelve

The press had been briefed on Hines's call, so all Tabitha had to do at the press conference was read a brief, simple statement, then handle routine questions. She breezed through the statement. However, when Officer Hammel played the tape for the media, the same chills washed over Tabitha that had seized her when Hines first called. With them came the same doubts.

She tried to push them away. She needed every ounce of confidence to deal with reporters groping for any angle.

But what if she did something wrong, said something she shouldn't? What if Hines spotted a police officer around her or the hospital? There were so many things that could go wrong, and she had so little experience.

You can't do anything right.

Her father's voice drowned out the question the female TV news reporter was asking.

Tabitha shook her ghost away. "I'm sorry. Could you repeat that?"

The beautiful redhead rolled her eyes. "Have there been any more leads as to Branson Hines's whereabouts?"

Tabitha glanced at Jake, turning the microphone over to him for the first time during the press conference.

He stepped forward. "The Mission Creek Police Department is working around the clock on that. We'll let you know when something develops."

Clamor followed, and Jake stood back. He always let Tabitha control the flow of the press conferences, though so far, he'd been the one to end them.

Tabitha pointed to a distinguished man behind the redhead.

"What are the chances that you'll find the hostages alive?"

Tabitha controlled a shiver, but just barely. "What do you mean by chances? Do you want a percentage? How can I give you that? I don't know Branson Hines as well as you people do, with all the research you've done."

"Surely the police have done research on him," another male reporter shouted from her left side.

"We probably know more about the man than you," Jake assured them, "but I'm still not going to call that shot. Too many variables. As Miss Monroe said in her statement, however, we're optimistic. Hines's call shows that he's willing to talk."

"How do you figure that?" a reporter asked.

"Yeah, he wouldn't let *her* talk," another said.

Jake shrugged. "It's a classic first step. Hines is playing it smart. Playing by the rules. As long as he does, we will, too."

Noticing that her hands were shaking, Tabitha angled herself so her back was hidden, then clenched them behind it. She was more than willing to let Jake have the spotlight. He was keeping to the script, giving Branson Hines as many strokes as possible, encouraging him to call again and negotiate.

The next question, however, was for her.

"What about the other hospital employees? How are they taking the kidnapping?"

Tabitha took a deep breath, then plastering a smile on her face, she stepped up to the podium when Jake moved back. "I'm surprised you haven't interviewed them all by now."

There was a bit of laughter, then a shout, "We have, but they're not talking. You scare them off us or something?"

"You scare them just fine on your own," she said, drawing another tittering laugh. "The hospital employees were asked to let the media get its information through me. However," she said over shouted questions, "they were not threatened with losing their jobs or anything punitive. They're simply loyal, and I appreciate each and every one of them."

A reporter she'd been avoiding pointing to because of the hostility in his eyes shouted over the others. "How can we assure the American public that you're doing everything you can, when you've never handled a kidnapping before? How do you know that you're doing anything right?"

You can't do anything right.

Tabitha's face suddenly felt cold as the blood drained away. She gripped the sides of the podium and forced air into her lungs so she could speak. "How can anyone know that what they're doing is right in this kind of situation?"

Jake gripped her elbow and gently urged her aside. Keeping his hand on her, he spoke into the microphone. "That's all for today, folks. Unless something happens, we'll have another press conference at ten tomorrow morning. And remember the riot act I read you this morning. No phone calls to Miss Monroe's home or office, and I'd rather you didn't hang around her house. She's not going to give you any statements, either way. Good night. Pray for the hostages.

"Wait right here," Jake said in her ear. "I need to speak to Chief Terry."

She stayed exactly where he left her, trying to regain her equilibrium. What was wrong with her? She thought she'd put her father's ghost away a long time ago. Why had he come back? Was it because she was dealing directly with police for the first time since she'd left home?

Jake shook Burl Terry's hand, then placed his hand on

the small of her back and nodded toward the steps. "Let's wade through the sharks."

He speared them through the crowd of reporters as efficiently as he always did. There were only two uniformed police officers in the hall, where this morning it had been lined with uniforms. But Tabitha knew some of the men hanging around were also officers in street clothes. Jake had the changes in place an hour after Hines had called that afternoon.

He nodded to several men as he guided her to the elevator, but didn't say anything to her until the door slid closed on them, alone.

"What was that back there?"

"What was what?" she asked, automatically covering her surprise at his question.

Had he noticed her distress on the podium? Was that why he ended the press conference so abruptly?

His eyes narrowed. "You turned white as a ghost when that reporter asked if we were doing everything right."

"I don't know what—"

"Don't try to tell me it was nothing. You were shaking when we stepped down from the podium. Hell, you're shaking now."

"I—"

The elevator door opened. Grateful to it for saving her, she walked out.

At the door to her office, Jake stopped. "I need to check on my men."

While they'd gone to lunch, his men had moved the command center to an empty office two doors down the hall, where they would be less visible.

"All right." Tabitha was even more relieved. She'd have time alone to get over her surprise, get over her fears, boost her self-confidence.

She went into her office and sank into her chair. She

closed her eyes and let the familiar sounds soothe her psyche. She hated knowing Jake saw her lapse, hated him seeing her vulnerability. How would he use it?

"You okay?"

Her eyes sprang open. Jake stood in the doorway.

She straightened. "Yes, of course."

He shook his head and closed the door. "Lean back and relax."

She gave him a crooked smile. "Easy to say."

He came around the desk, behind her chair, then put his hands on her shoulders. "Lean back."

"What are you doing?"

"Helping you relax." And he began to knead her tight muscles.

As Jake massaged her shoulders, Tabitha slowly sank into his strong hands. When his thumbs hit the tendons on the back of her neck, she couldn't stop a moan of pleasure.

"Enjoying yourself?"

She could hear the smile in his voice. "Mmm. You're pretty good at this, you know."

"So I hear."

"From whom? How often do you do this?" She recognized the feeling that made her stiffen—jealousy. Jeez. She was in deeper than she thought.

"This is my second time."

"You mean yesterday?"

"Mmm, hmm." He massaged harder, so she had to relax again in self-defense. "As for who I heard it from... Ooh. Ahh. Oh, yes. Right there. Yes!"

His silly mimicking of the sounds she'd been making made her giggle. "You make it sound like I'm having sex."

"Is that what you sound like, kitten?" he asked softly, close to her ear. "Are those the noises you make?"

Sex had never made her feel half this good. But if Jake could make her moan with just a massage... The possibilities ran through her mind. She shivered deliciously and relaxed even more.

He straightened and continued kneading her tension away. "You should do that more often."

Her eyes popped open. Could he read her mind? "Do what?"

"Giggle."

"I didn't giggle." She couldn't remember ever giggling. Giggling was caused by silly fun, and she was neither silly nor fun. "Did I?"

"Yes."

"Well, imagine that."

She sighed with pleasure as his thumb dug into the base of her skull.

"Tell me about it, kitten." His voice was deep, low. "Tell me why you freaked downstairs."

Tabitha frowned. She should have known the massage wasn't free. "I didn't freak."

"Then tell me why you never giggle."

Tears sprang to her eyes. No one had ever noticed that, including herself.

Why did Jake notice? People generally noticed things a person did, not things they didn't do. But more importantly, why did he care?

He couldn't know about her father? Could he?

Of course he could. She'd witnessed the thoroughness with which he gathered information about people who seemed insignificant to the kidnapping, like the hospital employees they'd interviewed. She'd been amazed at the details he'd known. It only made sense that he would have done a background check on her, too.

Dread ran through her like poison. "Do you know about my father?"

His hands stopped kneading her shoulders, then he slowly turned her chair so she faced him. Placing a hand on either arm of the chair, he squatted in front of her. "I know how he died, and why. That's about it."

She searched his earnest, interested face. "How did you find out?"

"I have my ways."

"The police network." She couldn't keep the bitterness from her voice. "Yes. I remember."

He shrugged. "Every profession has its networks. I'll bet you know other hospital administrators all over the state, if not the country."

Her chin lifted slightly, but she didn't acknowledge the truth in his words. "Why did you find out?" she asked.

"I wanted to know why you hate cops so much. At first, it was because I needed to know if that was going to get in the way of our relationship."

"What rela—"

"Our *professional* relationship. I needed to know if your attitude was going to hamper the situation in any way."

"I would never let my feelings get in the way of my employees' safety."

He took her hands in his, holding on when she would have pulled them away. "I know that now. I didn't then."

She studied his face. "And now?"

"Now?"

"You said at first that was the reason. What is it now?"

He twined his fingers with hers. "Now I want to know because I care about you."

"Care." She liked the sound of that, but didn't like that she liked it. "What does that mean?"

He shook his head helplessly and shrugged. "All I know that it means is I want to understand you, and that means knowing about your father."

Obviously he was as confused as she was about the attraction between them. He cared. She cared, too. Was it love? Could fate be cruel enough to make her fall in love with a cop?

"I told you about my parents," he said. "It's your turn. You need to. It helps to share."

Tabitha swallowed the lump of emotion blocking her throat. "I don't know if I can."

"That's because you're not sure if I really want to know. I do." He shifted, placing a knee on the floor. "You're not sure if I'll use it against you. I won't."

Tabitha was afraid of more than the reasons behind his curiosity. She was afraid of how much she wanted to tell him.

How would he react? He would be horrified, no doubt. Everyone was, in these kinds of situations. He would be defensive of her, for her, but then he would look at her differently.

Scott had. That was when their relationship had deteriorated. Not quite the same relationship she'd had with her father, but abusive all the same. That was when Scott had begun to loosen the full rein of his kinky passions. It was as if Scott had decided after she told him that she wasn't worthy of his love.

Jake might feel the same way.

Tabitha drew her hands from his. On the other hand, if he was like Scott, it would be better to know now, before she got in too deep.

She ignored the voice inside that said it was already too late, that she was in scalding hot water way over her head. "Well, then, you'd better get comfortable, because it's a long story."

He squeezed her knees since he no longer had her hands. "I'm okay."

She shook her head. "You can't be, like that. Go sit in a chair."

He stood and grabbed one of her hands. "Come on, then."

"Where?" If she was going to do this, she needed to sit here in her own chair, where she was comfortable, where she was safely untouched.

"The couch."

She glanced at it, mostly as an excuse to look away. "Why?"

"So I can hold you."

There was that lump in her throat again. "Why?"

He grabbed her other hand and pulled her to her feet. Since he didn't step back, she landed smack against his hard chest. "Because I want to."

She tried to swallow the lump. It didn't go away. "Oh."

"Because I wanted to hold on to you when I talked about my parents."

She'd wanted to, too. "We were in public."

"I know. But that didn't stop me from wanting you to."

Tabitha squeezed her eyes closed tight, then with a sigh of resignation, she slipped past him and led the way to the couch. She sat on one end.

He sat in the middle, close enough to touch her but far enough away to see her face easily. "Okay. I know he abused prisoners. And I know that officers who are abusive at work can be abusive at home, as well."

He did know. Somehow, that made it even harder.

"I...my father...we were..." She shrugged. "I don't know where to start."

"How about the beginning?"

"Don't you need to check on your men or something?"

"I just did. They'll tell me if something happens."

"I don't want to bore you."

He eased closer and took one of her hands. "Tabitha, this isn't as hard as you think it's going to be."

For some stupid reason, her eyes filled with tears. "I've only told one person ever, and he..."

"He what?"

"I guess he just didn't care."

Jake's other hand cupped her chin, his thumb tenderly rubbing her cheek. "I care. Please tell me."

She sighed raggedly. "I guess it started when my mother died."

He released her chin. "When was that?"

"She died when I was born."

He winced. "You never knew your mother?"

"No. But the only relevance that has to the situation is that my father blamed me for her death. He loved her very much, you see. Or said he did. I can't imagine him—" She shook her head. "Never mind."

"Oh, no, you don't." He squeezed her hand. "We're not going to have any *never minds*."

"I just..." She'd never said these words out loud. She took a deep breath and hurried through them. "I've wondered if he was as abusive with her as he was with me. I've wondered if she *wanted* to die."

Jake felt as if he were being torn in two. He'd never felt so much hate in his life. And he'd never felt so much love.

He knew in that moment—with crystal clarity—that he loved Tabitha. He didn't know what that meant exactly, or where it would lead either of them. Right now all he could deal with was her pain. He could feel it as surely as if Albert Monroe had struck him.

He gathered her into his arms, fitting her close against his body. Because she didn't resist, because she wrapped her arms around him, he placed a kiss on her soft blond hair. "When did it start?"

"I don't know," she said softly. "I can't remember a time when he didn't hit me. The only reason I survived when I was a baby is because I lived with his sister until I was four.

Aunt Lizzie had three children of her own when she took me in, and then four more after. My father dumped me on her doorstep when he brought me home from the hospital, then took me to live with him when I was four."

"Why didn't he just leave you with your aunt?"

"Because I was old enough to work around the house."

"At four?" Jake cursed under his breath. "And did you?"

"Of course. I'd been trained well by Aunt Lizzie. She…"

He grimaced, but finished when she couldn't go on. "She hit you, too?"

She nodded against his chest. "Her own kids, too." She cleared her throat. "I thought that was just the way it was. I thought everyone was raised that way, until I went to school and began to make friends."

He tightened his hold on her. "Oh, kitten, I'm so sorry. I can't believe I thought I had it rough. My parents adored me, gave me everything I wanted. I can't imagine what you went through. Why didn't you fight back, when you found out it wasn't normal?"

He felt her shiver. "The one time I tried, I wound up in the hospital."

"Damn." He stroked her soft hair. "I wish I knew what to say to make you feel better. I wish there was something I could do."

"There isn't anything to say." Her voice was bleak. "There's nothing you can do. It happened, and it can't be changed."

He wondered if telling her that he loved her would change anything. Or would it just scare her even more?

"I thought I'd gotten past it all, forgotten him, but this situation has brought it all back."

"Why?"

She moved in his arms, leaning back so she could see him. "His favorite thing to say to me was 'You can't do anything right.' I guess I'm—'' Her voice cracked, so she cleared her throat.

Control. Always in control. It took on new meaning in Tabitha's case. He wished she would just burst into tears, cry all over him.

''I'm afraid he's right,'' she continued in a whisper.

''He's not.'' Jake's hand was trembling with rage, but he stroked her cheek with gentle tenderness. ''He was wrong about everything. You are beautiful and smart and capable of anything. You've done *everything* right.''

''Then why don't we have Cait and Dr. Walters back?''

''These things take time. Don't worry. We'll get the hostages back, safe and sound.'' He was more determined than ever. He'd hunt Hines down himself if he had to.

Her smile was shaky and sad, but at least it was a smile. ''Because you'll rescue them.''

''I'm thinking you'll be the hero here.'' His voice was husky. ''I'll just lead the cavalry.''

She searched his face. ''Jake, I...''

''Yes, kitten?''

She sighed and closed her eyes. ''Maybe I'm just tired.''

''Let's go home, then.'' Funny, how that word meant something now. Before, the place he'd lived was just an apartment. He hadn't had a home since his parents died. But now wherever Tabitha lived was home.

Her eyes popped open. ''Can we? It's just a little after five.''

He nodded. ''Hines has called once today. He won't call again until tomorrow. Maybe not until the day after.''

When she didn't move, he leaned down and kissed her.

She sighed and dragged her fingers through his hair.

''Are you going to stay with me tonight?'' she asked when he drew away.

He searched her eyes. If he stayed, he wouldn't be able

to keep his hands off her. He knew it, and from the look on her face, she knew it, too. "Do you want me to?"

"Yes," she said without hesitation. "I do."

Jake kissed her again, with much more passion this time. She responded in kind, giving back as much heat as he gave her.

Somewhere from the back of his mind came a faraway voice, reminding him that this was not a woman with whom he could have a casual fling, then just as casually leave.

Jake pulled back and peered down into her lovely, flushed face. She looked so sexy, so soft, so vulnerable.

But was she enough to satisfy him for the rest of life? Was she enough to make him give up his ambitions of rescuing the world, as she'd put it?

And what might be more to the point—was he enough for her?

Her eyes fluttered open, and she smiled at him with a sexy sigh.

His heart performed a somersault in his chest. Never in all his thirty-six years had he felt this way. All he wanted to do was show her how much he loved her. He wanted to show her the joys of intimacy. He wanted to make her giggle every day. He wanted to rescue her.

Jake smiled. She was right. He had a rescue complex. He wanted to rescue her from her terrible childhood, erase the memories of pain, of rejection and replace them with memories of love, memories of him.

"What is it?" she asked.

He hesitated, then said, "I want to make love to you."

She shivered but didn't look away. "I know."

"I want you to touch me everywhere."

Her breath caught. "Can I?"

He groaned and leaned his forehead against hers. "You witch. I thought you were afraid to touch a man."

"But you want me to. You just said so." She moved her hands on his chest.

He shivered when they rubbed across the sensitive nubs.

"See?" She went back over them with her fingernails.

He moaned.

She giggled. "You like it."

He stared into her hot blue eyes. "Very, very much."

When she turned her hands around to do it again, he stood and pulled her to her feet. "Get your things. We're going home."

Thirteen

The scene at Tabitha's house was much less chaotic than the day before. There were a few of the more aggressive reporters hanging around, but they stayed off her lawn, no doubt thanks to the officers who took up position around the perimeter of her property. The reporters shouted questions at Tabitha and Jake as they walked into the house, but only halfheartedly. They'd apparently learned that neither she nor Jake were going to give them an interview.

The next time she looked out the window, most of them were gone.

Tabitha expected Jake to lead her to the bedroom as soon as they entered. He didn't, however. He surprised her by picking up the cat, who had come running to greet them.

"Looks as if Billy's taken to you," she said as she scratched the cat's head. "And I thought you didn't like cats."

Jake stroked the purring cat's back and grinned. "Since I've discovered a certain affinity for kittens, I figure cats can't be all that bad."

She felt blood sting her cheeks at his words and arched her eyebrow to cover it. "Cats and kittens both have claws."

His green eyes glowed. "I know."

His look made her remember his pleasure when she had scraped her nails across his chest at the hospital. "I'd better see if he still has food in his bowl."

He took her hand with his free one. "Are you afraid?"

She looked into his now serious face. "A little. Are you sure you—"

"Absolutely." He let the cat down, then straightened and caught her jaw with one hand. "Are you?"

"I want to, but I have to tell you…"

"Tell me what?"

"I'm probably not going to be very good at it."

He laughed out loud.

Hurt more than angry, she spun around, but he caught her before she'd taken two steps.

He took her face between his hands. "Kitten, if you were any better, I'd have been a very embarrassed man this afternoon."

A tiny thrill passed through her, knowing she had that much power over him. "Really?"

He chuckled. "Yes." Then he kissed her soundly. "Damn, you *are* a witch. I'm trying to be good and wait at least until dark."

"Why?"

"Because I want to make sure everything's quiet. Because I don't want my men walking in on us, thinking we're eating supper or something equally innocuous. Because once I start, I want the whole night. Because you're so— Oh, hell." He backed her into the dining room wall and, grabbing her bottom, lifted her against it and captured her mouth with a frenzy that took her breath away.

Surprised, off balance, she wrapped her arms around his neck and her legs around his hips.

With a low growl, he shoved her skirt, which had ridden up to her hips, all the way to her waist and ground his hardness into her.

Tabitha gasped. She was ready for him. She could feel her wetness.

"Damn," he breathed against her ear. "You're wearing a thong ag—"

The doorbell rang, making their heads jerk toward it.

"Damn," Jake spat. "I knew it."

Tabitha breathed hard as Jake eased her legs down.

"All this stopping and starting is killing me." He kissed her one more time. "You okay?"

She nodded.

The doorbell rang again.

He adjusted his pants, then cussed all the way to the door. He flung it open. "You'd better have a damn good— Oh. Hi." He glanced back at Tabitha. "It's Marie."

"Marie?" Tabitha stepped to the door to find her secretary standing on the porch. "Well, come on in."

Marie smiled expansively as she looked Tabitha up and down. "Oh, no, honey. I don't want to disturb you. Harry's waiting for me in the truck." She nodded at the vintage Ford sitting in Tabitha's driveway, then picked up a bucket at her feet. "Harry just thought you might like a nice mess of fish tonight, is all. We kept up with things on the radio, so we know you had a hard day, what with that evil man calling and all. Anyhoo, Harry caught his limit today. Nice fat bass."

Jake took the bucket from Marie. "Well, isn't that nice. We were just...discussing what we were going to fix for supper."

Marie's eyes sparkled, and she winked at Tabitha. "I can see that."

Tabitha barely restrained herself from touching her hair to see if it was standing on end. "Thanks, Marie."

"My pleasure." She turned to leave. "Before you can argue, I'm telling you now that I'll be in tomorrow. See y'all in the morning," she called over her shoulder.

"What was that all about?" Jake asked as he waved to Harry in the truck.

Harry waved back.

"I don't know." Tabitha turned to the mirror in the entry.

Her hair was a little mussed, but not so bad that anyone could tell what they'd been doing. "Sometimes I think she's psychic."

She peered in the bucket. "You're going to clean them, right?"

He chuckled. "Yes, ma'am."

Jake dug a sharp knife from the proper drawer—he already knew her kitchen, Tabitha noticed—picked up that morning's newspaper and took the bucket outside.

While he did that, Tabitha fed the cat rubbing against her legs, then cleaned his litter box. When she took the refuse outside to the trash can, she had to fight Billy away from the back door. He'd evidently smelled what Jake had carried through.

She found Jake squatting over newspapers covered with fish heads and guts. A police sergeant, by his stripes, stood over Jake.

"I see you have supervision," Tabitha said with a smile. "Hello, Sergeant."

The sergeant tipped his hat. "Evening, ma'am."

"Come to help?" Jake asked.

She shivered as she dumped her load in the can. "That's okay."

"Not a fisherwoman, I take it?"

"Not in this lifetime." She hurried back inside, again keeping Billy back. "You'll get some, don't worry. But it will be cooked."

"Meow."

"You can complain all you want to, but I've smelled the breath of cats who've eaten raw fish."

Billy rubbed against her ankles.

"That's not going to help, either." She started for the refrigerator, to fix some vegetables, then stopped. "If we're going to fry fish, I need to change."

Switching direction, she peeked out the kitchen window.

Jake was still talking to the sergeant, probably giving him instructions for the night. He only had a couple of fish cleaned, so she probably had time to change without him walking in on her.

Why was she worried about that? He was going to see every inch of her body in just a little while.

She giggled, then rolled her eyes. "Jeez. This needs to stop. I'm not a teenager."

Tabitha headed toward the bedroom, the cat at her heels. "A pair of jeans and a T-shirt won't do," she said to Billy. "I need something a little sexier, don't you think?"

"Meow."

Tabitha smiled and rubbed Billy's head when he jumped on her bed. "You're fun to talk to, you know it? Maybe I need to get a cat."

Billy lay down and started purring immediately.

Tabitha stroked down his back, all the way to his tail. "Yes, I definitely need a cat. Jake won't be around forever, after all."

Now why had she mentioned that? She hadn't thought about what she was doing in relation to Jake's plans.

She sat down on the bed next to Billy, absently stroking him.

Was she doing the right thing, making love with him?

Every instinct in her body said she was.

"I'm in love with him," she told the cat, who blinked with indifference. "How about that kick in the pants? I'm in love with Assistant Police Chief Jake White—a cop. And not just any cop. A supercop. A cop who's going to leave Mission Creek when his contract is up, whenever that is. A cop who needs to be rescued from his own rescue complex, but won't even admit he has one."

Even with all that against him, Tabitha felt closer to Jake than anyone, ever, in her life.

She knew that people in crisis situations often fell in love.

Or thought they did. Those relationships rarely lasted, because they were based on shared trauma, not real emotions.

"Is that all this is, Billy? Do I think I love him because he's helping me through this? I just met him yesterday. Two days. How could I possibly be in love with him?"

But it seemed more like two months, with all they'd been through. After the long, exhausting hours they'd spent together, she knew this man. She knew his goals. She knew his sexual appetites. She knew what drove his need to rescue every victim in his case file.

"That's what intimacy is, isn't it?" she asked Billy. "Knowing someone. Knowing everything about them."

How long could it last, though? Even if their relationship lasted, Jake was leaving. And he hadn't said anything about taking her with him. He hadn't said anything about loving her.

But he had said he cared.

"You know what, Billy?" Tabitha stood. "I don't care how long it's going to last. No one can know that, right? Even if he doesn't love me, I want this. I want him for as long as I can get him. I've never felt this way and, by George, I'm going to milk every moment."

She turned into the closet. "Now, what am I going to wear?"

"I don't think we'll be—" Jake stopped as he walked through the door.

"Close the door!" Tabitha ran and shut the door behind Jake just before Billy got there.

She needn't have worried. Billy stopped at Jake's feet, meowing and rubbing himself against Jake's legs.

"Is this the same cat who wouldn't give us the time of day last night?" Jake asked.

"You have fish."

"Ah, that explains it." He set the plate piled high with

filets on the counter, then washed his hands. He glanced around the kitchen. "I see you've already got things started."

She nodded. "I hope you don't mind corn again. I creamed it."

"I love corn."

"That's good. We're having slaw, too." She couldn't believe they were talking about vegetables when all she wanted to do was continue what they'd begun in the dining room. They were alone now. Wasn't he going to say anything? *Do* anything? She sure didn't know how to start it. Maybe she should have worn something sexier.

Since she didn't want to be *too* obvious, she'd opted for her tightest pair of jeans and a white cotton muscle shirt that fit her like a second skin. What made the outfit sexy—or so she'd thought—was that she wasn't wearing a bra.

"Sounds good," he said. He turned to a large iron skillet on the stove top. "I'll just get started breading the fish."

A thump made them turn in time to see Billy scampering along the countertop toward the fish.

Jake swooped them out of his way just in time.

Tabitha scooped up the cat. Flipping him over in her arms, she rubbed his belly to make up for his being denied the fish. "You'll get some later, silly Billy. I promise. But for now you're going in your crate. That was attempted robbery. You have to be locked up." She lowered her voice to a loud whisper. "There's a by-the-book cop here, you know. He'll insist."

"Very funny."

She touched her nose to Billy's. "Cops have no sense of humor."

After she put Billy in his carrier, she helped Jake with the cornmeal breading.

Jake insisted on the task of frying them.

Since he wore nice dress slacks, Tabitha pulled out an

apron and tied it around his waist. "If you're going to act like a stubborn cook, you're going to dress like a stubborn cook."

He held up a corner of the lacy apron and batted his eyes. "How do I look?"

"Very..." Sexy. Hot. Strong. Touchable. All of the words applied, but she said none of them because he hadn't mentioned sex since he'd cleaned the fish. Far from making him seem feminine, the contrast between his dark masculinity and the frilly apron showed how confident he was in his maleness. "...pretty." She cleared her throat. "I need to make the slaw."

Once that was done, all Tabitha had to do was occasionally stir the corn to keep it from sticking.

"What about hush puppies?" Jake asked halfway through the frying.

"I don't know how to make them," she said.

"Have an onion?"

She nodded.

He gave her directions and set her to work.

"Where did you learn so much about fish frying?"

"I helped with the Houston PD's annual fish fry. We raised money for crime victims."

"And how much actually got to crime victims?"

He stared at her, his stillness as forceful as his usual state of constant movement. "Didn't your father have any redeeming qualities?"

She turned away. "He had a beautiful tenor voice and sang in the choir at church. But, then, he also sang Christmas carols with some of his cop buddies to raise money for a policeman's fund. But they were the only policemen who benefited. They used the money to pay their tabs at the bar they went to all the time."

She felt him come up behind her.

"Tabitha, look at me."

She slowly turned and peered up into his intent green eyes. "Every penny of profit went to crime victims. I'm not your father."

"I know, Jake. I'm sorry. I didn't mean to imply—" She gasped as he set his hands on her waist and lifted her to the counter.

Separating her legs with his hips, he positioned himself against her, wrapping his arms around her and taking her mouth in a bruising kiss. When her breath was coming hard, he trailed kisses down her throat.

"You changed clothes," he said.

She smiled. "You finally noticed."

"I noticed the instant I walked in the door."

She threw her head back to give him better access. "You didn't say anything, so I thought—"

He growled against her ear. "Don't think so much."

"Well, I'm having difficulty at the moment."

He chuckled. "Good. You're going to have a lot more difficulty later."

"I am?"

"Yep. I'm going to peel your tight jeans off you like an onion skin, then I'm going to nibble on your legs, starting at this big toe..." He reached back and caressed the big toe of her bare right foot, then trailed his hand along the inside of her leg. "...all the way up, and then down the other leg."

She shivered. "And then?"

He chuckled again and pulled her tighter against his hardness. "You can't know everything."

"Why not?"

He bit the lobe of her ear.

The shiver that hit her this time racked her entire body.

"But I want you to know one thing," he whispered in her ear.

"What?"

"I won't hurt you, Tabitha. I will never, ever hurt you. I

won't do anything you're afraid of. If I do something you don't like, tell me." He drew back far enough to see her. "Okay?"

"Okay." She was only half aware of what she was promising.

He glanced down and drew in a quick breath.

She followed his gaze and saw her hard nipples poking through her shirt.

His open hands followed her curves upward from her hips, but all he did was cup the underside.

She thrust her chest out, wanting more.

"Damn." With a sudden movement, he pulled back and set her on the floor. "The fish need turning." He gave her a quick kiss, then turned back to the fish. "Chop that onion, woman."

Grabbing the edge of the counter to keep her balance. Tabitha blinked. How could he turn his desire on and off so quickly, so completely?

Miffed, she stirred the corn one last time, then turned off the burner. With the spoon still in her hand, she smiled. Time to see if he could take a little of his own medicine.

She asked him a question about his job and as soon as she had his attention, she began to lick the spoon in long, lazy strokes.

His answer trailed off as his eyes followed every movement. Just before his eyes began to burn, he yanked his gaze away and finished answering her.

Frowning, determined, she reached up into a top cabinet for a serving bowl for the corn. She could feel his gaze on her, but he didn't move from the fish. When that didn't work, she broke off a bite of cooked fish and walked over to Billy's crate in the corner. She bent over, with her butt high in the air, and fed it to him.

"Woman, if you ever want to eat tonight, you'll stop what you're doing right now."

She twisted to find his gaze on her, hot and wanting.

Finally. She widened her eyes deliberately. "What am I doing?"

"You're trying to seduce me."

She straightened. "Is it working?"

"What do you think?"

"I think," she said, walking slowly toward him and swiveling her hips with each step, "that you're ignoring me."

"Ignoring you?" He snorted in disbelief and shook his head. "One thing you don't have to worry about is seducing me. You've done a damn fine job already."

"Really?"

"Yeah."

"Well, you're the one insisting on eating."

His gaze traveled down her body. "Oh, I'm going to eat, all right." He shook the moment off. "And so are you. You're going to need every ounce of energy you can get."

Satisfied, Tabitha asked, "When is the fish going to be ready?"

He lifted the last piece out. "It's done. Now I just have to cook the hush puppies."

"I'll fix some tea."

They began their meal ten minutes later. To keep from talking about what was uppermost on their minds, Tabitha led the conversation to mundane topics. She gave Jake a litany of the work she'd done on the little house. He pretended he was interested.

Tabitha half expected Jake to start their sexual encounter as soon as they finished eating, but instead he insisted on clearing the dishes. He washed them while Tabitha dried and put away.

When that was done, he called his men at the hospital, then checked on the men outside.

Tabitha let Billy out of his crate and petted him to keep herself from screaming in frustration. The orange cat rolled to his back. He lay alongside her leg, his purring nearly drowning out the air conditioner.

Finally, just as it was getting dark, Jake reentered through the back door. He locked it, then searched for her. The living room was the last place he looked.

"Ready for bed?"

Fourteen

Tabitha went still. The only part of her moving was her heart, which beat double time. She cleared the lump from her throat. "Yes."

Jake smiled. "Me, too. It's been another long day." He walked to her and held out his hand. "Shall we?"

She couldn't smother a giggle as she placed her hand in his. "You sound as if you're asking me to dance."

She gasped when, as soon as she stood, he lifted her in his arms.

He grinned. "Is that better?"

She wrapped her hands around his neck and held on tight. If she'd ever been picked up by anyone, she couldn't remember. It was a definite loss of control and, as such, unnerving. "I don't think so."

He stopped in the hallway. "Give me my macho moment, okay?"

She smiled. Trust him to make this fun. "Okay, Mr. Macho. Carry me away."

"Oh, I plan to, kitten. Don't you worry."

He turned sideways to fit her through the bedroom door. Instead of laying her on the bed, however, he stood her next to it. He folded her in his arms and kissed her tenderly, then passionately, then sweetly, then deeply. He varied the kisses until, mindless with wanting him, she began to clumsily undo the buttons of his shirt.

"Not yet." He took her hands away and pulled them around his waist. "We have all night."

"All I care about is *now.*" She found the waist of his pants and worked her hands beneath. She smiled when she felt the silk of his boxers. "I want you now."

He closed his eyes on a shiver and kissed her forehead. "Damn. If you don't stop it, I'm going to take you right here and now."

"Okay."

"No." He pulled her hands out from the back of his pants and put them behind her back. "I want our first time to be all for you. I want you screaming my name."

"Screaming?"

He nodded.

She giggled. "Won't that bring your men running in?"

"Witch." He took her mouth again, hard and deep. Holding her hands behind her with one hand, he twisted enough so he could run his free hand up her side to cup her breast.

She gasped to finally feel his hands rubbing across the nubs that had been wanting his touch all evening.

"You drove me crazy during supper," he said. "Your nipples stayed erect the entire time."

"That's because you had me on the edge the entire time."

"The edge of your seat?"

"The edge of frustration." She tilted her head back so she could see his face. "What have you done to me? I've never felt this way. I've never wanted a man so much I want to rip off his clothes."

He growled for an answer, then released her hands so he could use both of his. He yanked her top off over her head, then stopped on a quick breath when her breasts were bare. "Oh, my God. Tabitha. I knew you'd be beautiful."

He slowly, almost reverently, pushed his hands upward from her waist, watching his progress intently.

Tabitha's breath caught when he finally cupped her breasts, dragging his thumbs across the sensitive tips. Grabbing his bottom, she ground her hips against his. The pressure felt good but wasn't satisfying. So she reached for the button of her jeans. Her hands were immediately pulled away.

"That's my job."

"Then do it. Please! This isn't enough."

He smiled with pure male satisfaction, but instead of obeying her, he bent and dragged his tongue across her nipple.

Tabitha convulsed with pleasure, instinctively leaning back over his arm to give him better access.

He held her upright in his strong grip, laving her breast with his mouth. Then he sucked it in, drawing it out to the nipple. He bit lightly, just enough for her to feel the edge of his teeth.

"Jake, please."

Jake's tongue drew a wet path down her stomach as he slowly dropped to his knees. Placing his hands on the waistband of her jeans, he unbuttoned them, then slowly slid down the zipper. As her belly button was bared, he dipped his tongue inside.

Tabitha set her hands on his shoulders to maintain balance.

With the intensity of a man concentrating on a difficult but interesting job, he peeled her jeans down her hips.

He growled when he got to the waistband of her red silk thong. "More red panties just for me?"

She gasped when his teeth snapped the elastic. "I aim to please."

He pulled her jeans down her thighs, but stopped when they were at her knees. He ran his hands up the inside of her thighs. When they were about six inches from the place she wanted them most, he touched the inside of her left thigh and looked up at her. "You have a mole on your thigh."

She shook her head. "It's a birthmark."

Apparently the difference didn't matter. He kissed it fervently, then yanked her jeans the rest of the way off.

Tabitha lifted each foot in turn to help, then sat on the edge of the mattress when he urged her back.

True to his words, he lifted her right foot. Starting at her big toe, which he sucked, Jake kissed and licked and nibbled his way slowly up her thigh.

Tabitha had never felt anything so sensuous. Her heart beat faster, the closer he came to her moist, throbbing lips. Then without touching them, he passed over her panties to the left thigh.

"Jake!" She fell back to her elbows.

"Yes, my kitten?"

"What are you doing?"

"It's called foreplay. Ever hear of it?"

"I've...heard of it."

She must not have been as successful as she'd wanted to be at keeping the meaning from her reply, because he lifted his head and met her gaze. "Don't tell me no one has ever kissed you like this?"

She gave a small shake of her head. "It's driving me crazy."

He smiled. "It's supposed to. Lie back and enjoy."

But she didn't lie back. She wanted to watch. There was something naughty—and thrilling—about seeing a man's head between her legs. A full-dressed man, at that, when all she wore was a skimpy pair of panties. But he wasn't just any man. He was the man she loved. That turned what might have been naughty into the most natural thing in the world.

Wanting to touch him but unable to reach, she lifted her right leg and ran her toes across his shoulders, then down his back. He arched into it, letting her know he enjoyed her touch. That thrilled her as much as anything.

"I want to touch you," she whispered when he was at her knee. "Please. You promised I could."

"I'm not finished yet."

"Hurry up!"

"No. You've never experienced foreplay." He nibbled along the inside of her calf, tickling her just enough to make her muscle twitch. "And I want to experience you."

"Torture me, you mean."

"Exquisitely."

Exquisite torture. Her elbows weakening, she finally slipped to her back onto the bed. What an apt description.

"There are other parts of me— Oh." She drew in a breath as his tongue moved back and forth on the arch of her foot. "There are other parts that want to be tortured."

"Are there?" He finally stood, his eyes traveling up her bare body.

Feeling wanton, and wanting to torture him, too, she stretched like a cat. "Mmm."

"Such as?" He reached up to pull off his tie.

"No!" With more energy than she thought she had, Tabitha sprang to her knees and threw his hands aside. "That's my job."

He smiled slowly. "By all means."

She slowly guided the tie from its knot, then slid the silk from his collar. Leaning to the side, she carefully laid it across the footboard.

He ran his palm over her hip as she did, sliding across her bottom.

She felt the muscles of her butt move against his hand as she straightened, drawing a moan from him. She smiled, then slowly unbuttoned his shirt, stopping now and then to play amid the hair on his chest.

She let his hand stroke her bottom until she needed to undo his cuff. Keeping his palm in contact with her skin, she pulled his arm around her body, settling it against her pelvic bone as she undid the button.

He set his other hand on the other side of her hip and

slipped her panties over the curve of her bottom. His eyes burned green fire as he bared her pubic mound. One hand returned, the fingers digging into the hair, one finger slipping inside.

"You're so wet."

Her hips jerked in reflex toward him, not away. But since she wanted to give him as much exquisite torture as he'd given her, she pulled his shirt off his shoulders, dragging his hand away. "Not yet."

His fiery gaze met hers. "Isn't that one of the 'other parts' I'm supposed to torture?"

She smiled. "Not until I do a little torturing of my own."

With that, she bent and took one of his flat nipples in her mouth. It wasn't easy, but he reacted every bit as strongly as she had. The small nubs puckered under her tongue and he sucked in a tiny gasp.

He let her move to the other side before he drew one arm from his sleeve and grabbed her around the waist. He stripped her panties completely off, then placing a knee on the bed, he carried them both down, his hard body landing on top of hers.

She glared at him. "I wasn't finished."

He shrugged out of his shirt. "Too bad. I nearly was."

When he'd tossed his shirt off the bed, he took her mouth with a ferocity she'd never felt. But she loved it. She wrapped her arms around his neck and held on, responding to his wildness with her own, plowing her fingers through his thick hair, arching her hips into his.

He moaned, then with her cooperation, parted her legs and settled between them.

They groaned in unison.

Tabitha giggled, then gasped when he thrust his hardness against her. "Take off your pants, Jake."

He rose to his knees, his hot gaze looking down at the moistness bared to him.

Tabitha didn't care. She watched him as intently as he did her, willing his hands to work faster.

Finally, he lowered his pants, baring his thick, hard maleness.

She gasped and, rising to one elbow, she reached out to stroke the velvet length. "Oh, Jake, you're beautiful," she breathed, running her thumb over the tip.

"More torture, witch?"

She smiled. "Can I?"

He groaned and dropped to the bed, lying half on top of her. As he covered her mouth with his, he cupped her breast, making her arch into his touch, then ran his hand down her stomach.

She parted her legs for him, but he still didn't touch her where she was now giving him tacit permission. He dragged his fingers down one thigh, then up the other.

Tabitha didn't know which sensation to concentrate on. She dug one hand into his hair and with the other scraped her nails along the inside of his forearm.

Finally his hand settled on the mound throbbing for his touch. One finger slipped into her wetness, flicking between the heated lips until it touched the nub pulsing with every heartbeat.

Tabitha's whole body jerked in reaction.

"There?" he asked against her lips.

"Yes. Oh, yes."

He flicked harder, faster, making her buck against his hand. He held her tight enough to stay in place, but loose enough to allow her movement.

Tabitha felt the train coming, rumbling along the tracks of her body until it hit with sudden, violent impact. Grabbing hold of his shoulders, she spasmed against him, over and over, toward the exquisite torture and then away. But it followed, relentless, forcing her higher and higher into paroxysms of pleasure that finally burst into a tunnel of light, lit by a thousand burning stars.

Jake held her tight, rocking her in his arms.

"Oh, Jake. I've never felt anything like that before. It was an orgasm, wasn't it?"

He laughed in pure delight. "An amazing one, if I'm not mistaken." He kissed her thoroughly. "You're a sensuous little kitten." He pushed back a strand of hair from her face. "You're *my* sensuous little kitten."

Tabitha couldn't believe what she'd just experienced. She didn't know pleasure like that existed.

"Shall we see how sensuous?"

She peered into his intense green gaze. "What do you mean?"

His hand drifted down her stomach to touch her there again and immediately set her off once more. She convulsed against him, writhing under his inexorable torture like a wild wanton. Her release was every bit as intense, every bit as astounding.

As she relaxed in his arms moments later, Jake began again. His hands and his mouth took her on a frenzied journey until, sweating like she'd run six miles, she finally screamed his name.

Only then did he drive inside of her, bringing her to climax again. But this time it was different. It came from within and without—all over her body.

Then he rolled them over, positioning her on top of him. She immediately began to move, riding him like a bucking bronco. She couldn't help it. He was hitting some marvelously sensitive spot deep inside her. Her entire body convulsed, and each convulsion took her down again, onto his hardness, over and over and over, until she stopped suddenly with a cry and leaned hard on his chest, panting as if she'd just added another five miles to her run.

"Jake, are you trying to kill me?"

He rolled over again, drawing her knees over his shoulders. "Complaining?"

He began to thrust.

"Complain? Me? Never. Oh, you're doing it again."

His thrusts grew harder, faster until he drove into her with a cry, then pulled out and drove in again.

Finally he was still. He stayed inside her, keeping their positions intact while the world settled back around them. Tabitha felt him throbbing inside of her. Or was she throbbing against him?

It didn't matter. She was exhausted, weak and deliriously happy.

Finally Jake disengaged and stretched out beside her. He slipped his arm beneath her head and turned her toward him.

"Damn," he breathed as he kissed her. "How many orgasms can you have?"

"I don't know," she said in a weak voice. "Probably just beginner's luck."

Instead of chuckling at her joke, he kissed her soundly, then said, "All I can say is that you've been involved with some very stupid men."

"Yes," she murmured. "He sure didn't know what he was doing. Not like you. I've never felt anything so intense in my life."

He grinned. "Is that a thank-you?"

She smiled back. "Thank you." She hugged him close. "Thank you!"

He chuckled as he rocked her back and forth, holding on tight. "I enjoyed it every bit as much as you did."

"You did?" She pulled back so she could see his face. "I was beginning to feel very selfish. Maybe next time you can have as many as I did."

"I wish. Men aren't built the way women are, kitten. We have to rest too much in between."

"That's too bad," she murmured, snuggling against the strong arm serving as her pillow.

He stroked a hand down her body. "Go to sleep now. You deserve it after that."

"You said all night," she complained weakly.

"And I meant it. Believe me." He kissed her temple. "But sleep for now. We both need it."

Tabitha didn't want to. She wanted to be awake every minute she spent in his arms. But so many orgasms had loosened a knot inside her, relaxing her beyond what any meditation or Oriental exercise ever had.

Just as she began to enjoy the throb of his heartbeat against her neck, it lulled her to sleep.

Tabitha woke suddenly to a dark room. At some point Jake must have turned off the lamp. Jake. She shivered. She couldn't believe the experience he'd given her.

She would have put it down to a dream, but she could feel his heat cuddled against her. One arm still served as her pillow and the other lay on her waist. His chest rose and fell against her back with even breathing.

"Good morning." He kissed her shoulder.

She twisted toward him. "You're awake?"

"Yeah."

"What time is it?"

He lifted his head, then dropped it. "Two-fifteen."

"Late," she murmured.

"Or early," he said. "Depends on how you look at it."

"I guess so."

He trailed a hand along her arm, making her shiver. "Cold?"

"No." She could feel his smile against her shoulder. "How long have you been awake?"

"I don't know. Half an hour, I guess."

"You didn't get up?"

"What for?"

"I don't know. To go out and check on your men. To call the ones at the hospital. To move."

"I don't want to move. I don't need to move," He lifted himself to his elbow and turned her so she was flat on her back. "How about that. I guess what they say is true—sex is the best destressor known to man."

She smiled ruefully, stretching her neck toward him as he began playing with her hair. "It's pretty good for women, too. Especially when *man* wears them out."

He chuckled. "Complaining again?"

She sighed. "No."

"You're amazing, you know that?"

"I am?"

"Hell, yes." He tightened his arms around her, snuggling close. "I've never been with a woman who had that many orgasms."

She twisted so she could see him. "Did I do something wrong?"

"No, of course not." He chuckled as he hugged her close again. "I can't believe you asked that. It didn't feel wrong, did it?"

"No. It felt wonderful. Although that word doesn't really describe the experience. I don't think you can. It was...indescribable." She giggled. "Indescribably delicious."

"Glad to have been of service, madam." He nuzzled her neck and whispered, "And thank you."

"Thank me? For what?"

"For trusting me. For letting go of your control enough to experience multiple orgasms. You've given me a very rare and precious gift."

"Oh, come on. It can't be that rare. I'm sure lots of women have them. I mean, I did, and I didn't even know what I was doing."

He pressed a kiss onto her shoulder. "Maybe I've just never been with the right woman."

Tabitha frowned. His words felt so good. Too good. "I wouldn't get used to this method of destressing, if I were you."

He stilled. "Why not?"

"You're leaving, so it won't be an option much longer. When is your contract up, by the way?"

"A little over a year." He ran a finger down her jaw. "Although," he said, lowering his mouth to hers, "at the moment, leaving Mission Creek is the last thing on my mind."

He wasn't leaving?

Tabitha froze for half a second, then returned his kiss fervently to cover her sudden confusion. She didn't understand why his words were such an unwelcome surprise. She wanted him to stay, didn't she? She loved him and wanted him to love her enough to live here in Mission Creek with her the rest of their lives.

Didn't she?

She didn't know. She hadn't considered the possibility before. Intimacy for a little while could be tolerated, and if what she experienced earlier continued, it could even be enjoyed. But intimacy for a lifetime? Could she handle that?

Her fears faded with Jake's caresses and kisses, and were gone entirely by the time he sent her to the stars. As she lay spooned in his arms, sweating, exhausted, she knew she wanted him to stay. In fact, she desired it with every exhausted cell in her body.

"Go to sleep, little kitten," he murmured against her temple. "We've only got a few more hours to sleep."

She lay there several moments, enjoying the feel of his arms around her. His breathing was shallow and even by the time she worked up the courage to whisper, "I love you."

Fifteen

Tabitha grinned at the off-key strains of "Desperado" muffled by the shower. She wouldn't have pegged Jake for a shower singer. But the song definitely fit.

After last night, though, she was hoping he'd changed from desperado to desperate for her. After having tasted the sensual delights he'd awakened in her, she couldn't imagine doing without. In fact, the only thing keeping her from joining him in the shower—though she'd been loved thoroughly the night before and again that morning—was the fact that they were already running late for the press conference.

Tabitha hummed along with Jake as she entered the kitchen. She wondered if he'd learned the song from the Eagles, or from any of the countless number of singers who'd remade it.

The phone rang, freezing her thoughts. Hines?

It wasn't her home phone ringing. Like Jake's singing, the ring was muffled. The cell phone?

It rang again as she dug through her purse. Definitely the cell phone.

First she plucked out the one Jake had given to her and looked at the display. Nothing.

She shook her head in relief. Her personal cell phone was the one ringing. It was probably Marie.

Tabitha pulled it out of the bottom of her purse. Local call. Hmmm. It wasn't Marie. Her number was programmed into the phone and should display. But Marie could be calling from one of her kids' houses.

Tabitha punched the talk button. "Hello?"

"I've seen you with your cop boyfriend," a nasal voice spat.

Her heart stopped. "Branson Hines."

"So you recognize my voice. Good. Shows you got a little sense anyways."

"What do you— I mean, where are Cait and Dr. Matthews?"

"Like I'm gonna tell you. Your cop boyfriend there?"

"Boyfriend? I don't know what you—"

"Save it, sister. I know you and that tin-star Houston cop are thick as thieves. Don't lie to me now. I might just have to—"

"No! Don't do anything rash, Mr. Hines. Don't do anything we'll *all* regret." Tabitha stepped into the living room, away from the sound of the shower. "Chief White isn't here. You told me to get rid of the police."

"Okay, well, just making sure he ain't hanging around, undercover like. 'Cause if you think he can save your friends, you got another think coming. You're the only one who can save 'em, and only if you follow my directions to the letter."

"I understand."

"You listening hard?"

"Yes." She searched for paper and pen, but there wasn't any handy. They were in her office, too close to the noise of the shower.

"You bring me a baby and meet me this evening, right after sunset."

"Where?" She listened intently, trying to hear above her pounding heart. She had to remember everything he said. Her cell phone wasn't being recorded.

"Drive out to the Lone Star Highway."

"East or west?"

"West. Toward Highway 16. Turn left on it, then go 'bout four miles. There's a dirt road off to the right. It's easy to miss, so look real hard. Drive down it until you see headlights flashing at you. You'll just be rounding a hill. Drive straight at me, real slow-like. Understand?"

"Yes."

"No cops. If your boyfriend follows you, he'll be dead, you'll be dead and your friends will be dead."

She swallowed hard. "I understand."

"You swear you're gonna bring me a baby?"

"I don't have any choice, do I?"

"Not if you want to get your doctor and nurse back alive."

"How do I know they're alive now?"

"I thought you might be asking that. Here."

"Hello?" The feminine voice was weak, hesitant.

"Caitlyn. Is that you?"

"Tabitha?"

She sounded dazed. Was she drugged?

"Are you okay, Caitlyn? Is Dr. Walters with you?"

"He wasn't allowed to—"

"That's enough," Hines growled. Then his voice was closer. "Sunset. If you ain't here, one of them's gonna be dead."

With a definite click, there was silence.

Tabitha punched the end button automatically, then stared at the phone, panic racing through her.

What did she do now? Tell Jake.

She walked toward the bedroom, intending to do just that. But she stopped in the kitchen. The shower was still running, though her heart was beating so loud she could barely hear it.

Jake was totally unaware anyone had called.

If your boyfriend follows you, he'll be dead, you'll be dead and your friends will be dead.

Tabitha gripped the countertop, willing away the panic that threatened consciousness. She couldn't give in to terror now. She had to think rationally.

If she told Jake, he would definitely organize the entire Mission Creek Police Department to descend on Hines. Police cars with sirens, flashing lights. Helicopters. Hines would hear, for sure. He'd kill Cait and Dr. Walters. He'd kill her, too. And Jake.

Tabitha forced herself to breathe.

On the other hand, the conversation wasn't recorded. She was the only one who knew that Branson Hines had called.

If she didn't tell Jake, he wouldn't follow. He wouldn't get killed. She wouldn't get killed, and Cait and Dr. Walters wouldn't get killed. If she did everything right. A very big "if."

But if she didn't tell Jake, she'd have to do it on her own.

You can't do anything right.

Tabitha pressed her hand over her heart to stem the panic caused by her father's lingering curse. Who was she to rescue anyone? What if she blew it? What if she said something she shouldn't? Moved the wrong way?

They would all be killed.

But Jake wouldn't.

Funny. He was the one with the rescue complex, and here she was thinking she needed to rescue him. Was she nuts?

No, she wasn't crazy. Jake *did* need to be rescued—from himself, from his own rescue complex. He needed to be shown that he was a man, not a cop. Or rather, that he was a man who happened to be a cop. He needed to be shown that someone loved him as much as his parents had. Someone cared whether he lived or died. Someone cared what time he came home at night. Only then could he come down off his white horse and be a man.

Suddenly she saw with crystal clarity the rightness of her plan, the absolute beauty of this thing she could do for the man she loved.

No one had ever thought about rescuing Jake. Cops were there to rescue other people, right?

But cops were people, too. They didn't always do things right, either. Like that kidnapping case Jake told her about where both the kidnapper and hostage were killed. Jake became a cop in order to save the world. But he hadn't been able to save those people, and he wasn't able to save himself. In fact, he didn't even know he needed saving.

But she knew, and she had an opportunity to do for him what he couldn't do for himself.

You can't do anything right.

She squeezed her eyes closed, then started with a gasp when Billy jumped on the counter. She petted him absently, thinking about ways she could get Caitlyn and Dr. Walters safely away—and how she could make Hines believe she was stupid enough to risk someone else's baby.

Then Billy started purring.

She focused her eyes on his orange fur, remembering how he lay still, on his back, like a baby, as long as she kept rubbing his tummy.

She picked Billy up and hugged him.

She *could* do this, and do it right. She had to…for Jake.

Jake left the bedroom, feeling good in the fresh clothes his men had brought him, feeling good about last night. He couldn't believe how responsive Tabitha was to his touch. Making her feel good made him feel good.

He entered the kitchen and stopped.

Tabitha stared down at Billy in her arms, her face pale.

"What happened?" he demanded. "Did Hines call?"

"What?" She shook her head, as if shaking off deep thoughts. "Oh. No. It's just that..." Her gaze slid away, and she smiled ruefully. "I'm out of coffee."

Two strides took him to her. He lifted her chin. "You're white as a ghost."

She tugged her chin away so she could set Billy on the floor. "I need coffee first thing in the morning. I'm an addict, okay? There, the truth comes out. You're involved with a caffeine addict."

Jake chuckled and forced himself to relax. The stress must be getting to him. He was seeing ghosts everywhere. "Two seeds in a pod. I have to have my morning coffee, too. Come on. I'll buy you breakfast at the hospital cafeteria."

She agreed distractedly, then suddenly stopped. "But we have to get through a press conference first."

"Afterward is too late?"

She set a hand on her hip. "Hey, you're the one who kept me up half the night."

He grinned and leaned toward her. "Complaining again?"

She yanked on his tie, pulling his mouth onto hers.

They shared a kiss so hungry, Jake was hard by the time he broke it off. "Damn, woman. You trying to make me call off the press conference altogether?"

She brightened. "Would you?"

"Do you want reporters camping out on your doorstep?"

She twisted her lips. "Point taken."

"We'll stop by a fast-food place and grab coffee and biscuits."

"Coffee will be enough for me. I can't eat."

"Oh, yes, you can."

She wrinkled her nose at him. "Cops are such bullies."

"Only when we have to be. You ready to go?"

"Let me grab my purse."

After the press conference, they settled into the familiar pattern of waiting. Jake tried to leave Tabitha alone as much as possible. She had work to do.

He did, too. State-of-the-art surveillance equipment had finally arrived from Houston, and he spent the rest of the morning overseeing installation.

But he couldn't stay away from her. He found excuses to wander past Tabitha's office, just to catch a glimpse of her beautiful face.

"You've got it bad, don't ya, honey?" Marie asked the third time he came in to ask her a question.

Jake glanced away from Tabitha's door. "Got what bad?"

"You sure as heck aren't coming in here to see me."

"But I—"

"Go on in there to her." Marie shook her finger at him. "Those secret smiles give it away every time."

"Give what—"

His words were cut off by the phone ringing. His eyes cut to Tabitha inside her office.

She looked up expectantly.

"Oh, it's just Wendell Nordan," Marie said with a glance at the caller ID. "He's the paper goods rep from Dallas."

Marie rang the call back to Tabitha, who took it calmly.

Jake watched her for a minute. Was she *too* calm? Yesterday she'd been so nervous she'd jumped every time the phone rang.

The look that he'd caught on her face that morning popped into his mind, and with it his suspicion that Hines had called.

Jake stepped into Tabitha's office, over to her desk.

She smiled at him as she talked to the salesman, but there was a brittle quality to her smile.

The call was brief. When Tabitha hung up the phone, her hand shook ever so slightly.

Jake relaxed. Nerves. Just nerves.

Tabitha looked up with widened eyes. Another sign of nerves. "What's wrong?"

He leaned down and kissed her. "Nothing, kitten. I just need a kiss."

She sighed, as if relieved. Her smile was genuine this time. "That feels good."

He kissed her again, then left her to her work.

Marie's grin was as wide as the Texas sky. "I knew it."

He grinned back. "So sue me."

He walked back down the hall.

He was seeing ghosts again. If Hines had called, his men would have picked up the conversation. Even if somehow they hadn't, Tabitha would have told him. What reason would she have not to?

Still he couldn't shake off his doubts. His gut told him something wasn't right—and his gut was rarely wrong. He just couldn't figure out exactly what his gut was trying to say.

Jake had his men order sandwiches for lunch, then took one to Tabitha on the excuse of making her eat. He even managed to work in a little cuddling. Though he didn't take it as far as the night before, Tabitha was as responsive.

Although… Was there just a hint of desperation to her caresses?

He couldn't tell, couldn't put his finger on anything specific to explain his uneasiness.

Then, just as Jake was leaving to check on his men, Tabitha's phone rang. Marie had gone out to lunch, so Tabitha had to answer it herself.

Jake stopped at the door and looked back at her.

She picked it up without hesitation. "Tabitha Monroe. Can I help you? … Oh, yes, Mrs. Wainwright. Thanks for calling me back. Crystal's out of town, so I'm making calls to reschedule the fund-raising meeting.''

Jake froze. She had no reaction at all to the phone ringing. Yesterday she'd nearly jumped out of her chair.

Still, it wasn't conclusive evidence. So what would be?

Maybe if he checked her caller ID.

After getting Tabitha's house key from Dan Hammel, who'd used it when he installed surveillance equipment there that morning, it took Jake twenty minutes to ascertain that Hines hadn't called her home phone. The one call coming there had been from the hospital.

It took a little longer to get to her cell phone, since it was buried in her purse which was buried in her desk.

They were leaving her office for the afternoon press conference when Jake stopped just as they stepped on the elevator. ''Damn. I forgot my notes on the search areas. You go on down. I'll be right behind you.''

She nodded distractedly. ''All right.''

When the elevator slid closed, he spun around and headed straight for her office.

''Forget something?'' Marie asked as he walked through.

''Yeah. I'll just be a minute.''

He didn't close the door behind him. Walking behind Tabitha's desk, he pulled open the right bottom drawer and grabbed her purse. Fishing out both cell phones, he checked the one he'd given her, the one his men could record. No calls.

He quickly found the incoming call history on her private cell phone. The last call was at eight-eleven that morning. It was from a ''local call,'' but didn't list the number.

Jake's hand gripped the phone so hard his knuckled turned white, as white as little Miss Feng Shui had been that morning.

She'd lied. Hines *had* called her.

He stared at the phone in disbelief. Why wouldn't she tell him? Did she think she could handle a violent criminal like Branson Hines? He had an arrest record as long as Jake's arm. The man was crazy.

Jake tossed both cell phones back in Tabitha's purse, then threw it in the drawer.

And she'd told him *he* had a Superman complex. Hines had no doubt told her he'd kill the hostages if the police were involved, and she obviously didn't trust *cops* to get her employees back alive.

Which really meant she didn't trust *him.*

Jake dropped into Tabitha's chair, feeling as if his heart dropped even further, into some dark corner of his soul where he'd never find it again.

After last night he'd thought that maybe she'd begun to care for him, that she'd begun to trust him. That maybe she'd realized he was a man even though he wore a badge. A man who wanted her, needed her.

For the first time in his life he didn't feel a pressing need to be on the job all the time. He didn't feel as if he would be missing something if he wasn't there. Last night he'd been content to lie in Tabitha's arms all night. With any other woman, he would have been up ten times, checking on the situation, on his men.

He closed his eyes and banged his head back against the chair.

This morning he hadn't even kept an ear out for the phone while he showered. He'd sung, for God's sake.

She'd done that for him. She'd made him relax, made him see that there was more to life than dragging criminals off the street, made him forget all about crime for a little while. She'd made him trust her, made him want to be with her twenty-four/seven.

But he obviously hadn't touched her in any way. She still

saw him as one of the cops she hated. She didn't see Jake the man.

He wanted to call her on it, wanted to see her reaction to him figuring out that she'd talked to Hines. But he couldn't say anything.

No doubt Hines told her to meet him alone. Jake didn't know why she thought she could pull this off by herself, didn't know why she would even want to, but he had to let her think she was doing it.

In one of his first kidnapping situations, years ago, he let the father take the money in. Because the man knew dozens of police officers were hidden, watching him, he kept looking around for them, clueing the kidnapper in to their presence. Eight people were killed that day, including four officers.

Jake had never forgotten that lesson.

"You okay?"

Jake looked up to see Marie in the doorway. He shook off his dejection. He had to seem normal. "Yeah. Just thinking."

She nodded as if she only half believed him. "Good things, I hope."

Jake didn't release the bitter laugh that bubbled to the surface. "Yeah, well, guess I need to get down to the press conference. Thanks for waking me up."

"What time are we going home?" Tabitha asked.

Jake studied her carefully averted face. She'd been quiet since the press conference. In fact, this was the first thing she'd said since then that wasn't answering a question of his. "I don't know. Why? You tired?"

She shrugged, but the movement was jerky. "Billy's probably getting hungry. He needs to be fed."

Jake had been wondering how she planned to separate

herself from him. She needed to be alone so she could slip away and meet Hines.

Throughout the day Jake had been quietly arranging for backup. Since he didn't know the location, the force he was assembling had to be on standby, had to wait on his signal to move in when he knew where they were going.

The only thing Jake had been able to do to prepare Tabitha was to show her some self-defense moves on the pretext of being restless and wanting to kill time. At the same time he'd given her a can of pepper spray just in case something happened when he wasn't around.

Jake glanced at the window behind Tabitha. About an hour until dark. That must be the time Hines had told her to meet him.

Didn't kidnappers have any imagination? Hines was going strictly by the book. Dark or dusk was a favorite time of kidnappers for meetings because the light was so uncertain. Shadows distorted things, or made them disappear altogether.

He would have laughed at Hines being such a cliché, but he wasn't in the mood. "I still have a couple of things I need to take care of around here. Probably another hour or so. You want to go on home and feed him?"

"By myself?"

Jake probably wouldn't have heard the hopefulness in her voice if he hadn't been looking for it. "Now, kitten, would I do that to you? No, not by yourself. I'll have a squad car take you home."

The officers he'd already chosen had orders to let her slip away "unnoticed." Jake would be parked down her street in one of the department's unmarked vehicles, waiting to follow her.

"I don't want to leave my car here overnight," she said.

"Of course not. They'll follow you home."

"Okay."

"Be sure to let them search your house before you go in."

She nodded. "I'm getting used to it."

He watched her gather her things. This might be the last time he saw her alive. He wanted to shake her, demand to know why she was being so irrational as to meet Hines on her own, urge her to be careful.

Most of all, however, he wanted to know why she couldn't love him.

But he couldn't make her love him. Letting on that he knew would only distract her when she needed all her concentration to come out of this unharmed.

As she rounded the desk, he took her in his arms and kissed her hard. She returned his kiss fervently, wrapping her arms around him as if she never wanted to let go, which made it even harder to let her go.

Finally he pulled back and gently forced her to look at him. "Promise me you'll be careful."

She dropped her gaze. "I'm only going home."

He drew his thumb across her cheek. "I know." He dropped another kiss on her lips. "I'll miss you."

She stepped away from his arms. "You'll see me in just a little while, Jake."

God willing.

He walked her to the elevator and hit the down button. "There's a couple of squad cars patrolling the hospital perimeter. I'll radio one of them to follow you home."

"All right." As the elevator dinged, she searched his eyes.

"Something wrong?" he asked, giving her one last chance to tell him.

She stretched up on tiptoe and kissed him, then trailed a hand down his face. "I'll see you."

Unable to let her go, Jake hugged her tight. ''Why don't you just wait for me? I won't be that long.''

She returned the hug, then drew away. ''Billy needs to be fed.''

''Yeah.'' He tried to smile but didn't think he was all that successful.

The elevator began to close, and he reached out to hold it for her.

She stepped in, then turned to face him. ''See you later.''

''Yeah.''

As it closed, he thought he heard the words ''I love you.'' He quickly punched the down button to make it open again, but it didn't.

She was gone.

Sixteen

Branson Hines was right. The dirt road he'd described wasn't easy to find. Extreme South Texas consisted of dirt and scrub, so distinguishing a road from the rest of the dirt in fading light took all of Tabitha's limited concentration.

Finally spotting some ruts disappearing between two hills, she turned west just as the sun blinked its last. Utterly flat coastal plains stretched east from Mission Creek to the Gulf, but rolling hills undulated westward all the way into Laredo. Highway 16 seemed to be the dividing line.

Since she didn't know how dark Branson Hines wanted it to be when she arrived, Tabitha stopped her car just out of sight of the highway.

She glanced down at Billy, who stared at her from his crouched position in the passenger seat. He'd crawled out from under the seat just a few minutes ago. "I'm sorry, Billy boy, but you had to come. I need you."

She slowly reached to pet him. He blinked as she stroked his head, making her sigh with relief. "Good, you're not *too* freaked. You've got an important part to play in this fiasco, so you need to be calm."

Tabitha rolled her eyes. "A heck of a lot calmer than I am at the moment. You need to be my sweet baby. Can you do that, Billy? Your mom's life depends on it. No pressure or anything."

She laughed nervously at her weak joke, mostly to keep from screaming. "I wish Jake were here. Jeez. What am I doing? Why didn't I tell him? Why didn't I let him help me? Am I nuts? I don't know what I'm doing. I could ruin everything.''

The cat started purring just as Tabitha noticed it was full dark. ''Yeah, well, at least you're calm. That's something. It's too late to turn back now. It's all up to us.''

Taking a deep breath, she shifted her car into Drive. To keep Billy as calm as possible, she kept a hand on him, petting him, as they slowly bumped along the rough road.

She guided them over and around hills of varying size, wondering how far she had to go, how far she'd gone. ''What if I missed them? What if we're too—''

Headlights flashed from a relatively flat field as she rounded a bend.

Tabitha stepped on the brake reflexively, her heart pounding against her ears. ''Oh, Billy, what are we doing?''

She swallowed her fear. She'd made the decision to do this hours ago. It was too late to turn back now.

As she guided her car toward the shadows, her lights bounced off three people—two men and a woman.

''At least Cait and Dr. Walters are alive.''

Jake picked up his cell phone as he drove, on purpose, past the dirt road that Tabitha had turned down.

''She just turned onto a dirt road heading west,'' he said into his phone. He'd kept an open line on his cell phone since leaving Mission Creek. Since Hines could be monitoring police bands, he didn't want to chance a two-way.

Burl Terry was on the other end of the line, leading the rescue force following Jake.

''That's the drive to the old Miller ranch,'' Burl said. ''It was abandoned thirty-odd years ago.''

''Is there a ranch house?'' Jake asked. ''Or a barn or some type of shelter?''

''Nothing at all,'' the chief answered. ''Brush fire got

every stick of wood standing for about a five-mile stretch. No one knows exactly when."

Jake continued down Highway 16 for another hundred yards. Then checking the empty road in both directions, he turned off his headlights and drove back. "Any idea where Hines'll be waiting for her?"

"Not a damn one," Burl said.

"How far back does the road go?"

"Six or seven miles."

"Great. The hills are a blessing and a curse. If I go on foot, it could take an hour to reach them. If I drive, I could be on top of them before I know it."

"If I were a betting man—"

"Which you are." Jake turned off the highway onto the dirt road. Dusk was rapidly turning into night, though it hadn't quite made it there yet.

Burl ignored him. "I'd lay odds that Hines'll pick an open area, where he can see what's coming at him for a ways. There's a couple of flat stretches along the road. One about two miles in, the other about five."

"All right. I'll let you—" He hit the brakes. "Damn."

"What is it?"

"She stopped about a quarter mile in. Must be waiting for full dark. Hope my brake lights didn't reflect off any of these hills."

"Nah. Texas dirt is so dull it soaks up every ray of light that hits it."

Jake sat still for a long moment, watching the shadowy car ahead. All he could see was the back end. The taillights were glowing but not bright. She had it in Park.

"I guess I'm clear. I'll give you the heads-up when she starts moving."

The short drive across the rough field seemed to take an hour to Tabitha.

On the other hand, when Hines waved his gun, motioning her to stop, it was far too soon. Guiding her car perpendicular to Hines's truck so she could have it between herself and him when she got out with the cat, Tabitha shifted her car into Park, then switched off the engine.

"Turn off your headlights," Hines screamed in the now-familiar nasal voice. She'd been hearing it in her head all day.

She twisted the stick on the left side of the steering wheel, and the field went dark. That was both good and bad. Branson Hines's view of the "baby" would be that much more limited. But then, her view of him would be, too.

"Get out real slow-like, and hold up the baby so's I can see him. It *is* a him, ain't it? You wouldn't try to palm no girl off on me, now would ya?"

"It's a boy," Tabitha called back as she wrapped Billy in the baby blanket she'd managed to sneak out of the maternity ward. At least she didn't have to lie about that. Not that it would bother her. Hines had done much worse. And she was about to.

Holding Billy in the crook of her left arm, she mentally ran over her plan one last time. She made sure the top on the baby powder was barely on, then she arranged the blanket so the can of pepper spray Jake had given her that afternoon couldn't be seen in her left hand.

"What's taking you so long?"

"Babies need a lot of stuff. Plus I'm trying not to get him upset. You don't want a screaming baby on your hands, do you?"

"I reckon not. But get on outta there."

"All right. I'm coming." She opened the car door, grateful that she had remembered to set the inside light to not come on.

It wasn't easy getting out of the car while scratching a cat's tummy at the same time—with the same hand holding a bottle of baby powder with the top barely on. But somehow Tabitha managed not to upset Billy by dousing him with powder.

"C'mon, lady. We ain't got all night."

Tabitha hesitated on the pretext of adjusting the blanket, glaring across the hood of her car at the weasely little shadow there. She wanted to point out to Branson Hines that a man who had tortured an entire town for days could wait for a few minutes. But she didn't dare.

However, the anger gave her strength and bolstered her courage.

She could do this. She *would* do it.

"Caitlyn, are you okay?" Tabitha asked.

"Yes." But her voice was weak, scared.

"Dr. Walters?"

"We're fine, but what are you doing? You can't seriously be bringing a baby."

"Shut up!" Hines ordered.

The grunting sound that followed told Tabitha he'd hurt Dr. Walters some way.

"Hold that baby up so's I can see him."

"You can't see anything from there," she said. "It's too dark."

"All right, then. Come around the car, but real careful so's I can watch you. You," he called to Caitlyn.

"Yes, sir?" Cait said in a frightened voice that Tabitha had never heard. No doubt Hines had bullied—or beaten—them into submission. The little weasel had a lot to pay for.

"I'm gonna untie your hands so you can take the baby for me," Hines told Caitlyn.

"Oh, no, you don't." Tabitha stopped dead at the front of her car. "The deal is you let them go. I don't come another step closer until—"

"Who's got the gun, lady?"

Tabitha stared at him. Her eyes were getting accustomed

to the dim light now. She could see his wild, abnormally wide eyes. He was no doubt on drugs. No telling what he'd do. She shouldn't push him, shouldn't warn him that she would fight back in any way. If he was off guard, her plan stood a better chance of working.

"You're right," Tabitha told him, trying to sound contrite. "I'll hand the baby to Caitlyn."

All his senses on alert, Jake had seen Tabitha's headlights bouncing across the field. Calling in the forces, he hid his car in the shadow of a hill and sneaked across the dark expanse behind the cover of Tabitha's, blessing her for placing it between him and Hines.

He reached the cover of her car just as she was rounding the front of it, just in time to hear the anger in her voice as she questioned Hines's order that Caitlyn get the baby.

"Shut up, Tabitha," he whispered into the dark. "You're only going to make him mad."

Jake breathed a sigh of relief when, after a brief pause, Tabitha acquiesced.

"Good girl. Let's keep him occupied for five minutes. That's all it'll take for Burl to get here."

"Put the baby in the truck when she gives him to ya," Hines ordered.

"Yes, sir," Caitlyn Matthews said.

Tabitha stopped a few feet away from Hines. "Don't you want to see him first? He's a beautiful boy. I picked the very best one for you."

Jake cringed. He could hear revenge in the quietness of her voice. Damn. All he could do was get in position and hope Hines had enough sense to quit while the quitting was good.

But the man was too stupid. Licking his lips, Hines moved forward with Caitlyn, his eyes on the wiggling bundle in Tabitha's arms.

While his attention strayed, Tabitha caught Caitlyn's gaze.

"Damn," Jake whispered. "What are you up to? Just hold on. Please! Burl will be—"

Caitlyn froze for half a second, just enough to make her stumble.

Hines grabbed Caitlyn's arm. "Hey, you—"

Tabitha threw something at him that looked like white powder. It arced the air in slow motion, the cap whizzing past Hines's head as he ducked. Then she grabbed the blanket from around the so-called baby. Out sprang Billy. Tabitha threw the cat at Hines, too.

Billy screeched as he landed on Hines's head. Instead of hanging on and clawing, the cat used the man as a springboard for a flying leap into the night.

Squatting low, Jake ran to the front end of Tabitha's car. His heart hammered in his chest. His feet felt like lead weights.

"Billy!" Caitlyn cried, turning to where Billy had disappeared.

"Caitlyn," Dr. Walters called. "Wait."

She hesitated, spinning back toward the doctor.

It seemed to Jake that everyone moved in slow motion. Everyone but Hines.

He lunged at Tabitha. "You bitch! That weren't no baby. I'm gonna kill you."

Tabitha brought the pepper spray up, but couldn't get off a single spritz before Hines knocked her to the ground. Standing over her, his eyes wild, he brought the gun down in a wide arc.

Tabitha screamed and curled into a ball.

"Freeze!" Jake shouted, not even trying to keep menace from his voice. "Police."

Hines froze in midswing and cut wild eyes toward Jake. "Don't shoot."

"Throw the gun away," Jake ordered. "Now."

Hines straightened and tossed his pistol away.

"Put both hands in the air, and move away from her."

Hines stuck both skinny arms toward the sky and took two steps back.

"Miss Matthews? Dr. Walters? Are you okay?"

"Yes," Dr. Walters answered. "We're fine."

"Are you both untied?"

"Caitlyn is," Dr. Walters said.

Caitlyn looked at him sharply, but Dr. Walters's head didn't turn toward her.

"Yes. I'm untied," she said. "He untied me so I could take the baby."

"It weren't no baby!"

"Shut up, Hines," Jake spat. "Miss Matthews, would you please turn on the headlights in both of these vehicles? Backup is on the way, but they need to see where to come."

While Caitlyn complied, Jake kept his gun on Hines.

"Billy! Oh, thank goodness." Caitlyn switched on Tabitha's headlights, then lifted the cat from Tabitha's car. He'd evidently hidden in the nearest place that smelled familiar.

When the area was lit, however, Tabitha still hadn't moved.

"Tabitha?" Jake asked. "Are you okay?"

"Yes," she said, but the smallness of her voice worried him more than convinced him.

Jake could hear the backup forces moving in. His first duty was to subdue Hines and handcuff him. In lieu of that, all he had to do was keep his gun trained on the kidnapper for another two minutes, until Burl Terry brought in the troops.

But all Jake could think about was Tabitha. Had Hines fired a round he hadn't heard? Was she bleeding there in the shadows where the headlights didn't hit?

He had to know.

Taking two steps to the right, he squatted down, keeping

his gun and attention trained on Hines until his other hand touched the woman he loved.

He glanced down. "Are you all—"

"Watch out!" Dr. Walters shouted.

"No!"

Jake's head turned in time to see another gun in Hines's hand.

Jake straightened his arm and squeezed the trigger of his own gun, but fire slamming into his chest made his shot go wild. He gasped and went down to one knee.

Jake heard thuds and grunts behind him, but barely.

"Jake!" Suddenly Tabitha's arms were around him. "Jake, you're hurt!"

He leaned into her, vaguely aware of people streaming into the area. "I can't..."

"Oh, my God. Somebody help him. Please!"

His weight made her fall back, but she held on to him, taking the brunt of the fall. Even so, pain ripped through his chest.

"Dr. Walters, he's been shot. Help him."

Jake heard tears in Tabitha's voice. Opening his eyes, he saw them streaming down her face.

A strong hand lifted his arm. Jake wanted to scream at the pain, but the best he could manage was a low grunt.

A voice he recognized as Dr. Walters's cussed. "He's wearing a vest, but Hines's lucky shot got him right under the arm. We've got to get him to the hospital. STAT."

Burl Terry's grim voice came from above. "A helicopter's not sixty seconds away."

"Tell them to hurry," Tabitha pleaded. "You can't let him die."

"We're going to do everything we can," Dr. Walters told her.

Something soft was stuffed under Jake's arm.

"You need to let go of him, Miss Monroe, so we can lay him flat."

"No." Tabitha squeezed him, but not too tight. "I won't ever let you go, Jake White," she whispered against his ear. "I love you. Do you hear me? You can't die. I won't let you."

"Over here!" Burl called to someone.

But Jake didn't care who it was.

Tabitha loved him. Nothing else mattered.

Seventeen

Tabitha had never seen this side of a hospital.

Oh, she'd seen people who sat in the emergency waiting room, their faces pale, their eyes bleak as they waited—half hopeful, half fearful—for news about the loved one on the other side of the swinging doors. But she'd never had a loved one to be fearful for until now.

She'd never had anything—anyone—to lose until now.

The possibility of losing Jake now, when she'd barely begun to love him, was tearing her apart. She wanted to barge through those swinging doors, into the operating room where Mission Creek's best surgeon was removing the bullet, and—

And what? What could she do?

She'd already seen that Jake had the best care Mission Creek Memorial Hospital had to offer. She'd flown with him in the helicopter, issuing orders right and left about his care, never letting go of his hand, thinking somehow she could impart some of her strength to him, the strength to live.

Now all she could do was wait. And worry. And wonder.

What would she do if he died? How would she be able to get out of bed each morning knowing she'd never again see or touch or hold the only man she'd ever loved? The only man who'd ever loved her.

Though Jake hadn't said the words, Tabitha knew he loved her.

He'd checked on her before securing his prisoner. At that

moment he'd proved he was a man before he was a cop. A man who cared more about her than his job.

That moment had held absolute truth, absolute proof that he loved her. That same moment might have cost Jake his life.

Tabitha fought the stinging tears, feeling helpless and more alone than she'd ever felt in all her years on her own.

Now everything was up to Jake. Did he love her enough to live?

Finally, at 3:35 a.m., Mission Creek Memorial Hospital's chief surgeon pushed open the swinging door.

Tabitha stood, her stiffness testament to the fact that she'd barely moved for the past six hours.

Dr. Stephen Carmichael smiled. "He's going to be okay."

"Oh, thank God." Relief spread through her like a shot of morphine. She nearly passed out.

Dr. Carmichael caught her arm and led her to the nearest seat. Only when they were seated did he continue. "He's going to need a lot of care, even physical therapy, in the next few months. The bullet tore into the left cavity of his lung and there was a lot of bleeding. We gave him six units. But he's young and strong, so barring infection or any other unseen complications, I don't see why he shouldn't have a full recovery."

Tears streamed down Tabitha's cheeks. "I have to see him."

Dr. Carmichael held her in her seat. "He's still in recovery."

"I don't care." She met his eyes dead-on. "I'm going to see him."

"You can't—"

"Dr. Carmichael, I am the administrator of this hospital. I can go anywhere in this hospital I want to go."

He acknowledged that with a crooked smile. "He probably won't be conscious for several more hours."

"I don't care if he's not conscious for several more days. I will scrub anything you want me to scrub, but I'm going in there."

Dr. Carmichael nodded toward the glass doors to the emergency room to the media held back by Mission Creek police officers. "What about a statement for them?"

Tabitha frowned. As chief administrative officer, it was her job to update the press. But at the moment she didn't care. Her job wasn't nearly as important to her as it had been a few days ago. The most important thing in her life was lying in intensive care.

"You're chief surgeon, and you performed the surgery. Why don't you give them a statement?"

He shrugged, having done it before. "They'll ask about you, too. What should I tell them?"

"Me?" She considered the question for a moment, then smiled proudly. "Tell them I'm waiting at the side of the man I love."

Jake always came awake quickly, fully alert. So wandering in and out of consciousness as he shook off the drugs was disconcerting.

He smiled at the ten-dollar word. Tabitha was rubbing off on him. Although she'd say it wasn't a ten-dollar word, more like six, but for him—

"Jake?"

The sound of her voice brought him fully into consciousness.

"Are you awake?" Her voice was raspy, uncertain, exhausted.

His eyelids weighed a ton, but he willed them open. Bright lights stabbed into his brain, making him aware of pain for the first time. His whole body hurt, but his left side felt as if it had been ripped off. "Tabitha?"

Her beautiful face appeared in his line of vision, making him realize he hadn't turned his head. Her smile was bright, though tears made her bluebonnet eyes liquid.

"Hey, sleepyhead." She touched his face. "Would you like a little water?"

She was brilliant, his kitten. She knew exactly what he needed. "Please."

She twisted, then turned back. "Here. I'll drip it from the straw."

He took several strawfuls, but that much effort exhausted him. Afterward he couldn't keep his eyes open. But he wanted to know. "What happened?"

"Shh." Her cool hand stroked his cheek. "Everything's fine. You don't need to rescue anyone. Go to sleep. I'll take care of you."

Jake relaxed. "I love you."

"I know," she whispered with a soft kiss on his cheek. "I love you, too."

Jake felt a little stronger the next time he woke, and even stronger the time after that. Tabitha was with him every time he drifted into consciousness, making him feel cared for, safe.

Finally he woke feeling tired, but with no pain anywhere except his left side. He remembered being shot, but the only thing clear after that was Tabitha telling him she loved him.

Jake's lips were so dry they felt as if they were cracking. But he couldn't help smiling. Where was she? He turned his head stiffly.

Tabitha sat in the chair next to the bed, more or less. One arm was bent under her head on the edge of his mattress, the other stretched toward him, her hand resting on his arm as if she refused to let go of him.

Love swept over him in healing waves. He didn't care what he had to do, what promises he had to make, where he had to go or stay, he was going to make her his woman, any way she'd have him.

"I love you," he whispered.

Her head lifted immediately. She blinked. "What?"

"I said, I love you."

"Oh." Her face melted into smiles. "I know."

"You do?"

She nodded, then twisted and reached for a plastic cup from the rolling bed table. "Think you're strong enough to sip from the straw? You'll get more that way."

He nodded and drank the cup dry. As she refilled it, he asked, "What happened after I was shot? Will you tell me now?"

She guided the straw to his mouth. "You were airlifted to the hospital, then you were in surgery for six—"

"Not me. Who brought down Hines?"

"Oh, that. Caitlyn had untied Dr. Walters while you had Hines at gunpoint. When Hines shot you, Dr. Walters tackled him and wrestled his gun away. The other cops arrived just a minute later."

"They were right behind me. What about the hostages? How are they doing? How long has it been, anyway?"

"This is the second day. You slept most of yesterday." She set the cup back on the table and leaned against the edge of his bed. "As for Cait and Dr. Walters, they're in seclusion. I called them both and told them to take as long as they need to get over...whatever happened to them while they were captive. No one knows what that is. They haven't said anything to anyone."

"That's not unusual," Jake said. Wanting to touch her, he lifted his hand.

She laced her fingers through his. "You've had about a million visitors. I wouldn't let them stay long, but—"

"You said you know I love you. How? I haven't told you, have I?"

Her face softened. "Well, yes, but you didn't have to. I already knew."

"How?"

"When you bent down to check on me before you put handcuffs on Branson Hines, you proved you were more concerned about me than your job."

"You were lying so still."

Her smile was shy. "That's what I mean. For the first time in your police department life, you were a man before you were a cop. I knew right then that you loved me." Her eyes teared up. "But at the same moment I nearly lost you. Promise you'll never do anything like that again."

"I won't be able to, because I'll no longer be a cop."

She froze. "What? Why not?"

"Because you don't like cops, and I want you."

"Oh, no. You're not going to put that kind of guilt on me."

"I realized something that day as I watched you prepare to meet Hines without me, which is something we'll discuss in depth when I'm feeling better."

Her lips twisted. "What did you realize?"

"That the reason I felt the need to rescue other people was because I needed rescuing myself." He squeezed her fingers. "Somehow you knew that, and you rescued me."

"I did? How?"

"By showing me the goodness in people. By loving me."

"And you love me back." There was wonder in her voice.

"Very much."

She smiled into his eyes. "You're not going to give up being a cop. I won't let you."

"But you don't like cops."

She bent and kissed his lips softly. "I've recently discovered that cops aren't too bad. At least, a certain one."

"Marry me."

She straightened with a snap, her eyes wide. "What?"

"You heard me. We're going to get married."

A blond eyebrow lifted. "Oh, so it's an order now, not a question."

"Will you marry me?"

She searched his face, her own filled with wonder and confusion. "You're nuts. We've only known each other for a few days."

"I don't care. It took me thirty-six years to find the woman I love. I'm not going to let you go."

She stroked his cheek with a cool hand. "All right."

His eyes narrowed. "All right? Just like that you're agreeing to marry a cop?"

Her lovely face sobered. "When I first saw you, lying in the recovery room, so pale, so still, I knew I couldn't live without you. Not only was I going to make you live, I was going to make you live with me. If that means marriage, even this quickly, okay. I love you, Jake, and I want to be with you. You taught me what it's like to love and be loved. I'm not going to be satisfied without it now. And I'm not going to be afraid of it anymore." Her smile was brilliant. "So, yes, Jake White, I'll be your wife."

Jake tugged on her hand.

She bent and kissed him.

He sighed with happiness. "That's good, because I'm going to need rescuing again, you know. Especially if you're going to make me continue being a cop. I want to know that you'll be my backup for the rest of my life."

She scraped her nails along the stubble on his jaw. "My love, I'll back you up in anything you do. If you really don't want to be a cop anymore, that's okay. I just want you to be happy."

He found the strength to lift his hand to her face. "*You* make me happy, kitten. You have from the instant I saw you. I fell in lust with your mole, then I fell in love with you.''

''My mole is yours, Jake. And so am I.'' She kissed him. ''Always.''

* * * * *

You will love the next story from Silhouette's
LONE STAR COUNTRY CLUB:
DOCTOR SEDUCTION
by Beverly Bird

Available September 2002 (at Direct only)

Turn the page for an excerpt from this exciting romance...!

One

Everything looked just the same, she thought.

Caitlyn Matthews stopped her car at the Mission Creek Memorial Hospital and looked around. The automobiles and SUVs stacked side by side in the employees area were the same ones that had always been here. The American flag still snapped to attention with each hot gust of South Texas wind. The original hospital building looked strong and impressive, but the windows of the new maternity wing looked a little shinier than the others. Maybe that was her imagination.

She had worked within the hospital's walls for the past four years now. The sight of it should have filled her with a sense of normalcy, of hope. Instead, she realized that it was entirely possible she was about to throw up.

She unclenched one hand from the steering wheel to press her fingers against her lips. *What's wrong with me? I can't be like this. It's just not acceptable.* Cait took her hand away from her mouth with a jerky motion and laughed aloud at that thought. A lot of things she would never have allowed before had been creeping into her life lately.

Her life was a shambles, a disaster. It was in sharp little shards at her feet and she had no idea what to do about that. But she *did* know that having her life torn apart and tossed about for a few short days was not going to undo her permanently. She would just have to pick up the pieces and put them all back together again.

"Give it time," Cait said aloud. She had a plan. But first

she had to force herself to simply step inside the hospital again in the first place.

She got out of her dark blue compact Ford and locked the door behind her, then she jiggled the handle to make sure it was secure. Cait turned away from the car again like a marine drill sergeant. She made it through the front doors of the hospital just fine. But as it turned out, that was the easy part. The man she'd suddenly decided to give her virginity to after twenty-five otherwise chaste and uneventful years was right there in the lobby, staring at her.

It was unconventional, but Dr. Sam Walters prided himself on marching to a different drummer. He stepped off the elevator with a mission, towing the boy behind him by one hand.

Gilbert Travalini was nine years old, scared out of his mind and, in all likelihood, dying, though Sam had yet to give up the fight to turn that particular tide. Fresh new marrow would be transplanted into his bones at seven o'clock tomorrow morning. The match wasn't as close as Sam would have liked and there was a chance his body would reject it. But until that happened, Gilbert was still a motor head and Sam happened to own one very fine, candy-apple-red Maserati. Said Maserati was currently parked outside the hospital.

"Let's go," he said, tugging the boy into the lobby. "If all that stuff about speed was just some macho bluff on your part, better cough up the truth now before you wet your pants."

"You're going to let me ride in it?" Gilbert's blue eyes bugged.

"I'm going to do better than that. I'm going to let you drive it."

The kid stumbled in thrilled shock. "That's against the law," Gil said.

"Are you going to rat me out?"

"No! No, sir."

"Then come on. I've got thirty minutes before rounds and—"

And then she was there.

Sam's voice chopped off in midsentence and he came to a stop. He had a single, inane thought: This wasn't supposed to happen yet. They'd only gotten out of that underground basement room where they'd been held hostage a few days ago. He'd figured it would take Caitlyn Matthews a week to recover and get back to work. At least, it would take the average woman that long.

But little Miss Tight Buns obviously considered it her patriotic, God-given, Hippocratic, fussbudget duty to get back to work as soon as possible after the singularly worst event in her ultraorganized life, Sam thought. She'd probably do it if only to make *his* life miserable, Sam thought. His eyes narrowed as she came toward him. A petite, waifish blonde, her every stride was measured and precise. That little chin of hers was held high, and her sapphire eyes moved neither left nor right. Every germ within a fifteen-yard radius either saluted or ran for cover at the sight of her, Sam decided sourly.

His heart was pounding like a sledgehammer.

"What are you doing here?" he demanded when she came to a stop in front of him.

"I work here," Cait replied without looking at him. Then she bent over to look into Gilbert's eyes. "Running off on me, are you?"

"No, ma'am. Yes, ma'am. I'll be back, though," the boy said, clearly rattled.

Cait straightened again and transferred her attention to Sam. "Where are you taking him, anyway?"

"Nowhere." He felt like a kid, Sam thought—one just caught in the act by a particularly unpleasant teacher.

What was he supposed to do about this situation anyway? Sam decided this was all her fault. No matter that he should have known it would eventually come to this when he'd first taken it into his head to touch her in that underground room. He'd thought—for that one insane, stress-induced moment—that he would just taste her and that would be that. But he hadn't stopped there, because something amazing and overwhelming about her had swum through him and over him and driven him to a place where nothing else had mattered except the scent of her, the feel of her, her heat.

Now they were back at the hospital, back to being co-workers, and he couldn't seem to get his stride.